THE GODDESS OF 5TH AVENUE

Ten Thousand
Blessings
to
You!

Simone

THE GODDESS
OF 5TH AVENUE

A NOVEL

Carol Simone

HAYDEN

HAYDEN Publishing, a Division of Hayden Companies, Incorporated
117 Greenwich Street
San Francisco, California 94111
1-800-200-7441

www.haydenpublishing.com

HAYDEN Enlightened Communications is a trademark of Hayden
Companies, Incorporated.

The author would like to thank the following for permission to use excerpts
from their works:

"What Is the Heart?" From *The Glance, Rumi's Songs of Soul-Meeting,* translated
by Coleman Barks, copyright © 1999 by Coleman Barks. Reprinted by permission of Viking Penguin, a division of Penguin Putnam, Inc.

"I have come to rebuild what has been shattered. To rebuild love." From a
dharma talk given by Vietnamese Buddhist monk, poet and peacemaker
Thich Nhat Hanh.

"I am remembering forever, where we Belong." From *Life Span,* by Alma Luz
Villanueva, copyright © 1984. Reprinted by permission of the author.

PUBLISHER'S NOTE: This book is a work of fiction. Any references to
historical events, to real locales or to real people, living or dead, are intended
only to give the fiction a setting in historical reality. Other names, characters,
places and incidents either are the product of the author's imagination or are
used fictitiously, and their resemblance, if any, to real-life counterparts is
entirely coincidental.

Cover and text design by Addis

Printed in the United States of America

HAYDEN Publishing books, by arrangement with Beyond Words Publishing,
are distributed to the book trade by Publishers Group West.

Library of Congress Card Number: 00-112140

Publisher's Cataloging-in-Publication
Simone, Carol A., 1948–
    The Goddess of 5th Avenue / by Carol Simone.
    p. cm.
    ISBN 1-930880-00-6
    1. Goddesses—Fiction. 2. Women—Social conditions—Fiction.
3. Mysticism—Fiction. 4. Adult child abuse victims—Rehabilitation—
Fiction. 5. Civilization, Ancient—Fiction. I. Title.
PS3569.I4865G64 2001   813'.6
                        QB101-902113

For
the Quan Yin
in Everyone
&
For Marian Nestle

ACKNOWLEDGEMENTS
AND BOWS

With great love I wish to acknowledge the spiritual fire of Thich Nhat Hanh, Gangaji, Ann Hinkel, and the homeless woman of Fifth Avenue who sent me on my journey.

Jan Venturini, thanks for walking down Fifth Avenue with me on that auspicious day. A warm embrace to Leslie Arno who listened repeatedly to the channeling of this story as it came through me. You are always with me.

To Bob Longhi who opened up his home to me and revealed the exquisite femininity of Maui. And to the island of Manhattan (my first home) that, in my early years, inspired in me poetry, jazz and a sense of resiliency.

To my mother Margery, who taught me to love the animals and who championed my writing from the beginning. And to my father, who loved to tell stories. To my sisters: Nina, who brought me great strength as a child, and Connie, whose silent eyes taught me the power of the present moment. And to Naeemah, a born goddess.

To Tish Lampert, my oldest friend. You're the smartest writer I know. Mary Bartnikowski, you're the funniest. And Michael Price, you're a big fish who swims deep.

Stanlee Gatti, you are the rose in my heart. Thank you for introducing me to your mother Anne's Quan Yin smile.

Josie Hadley, Dorthy Tyo and Terry Attwood, you are my favorite triumvirate. Thanks for being.

To Patti and Tuck Andress, love warriors and true family.

To Anne Navarre Chaney, my late-night listener and confidante. To Dayle Schweninger, Mary Lautner, Susan Davis, Mary Tennes, Sheryl Peterson, and Catherine D'Allessandro. And to Colleen Murphy, and Jim Silva who helped me rediscover the energy to birth this old soul.

To my chère amie, Erin Sommerville, whose tremendous loving optimism and support has blessed my life for decades.

To the wise woman, Victoria McLaughlin. Thank you from all directions.

To Holly Hayden, thank you for your forthright words and actions, and Hillary Hayden, it's been a privilege watching you come into full bloom. Everyone associated with Addis Group, you're the greatest!

Thank you to Hal Zina Bennett, Rebecca Arno, Chip August, Tomas Yelda, Mike Yazzolino, Barbara Courtney, Stephanie Mahron, Isabel Geffner, Laura Bellotti, Barbara Rose Booker and Marlene Fern-Caldes for your input. To Lauren Maddison, whose intuition and editorial eye brought this book into a much needed form. And to Sandy Satterwhite, who stood by this project in the early days. Thank you for your good will.

Peter Guzzardi, you are an absolute joy to know, and I am honored I was given the opportunity to work with you. Thanks for deepening Billie's world. Poet, diplomat and friend, Al Young, your loving soul is dancing through the pages of this book. Jan Allegretti, your insight and delicate brushstrokes were invaluable to the Goddess.

To David and Storey Hayden—visionaries, muses, publishers and friends—whose energies inspire in me courageous action and a brand new understanding of the thrill of "going for your dream." Boundless love and thanks.

And, to Locke McCorkle, whose generosity and lightness of being allowed me to manifest this work. You have done the seemingly impossible, awakened within me trust and intimacy and a place in time steeped with peace. I love you with all my heart.

And, finally, to the energy of compassion that is known as Quan Yin. My connection to you is inexpressible through words. So I'll be quiet now. Namaste.

"What is the heart?

It is not human, and it is not imaginary.

I call it you."

—Rumi

PROLOGUE

I dangle my sunburned legs over the wet, black lava rocks of this secluded Hawaiian bay. A cool, ripe mango drips into the palm of my hand, and in this moment I am totally present in the turquoise afternoon. No plans, no goals, no telephone. In my fiftieth year I am finally nobody.

If my ex-therapist Dr. Janowitz could see me now, he would probably lapse into the dark throes of dismay. I'm quite sure he would not understand my behavior at all. In fact, he'd probably diagnose me as delusional, even psychotic. After all, just a few months ago I was a prosperous, respected, sought-after professional in the therapeutic community. I was confident that I knew who I was. Specifically, I was Billie "Never Stops to Take a Breath" Bartholomew, a Manhattan psychologist who thought she was saving the masses from the perils of mental chaos. But when I encountered Maria of a Thousand Flowers, a street person who unknowingly mirrored my shadow self, I discovered that I couldn't save a soul if my life depended on it. So I had my own kind of breakdown, or breakup, or perhaps break with everyone's expectations, including my own. I discovered that I didn't have a clue. I was lost and confused, hidden behind my perfect mask. I had no idea how hungry I was to be myself, or how disconnected I was from whomever that "self" might really be.

Then quite suddenly everything changed. I learned a wonderful, terrifying, soul-saving lesson about life. And in the end

I cashed in my IRAs, sold my luxurious East Fifties brownstone and the black Saab convertible I was nervous about driving in New York City anyway. I dumped my overstuffed Chanel make-up bag and Mont Blanc pens, my all-important police whistle and my dreaded Daytimer—filled with appointments—into a trash can across from Radio City Music Hall. A tortoise-shell hair clip, my black Carrera sunglasses and all of my furniture were waiting for my housekeeper on her cleaning day. A note from me explained it was all hers to keep.

Only months ago, this decision would have been unthinkable. As a therapist and as a person I was, well, stuck—a woman with a fabulous grin, besieged by the torturous memories of her past. Raised amid the chaos of molestation, alcoholism and violence, I was an old soul who knew at a young age that I had fallen onto the wrong planet, and that my parents, MollieO and Martin, were part of the crazy cosmic joke. If it hadn't been for my rebellious hellion of a sister, Callie, I wouldn't have made it to age twelve. From then on it was Aunt Lillian who championed me and taught me to see life as an incredible adventure.

When I finally began to open my eyes and hope for a bigger, saner world, an immortal tiger appeared, . . . I helped a woman die wrapped in a garbage bag on Fifth Avenue near Tiffany's . . . and a goddess entered my soul like a piece of violet silk, changing my life forever.

It's taken some time for me to get ready for my appointment with the goddess who lives beneath the ocean. Ever since I was a little girl I have avoided all kinds of deep water, fearing that I would be swept away into a sea of destructive emotion. But at the same time I also sensed someone watching over me, someone who was only a breath away.

And then the goddess Quan Yin appeared. It was she who inspired me to let go and dive into life. It was she who invited me to open my heart and leave this troubled world for a more heavenly destination: Lemuria, a continent destroyed by Atlantis a long, long time ago, floating now in a dimension far beneath the Pacific. Lemuria, a civilization that has mystically reemerged, and where, even today, peace prevails. Quan Yin beckons me now to Lemuria, a place where my soul can rest and remember its softness, a timeless domain where I will be an apprentice to a merciful goddess.

Why wouldn't I leave? Knowing how extraordinary it is out there, what could hold me here? Besides, my spirit is ready now, and I have a crumpled map of Lemuria here in my hand. I feel quite confident that I will find it.

I can feel Quan Yin's loving energy coming closer now, hear her soothing words beneath the surface of the waves. Softly she beckons . . .

> *I am the one who brushes my lips across your cheek as you sleep.*
> *I am the one who envelops you in light during the most perilous of times.*
> *I am the one who listens to your prayers whenever you call.*
> *Do not be afraid. I will never leave you.*

The sky is marbled fuchsia. I begin the slow wade in. Gently, the lackadaisical waves slap at my legs and hips; I can feel the angelfish and tang bobbing below. The exhausting world— where I feel driven to please everyone, where I lose myself in the endless discord and disorder, the half-baked relationships with men and my chatterbox "coyote" mind—lies behind me now. With each watery step I am letting go of everything.

At eye level, the island of Molokai wavers in the distance, dissolving instantaneously as the waves wash over me. For a moment I am unsure, struggling with the urge to turn back. But I sense Quan Yin close to me now, her loving arms outstretched and quietly waiting. I hear her whisper,

> *Keep finding me. Keep finding me.*

I take in a full-bodied, beautiful breath. And then I dive . . . deep . . . deeper.

My arms move through a myriad of blues, each hue deeper than the next. Communities of midnight blue neon fish want to swim right through me, but instead casually kiss my legs and arms. Turtles half my size pedal down a lower reef. An inquisitive octopus zooms in for a close-up. Sand swirls around me, settling down gently on my shoulders like tiny golden leaves. I am not afraid. I am shrieking with delight.

Something else is coming toward me now, swimming solidly with a surreal, celestial power. It dances through the currents like a humpback whale or a rambunctious mermaid. As it moves, it sparkles, lighting the depths like a cosmic highlighter. It heads right in my direction.

I begin to make out the form. I can see a lavish headdress, and layers of silk flowing off to her sides and back. The face looms closer but I am only aware of her eyes. Dark and embracing. The eyes of the goddess. Quan Yin.

> *I come to bring you courage.*
> *I come to teach you to forgive.*
> *I am the one who delivers you from the doorway of death*
> *to the gateway of everlasting life.*

Now my body is composed of rivers of moving light. I stream through Quan Yin's eyes as if they are portals to another world. A world where I am safe. She turns and swims ahead through the purple energy fields. She glides through a doorway.

Come in, Quan Yin whispers.

I swim right alongside Her Majesty. An island floats like a fetus in the distance, protected from every angle by an aura of sacredness. Although it is far away, it is massive. As we approach, I make out a pyramid positioned in the center, surrounded by palm trees and white stone structures. There are tender, gardenia scented breezes and fields of golden wheat blowing in the warm wind. We are moving closer. A feeling comes over me, something old and familiar—I know I have been here before.

> *This is Lemuria, the ending and the beginning,* Quan Yin tells me as she opens her magnificent arms.

My heart is turning over.
I am coming home.

Part One

SNAPSHOTS FROM MY TRUSTY BROWNIE

"**Goddess:** *A spiritual warrioress. The embodiment of love.*"
The Akashic Records, Eternity

"**Goddess:** *n. a female god.*"
The New Woman's Dictionary, 1972

"*Trust no one. Kill the goddess.*"
Graffiti, lower east side subway station,
Manhattan, 2000

1

MEET THE FAM

I was a tow-headed pudge ball born into wealth and prestige, passed from Rockefeller laps to Vanderbilt bosoms, clothed in scratchy Scottish kilts and little blue navy tams. By the age of three I was sexually undone. By four I'd been seriously shamed, and by five I was deep into denial and self-effacement.

If things had gone as planned there would have been six of us—twelve with the cats and dogs. Besides my older sister Callie, I nearly had two brothers. Mitchell died the day he was born and Bertram died two days after his birth. I think they both checked out the family scene while they were in MollieO's womb and decided to take a rain check. When Martin Jerome Bartholomew, our Father (never Daddy), introduced us to friends at the Russian Tea Room he would say, "This is my beautiful wife, MollieO, and these are my two makeshift sons, Callie and Billie."

Martin was habitually inappropriate, angry at everyone around him pretty much all of the time. Back then, people would have just called him a son of a bitch, and probably did behind his back. We didn't call him anything except Father or Sir, because most of the time we were scared to death that the wrong word would put us in the line of fire.

When he wasn't spewing venom, Father was shouting orders. "Where is the salt? I suppose the pepper mill is empty, too!" Or, "Goddamn it, MollieO, I keep you all dolled up in Chanel. Can't you clean the fucking bidet?"

Our toilets were spotless, not from MollieO's alabaster hands, but from our maid's overworked, double-strength latex gloves.

"Lupe!" MollieO would call out in as firm a voice as her soft drawl permitted. When I was little, Mother's drawl sounded quite exaggerated. But as I grew up and got used to it, I could hardly hear it. Where once I would have heard, "Ah thought Ah told y'all . . . ," now I heard, "I thought I told you to cleanse the toilette! Now look what you've done! Marty's all angry again. Damn it! Girls, hush up!"

We would sit silently, Lupe would ignore the criticism and Mother would close her eyes tight, waiting for the storm to pass.

Father did spend freely. He kept Mother up to her diamond encrusted ears in *haute couture* because his image was on the line. Their bedroom alone had three closets stuffed with her garments. One closet held nothing but fur coats. *Real* fur coats. Champagne chinchilla, blonde mink, and the nightmare of nightmares—full-length leopard skin. Despite the protests of her daughters, MollieO felt absolutely no compunction about killing cute furry animals for their skins.

"They're not like *our* babies, Binky or Big Boy or Roskolnikov. Really, girls, you make so much out of everything!"

Mother was, however, entirely devoted to her own animals. She gave them more attention than she gave us, for reasons we couldn't quite understand, but accepted. She wouldn't even let Lupe prepare food for her angels, even though the woman's culinary talents were good enough for the rest of us. MollieO herself cooked the dogs sirloin beef and basmati rice with a side dish of carrot purée.

Lupe was assigned the task of taking the dogs for their "doodle dumpies" six times a day—once between the dogs' requisite groomings, again after their bow-tying ceremony, then before their daily massages and pedicures. Out they'd go again after their mid-afternoon storytelling, an hour after dinner time, and once more before "sleepies" and discourses on the meaning of life delivered in MollieO's sweetest southern drawl.

When our huge black standard poodle Big Boy died, Mother created an elaborate altar in the living room to honor his soul. Between emotional outbursts and tears, she decorated a wreath with dog bones and miniature toys, and hung it reverently on the mantel. She lit mint candles and filled Big Boy's Hammacher Schlemmer food bowl to the brim with fresh treats. "I just know he's gonna come back," she said, "and he'll be hungry after his journey. Now y'all come sit with me in front of the fire. I just know he'll miss us. You'll see."

So I sat down on the purple velvet, overstuffed couch, folded my petite hands (all of us girls had tiny, thin hands) and patiently waited. Not so much for Big Boy's return from the grave, but for Mother to notice how my new penny loafers shined. Or how fresh I smelled in Canoe cologne. Anything for an arm around the shoulder or a loving glance. Neither was forthcoming. I told myself such desires were selfish. After all, Big Boy should be at the center of Mother's world this evening, or any evening. That's what one part of me thought.

But a more honest part fantasized how MollieO would feel if I was the one who passed away. I saw myself overdosing on fried chicken skin, onion rings and the other greasy food I hid in my closet to stave off anxiety. In my fantasy, when I did not dutifully show up for brunch, Mother would shout my name three times with great annoyance, then reluctantly climb the staircase. She'd swing my unlockable door wide open and discover me blue and bloated on the floor of my studio-sized clothes closet. "Oh, my poor darlin'!" MollieO would say, weeping uncontrollably. "What did I do wrong?" And then what? Would she create an altar in my name? And if so,

what would she set on the fireplace mantle to call *my* spirit
back?

As I returned to the land of the living, Callie's footsteps
echoed down the long hallway from her bedroom, then padded
across the lavender Persian rug. I saw with some surprise that my
sister was wearing a black armband. But then, she had genuinely
loved Big Boy. Mother made a place for Callie, cautioning, "Not
on my gown, darlin', watch where y'all sit. It's a Dior."

Maybe that was the problem, I thought to myself. She didn't
hug us because it would ruin her clothes, the clothes Father
bought her, the clothes she paid for in ways I hated to think
about. Even though I had been forced to conclude that Callie
and I weren't as important as dogs or clothes or male offspring, I
knew there must surely be some reason we'd been born, and that
we held some place in the hierarchy of my mother's needs and
desires.

That night MollieO's eyes softened as she noticed the armband, and she touched Callie's hand for just a moment. I think
that was the only time I ever felt the two of them connect, even
though Callie continued to wear the armband every day for
months. But when it came to grief or injustice, my sister always
had a greater attention span than our mother.

MollieO Bartholomew, *née* Smith, was consumed by her need
to be both beautiful and comfortable. Her life was a race to stay
ahead of memories of being born white trash in Nashville, Tennessee. According to her, she had been parented by "po' folk,"
but had never actually been one of them. "You know me, darlin'," she would say, "I'm always a cut above."

She and Aunt Lillian, her older sister, left home when
MollieO was fifteen. They hitchhiked to New York and began
their professional lives as garment workers, then tailors—but in
MollieO's case it was a short career. She was much too ambitious
and beautiful to sit in front of a sewing machine for ten hours a
day. She had full lips, perfect 32-C breasts, an eighteen-inch
waist and gorgeous legs that knew full well how to sashay across

a room. Her suggestive hips seemed to carry on a dialogue of their own with each and every admirer.

One cool September afternoon Father arrived for a fitting at his neighborhood tailor shop, and was waited on by this ambitious and enticing young thing. Who knows if it was the seduction of her drawl or the greed in her eyes, his fear about ending up alone (nobody wants to live with a rage-aholic) or his intuition that he could treat her any way he wanted and get away with it that tied this twosome together? Whatever the allure, within a month, as the copper leaves of autumn blew through Central Park, MollieO was giggling in a horse drawn carriage with Martin Bartholomew, a man who confidently announced to all that he had New York by the balls. Her kinda guy. A man who could give her everything she had been denied.

On Martin's side of the family was the Bartholomew clan, a brawling, boisterous lot who brought alcoholism and chaos here from the old country at the turn of the century. Large, ruddy-cheeked, red-haired males with determined blue eyes, and petite, repressed, freckled females moved into a seaport town in northern Massachusetts. Before you could spell cirrhosis correctly, they built a whiskey dynasty that rivaled Seagram's. Those credentials and a relentless drive for power brought the money and prestige and ruthlessness that defined my childhood.

Samuel Bartholomew, Martin's father, had come to New York as an attorney and worked his way up to Supreme Court Judge. On the way, he married an Irish girl who was half Jewish named Naomi Walker, a debutante who had become the belle of Manhattan. Naomi also happened to be a lesbian. Their union was a match made in Hades and, soon after, Father was born into an atmosphere of sexual frustration and alcohol addiction. Within a year of their betrothal, Naomi left Grandfather Samuel for a beautiful Ziegfeld Follies girl.

Before he lost his baby teeth, Martin became Samuel's sexual slave and whipping boy, destined to a childhood of verbal abuse and belt thrashings. I guess all the years of taking in his father's

anger imprinted layer upon layer of wrath on his young soul—
and relentless ambition, too. The only reason I know anything
about Father's childhood is that he confided in MollieO who
told Aunt Lillian who told me. That was the way it always was in
our family. If you wanted to know the truth, you went to Lillian.

At thirty, Martin Bartholomew was Manhattan's hardest hitting attorney. He defended the prosperous and the infamous,
anyone who could widen his outrageous reputation. Grandfather Samuel, not incidentally, was gunned down in front of
O'Flannigan's Pub on 43rd Street. Everyone who was anyone
attended his funeral, but no tears were shed.

By the time Callie and I were born, MollieO must have wondered more than once about the wisdom of the bargain she'd
made. The more diligently she designed the most opulent penthouse in all of Manhattan, the more Martin raged and whined
and disrupted our lives. We never knew when he was going to
explode or for what reason. On any ordinary day in our happy
home we could expect to watch roast beef juice drip down
the wall, or see MollieO jerked from the table by her ultra-
lacquered, sophisticated, high society "do" for overcooking the
lamb chops or forgetting the mango chutney, for Christ's sake.

"I said rare, goddamn it! PINK! Like your pretty little lips!"
He dragged her down the hall, his wing tip shoes solid against
the mahogany floors. His screaming went on for well over an
hour, and then the dreaded quiet took over our house.

"Do you think he'll kill her tonight?" I asked Callie in a
vacant voice, my hands gripped tightly over my knees.

"Unlikely," Callie said quietly. "He'll just tear her up a little."
We were always thinking in terms of dead or not dead. Naively,
we assumed that anything short of dead was preferred.

Callie's prediction was unflinchingly accurate. After Father
went down the street to buy the evening paper, we had our
chauffeur, Geoffrey, lift Mother out of her satin sheets, take her
down the service elevator to the garage and load all three of us

into the Cadillac limousine. There was something special about Geoffrey. Maybe it was his super protective, gargantuan frame— the guy was pushing six foot seven. It was uncanny how he was always there for Mother at the right moment. Once I asked Callie if he was sent to our family on a special mission, like a big blonde angel. She looked at me like I had totally lost it.

"It will be okay," he told us, masterfully navigating his way through the crowded city. "She's made it through every time before." And then he would pick her up like Rhett did Scarlett and kick open the Emergency Room doors.

The folks at the E.R. knew us well, but not as the Bartholomews. There, we were the Williams family—Meadow, Meredith and Maisie. Names with character. Callie made them up herself. Even in her semi-conscious state, MollieO would remind us, "Never tell them our real name, do you hear me? The *New York Times* would have a field day!"

Callie and I sat outside as the doctors sutured Mother's lower parts. "I can just see the front page of *The Daily News,*" Callie told me. "Manhattan Attorney Tears Up His Wife Over a Scorched Banana Flambé." She wrung her hands hard against her lap. "What an asshole! Why doesn't she ever stand up for herself?"

"Maybe she's afraid, Callie. That's why she takes all those pills."

She shrugged. "Great parents, huh? A junkie and a thug. If he does it again, I'm gonna fix his ass!"

I shuddered beneath my camel hair coat. I was eight, Callie was twelve. I knew that sooner or later she would keep that promise. That was why I loved her so.

2

THE DEED, 1953

I had always been a water baby. My earliest memories are filled with the colors and sounds of beaches and pools of all sorts. Romping in our pond and laughing at the turtles floating just below the surface, playing "froggy" as I swam through my mother's legs in the surf at Atlantic City, laughing wildly in a yellow rubber tub with Callie—all before I was big enough to hold on to both sides of the big black inner tube MollieO used to float on through all those lazy summer afternoons.

In those years the water held a special magic for me. One afternoon Callie and I were swimming in the teal waters of Key West when I had a rather "other worldly" kind of experience. She and I had been holding hands, chasing waves as they slid in and out on the sandy beach, when a mother wave rolled in and separated us, pulling me out into treacherously deep waters. Lost in a blanket of swirling sand and crushed shells, I was terrified. That is, until I felt someone very close to me whisper, *"Be still. Give into it."* The voice was soft and healing and my body surrendered to the force. When things calmed down and I could finally open my eyes, I searched for the one who had saved my little life. There was no one there. Later I told MollieO, who claimed I'd heard the very same words that she had screamed from the shore.

I could go on and on about my innocent water memories, but what matters is that those memories end abruptly at age three. Suddenly not the sea, not the shower, not even a seductive little rubber whale floating in an 8 P.M. tub could ease the repugnance I felt anytime I had to so much as stick a toe in the water. All at once my innocence had been taken, my joy swept away like so many particles of sand down the bathtub drain.

The fact that one day I simply could not enjoy the water any longer should have been the tip-off for my mother that something was terribly wrong. Of course, somewhere in my unconscious I knew my mother knew. Right after the first occurrence she secretly started cleaning the tub six and seven times a day. Our whole apartment stank of bathtub cleanser. Even now I have to leave a restaurant if I pick up the faintest whiff of bleach in the air.

There was a time when I couldn't talk about it at all, or even accurately recapture the cause of my aversion to water. The first time it all came flooding horridly back into my consciousness, I was beautiful and nineteen, standing in the shower after having "finger sex" with a boy for the first time. A razor was sitting on the edge of the tub and I remember thinking, *I think I'll cut my vagina out.* The phrase moved through me as easily as "I guess I'll call myself a cab," and yet I had never had a masochistic thought like that before. I put my hands up against the cool Italian tiles of the shower wall and closed my eyes. As I did, images surfaced of a "little me" in the tub, my father washing my neck, my chest, my belly, but not stopping there as he always had before.

My father, Martin Bartholomew, football hero, recipient of the Purple Heart, self-made millionaire, the toast of New York society. He was a man of six feet and one hundred seventy pounds who had his black hair, thick eyebrows and nose hair stragglers trimmed at the local barber shop on Lexington Avenue, where they provided the gentlemanly service of painting his square-shaped fingernails with clear polish. That was the Martin the world knew, and the Father that I loved. A neatly wrapped package that, when it came undone, could destroy lives.

Right before the deed happened, my parents had gone to Hawai'i on a business trip to a beautiful little bay on the north shore of the island of Maui. I knew Martin would bring me a great gift, but I had no idea what the ramifications would be.

They returned late one evening with souvenirs in tow. I opened the elegant box from one of Maui's finest hotels, and pulled out a green grass skirt and a miniature bra made from two coconut shells, like the one Ray Walston wore in *South Pacific.* I ran upstairs, and mother followed to help me put them on.

"Well, look at you, Billie!" she said as she tied the strings of the little bra behind my back. She put her hands on my shoulders and stood gazing at me in the big oval mirror that hung on my closet door. "You go downstairs now and show your father how absolutely precious you look. I can't wait to see his face." Then, lowering her voice, she added, "You know, he's been so wretched lately. . . ."

She took me by the hand and, like a good girl, I followed her down the stairs and back to the living room where father was waiting. As he put on Hawaiian tunes, I sat on the stool by the big leather chair, ready for my hula dance instructions to begin. He walked across the room, reached out his hand and pulled me toward him like Fred Astaire pulled Ginger, and then placed his hands on my hips. In that moment I felt safe, happy and secure. Father moved his arms in undulating patterns and helped me mimic the Hawaiian dancers. On and on I danced, closer and closer to Father, farther and farther from me.

Somewhere in the center of all the music and the movement, something in the pit of my stomach began to tighten. I felt my father's eyes watching me in a different way, an uncomfortable way. He looked hungry.

"Get ready for your bath, Billie," Father said. I heard my mother say she would give me my bath, but he told her to rest, he'd take care of it.

That was the first time in my life I felt afraid of water. I was convinced I couldn't keep my head above the surface, that I was about to drown and nobody would be there to save me.

"Please, Father," I told him with panicked eyes, "don't make me go in. Scary!"

"This is nonsense, Billie, lie back," he whispered. "I won't let anything happen to you."

But in those fifteen minutes everything happened to me, although much of me wasn't really there. I rose out of my body like my soul was heading toward heaven, free from the torturous world that lay far below. I closed my eyes and pictured an invisible world spread above me, a patchwork quilt of tangerine sky, conch shells, sea horses and little falling stars, where docile turquoise waves rolled through the center and dolphins dove just for the fun of it. There were thousands of white candles flickering through the quilted fabric where special prayers had been sewn in for people who were in need of protection. Surely one of them was for me. In the distance, I envisioned someone very gentle waiting to take me under her wing.

This was my hideout where no one could find me. I promised myself again and again that I would find my way here and walk through the door of heaven, even if it took forever.

3

ANGELS DON'T HAVE MOTHERS, 1954

It was the holiday season and the four of us were vacationing in Miami. By then Father was a phenomenal success as a high profile attorney, and he was growing richer and more respected day by day. He had serious "connections," as they used to say. So our hotel suite that night was wall to wall with famous people, movie stars, politicians, members of the Mob, and heavyweight social climbers all trying to rub elbows with The Man.

I was dressed in a pale blue sailor suit that scratched my chubby white thighs. At four years old I was much cuter than everyone else—at least that's what I was told. The problem was, I didn't feel cute. Actually, I hurt. Something was stinging between my legs, and I asked MollieO to help me.

"Mama," I said, grabbing her hand and leading her into her bathroom. I pointed to the large tube of ointment on the blue tiled counter.

"Not now, Billie!" MollieO snapped, her tone full of impatience. "I'm all dressed up, darlin'. Can't you see that? You don't want Mother to ruin her organza dress, do you? Now, get ready so we can make an appearance in front of our guests. Do you know who's down there? The mayor and the governor and the Vice President of the United States himself are down there, that's who."

She walked out to her bedroom and sat down at the wicker vanity. The ceiling fans were whirring high above the floral bed coverings. The potted palm trees in the corner swayed lazily back and forth. Everything was hot and sticky. I shuffled through the doorway and sat on MollieO's bed, watching her apply "Cherries in the Snow" to her swollen lips. Her lower eyelash was coming unglued in the heat, but she caught it delicately as it fell down her cheek. My legs were so chunky and dimpled I could barely cross them. Something down there was still stinging so it made me want to hide that area. I raced back into the bathroom, grabbed the ointment and brought it in to Mother again. I paused beside her. She was dabbing the tip of her pug nose with loose face powder that had already dusted her cleavage like new fallen snow. How beautiful she was. How regal. Her raven hair swept up into a French knot, her elegant neck and earlobes accentuated by emeralds, her tiny waist encircled by a sparkling rhinestone belt. Even her spiked pumps carried rhinestone stars at the toes.

"You can't tell I have one of those migraines, Billie, can you? I look decent, don't I?"

She picked me up in her arms and I rested my head on her bosom. She reeked of Joy perfume and lotion. I coughed and she put me down. I was still hurting, and I put my hand between my legs to show her precisely where.

"For God's sake, Billie, stop that! It's not ladylike. And how did you get that ointment again? I told you, *not now*." Mother grabbed the ointment out of my hand and tossed it onto the nightstand.

"Can't you see this is a big night for us?" She stopped and looked me straight in the eye, something I later realized she did only when she was on the edge. She grabbed me in her arms and carried me to the doorway of the living room where everyone was assembled.

Mother cleared her throat, but most everyone was too busy climbing Martin's personal influence ladder. Torch-toned lipsticks were being retrieved from tiny black beaded bags. Heavy silver lighters were flicking, and women pulled their heads back so that their slender cigarette holders could reach the flame. The mayor's wife idly poked through a carved glass bowl of melting chocolate grasshoppers as Cuban waiters in pink ruffled shirts with orange cummerbunds twirled around the guests with trays of smoked oysters, deep fried scallops, Lobster Thermidor and dark, seductive rum drinks. Cha-cha-cha.

MollieO took a deep breath and cleared her throat again. Finally someone turned toward Mother and the room began to domino in her direction.

"Good evenin', everyone. It's so lovely to see y'all," she said, working the room like Scarlett O'Hara. I was bobbing against her chest, clinging to her neck in an effort to contain my pain.

"We have a special treat tonight. My eldest daughter, Callie, has promised to sing for us in honor of our distinguished guests. Callie, where are you, sweetheart? Oh, and by the way, this is my darlin' Billie. She's rather shy." I pushed my face further into Mother's chest.

Callie emerged from the crowd in white crinoline with an open gardenia perched behind her ear. *Quelle chanteuse!* She sat at the piano that had been rented just for the occasion, extending her legs so her white patent leather shoes could reach the shiny brass pedals of the white baby grand.

Callie launched into a long introduction. Her tiny fingers were flying over the keyboard. We sat like stunned pigeons. Would this tiny starlet entertain us with a show tune? A Sinatra ballad? Something tropical in keeping with the ambiance of the party?

"This is a Bessie White original, entitled *Woman Song,*" she announced in her eight-year-old voice. Then Callie cut loose:

> *"Oh, a woman is a hard thing to be.*
> *Nothing comes her way easily.*
> *She lives in a cage*

Created by rage.
Oh, a woman is a hard thing to be."

Then, looking out at the audience, Callie shook her head and moaned, *"Lordy, Lordy. Oh, oh . . . ."*

As her fingers flew over the keys and her voice dragged sweet misery out of every note, I watched, hypnotized. The crowd began to look stiff and uncomfortable; some of the women's faces expressed recognition. I looked over at Martin who had all of a sudden begun to listen very closely. He had started toward Callie with that "I'm not going to put up with any shit" look on his face, when Mother met him half way and grabbed his hand. She was determined to avoid a scene.

By then, Callie was sweating and breaking into the second verse:

"A woman's life is a torturous thing,
Filled with a punch, a sting, and a diamond ring.
Oh, he hits her hard
And she calls him 'honey.'
She gives in to his rage
For all of that money.
Oh, a woman's life is a terrible thing."

Callie looked directly at MollieO as if to ask, "Do you hear what I'm saying?" By now a look of horror had swept around the room. One oblivious and tipsy spinster was singing grossly out of tune. MollieO couldn't calm Father any longer. He headed for Callie, who ignored his approach. *"Ohhh, ohhh,"* she moaned, searing the audience.

"Oh women, don't let your man shatter your dream,
Break your back and cause you to scream.
Choose a man who is kind,
Sweet talkin', refined.

Don't hide in your shell
Or life will be hell.
Oh, a woman is . . ."

With a lunge, MollieO interposed herself between father and daughter, pried Callie's fingers off the keyboard and rested her own hands on my sister's sunburned shoulders.

"Well," MollieO sang out in an almost shaky voice. "This daughter certainly isn't shy tonight!" Nervous laughter rippled through the crowd. Dick Nixon nodded with a tight grin.

"But she's still my angel," she told the crowd. I could see Mother's grip tighten on Callie's shoulders. It had to hurt, but Callie didn't flinch. "You are my angel, aren't you, Callie?"

Callie raised her head and replied just loud enough for MollieO's ears alone, "Angels don't have mothers." She stepped down from the piano seat, took me by the hand and we retired into the kitchen.

"Billie," asked Callie, "why do you keep touching yourself like that? What's wrong?"

"Nothing, Callie," I told her in my resigned little voice.

4

A DAY IN THE LIFE . . . EAST SIXTIES STYLE, 1955

Winter. Fall. Summer. Fall. Spring. Each crazy childhood memory meshes with the next. When you live in constant fear, that's how it is. The good blurs with the bad and you can't remember what moments of your life were wonderful, which were horrible, or whether it was all just insane. Holiday gifts may have come wrapped in gold ribbons, but the expectations that came with every box made even Santa's goodies dangerous.

It was another tense Christmas holiday, dark outside by early afternoon. We had all opened our gifts and were hiding out in our respective bedrooms, waiting for the big grandfather clock to strike the dinner hour. The embossed menu card was scrolled in Japanese style calligraphy. It read,

Merry Christmas Bartholomew Family
Lobster Bisque Laced in Brandy
Christmas Endive Salad
Poached Sole & Chablis Grapes
Soufflé Potatoes
Chocolate Truffle Cake
Mouton Cadet, Dom Perignon 1942

But, believe me, in apartment 33J there was more than one kind of soul poaching going on.

Father had dragged Callie out of her bedroom, enraged at hearing her wail along with a jazz rendition of "I'll Be Home for Christmas." He chased her around our penthouse, waving a sharp pair of scissors. Her freckled face was a blur of flushed fury and perverse laughter. After a few narrow escapes he caught her, pinned her to the wall and cut off her shiny, waist-long, auburn hair. Just what she needed—one more reason to plot her revenge.

Callie woke me up around 11 P.M. with madness blazing from her eyes. "Come with me, little sister. You can assist." My beautiful sibling resembled a Dickensian street urchin with that freshly sheared spiky hair, but her voice was absolutely clear. "Come with me," she said, pulling my little body out of my warm bed.

We tiptoed into the kitchen and Callie pulled a measuring cup off the shelf. A bone china cup fell and shattered on the Italian tile floor.

"That's one of MollieO's prize cups," I whispered sternly. "She'll be furious!"

"Mother has more china than the White House. She'll never miss it. Come on!" With Callie leading the way, we worked our way down the Persian carpeted hallway to her immense room strewn with disheveled clothing and into her black stripe wallpapered bathroom. The whole place smelled like Clearasil. Callie crouched over the toilet and began to pee. She filled the measuring cup, handed it to me and wiped herself. I was dumbfounded.

"Tomorrow morning I'm going to get up early and make breakfast like a *good girl* and when that bastard starts screaming for his freshly squeezed Valencia orange juice I'll be ready. I'm going to whip up a special blend just for him."

"No, Callie, no!" I managed to spit out. "You could kill him."

"All the better," she said giggling. And then, glancing at me, she added in a very confident tone, "Urine can't kill anyone. It's filled with nutrients. Besides, he'll never know. Run back to bed. Stop worrying."

To tell me to stop worrying was like telling one of MollieO's dogs to stop humping. It was inborn. I could worry about anything and anyone. I had a gift for it. But I also knew how to cover up, how to *lie,* a word that is part of the given name of every female in our family. Each one of us was a master of deception. We had to be.

I lay in bed sleepless, balled up in fetal position all night. I thought of the jackknife that Callie kept on top of the nightstand next to her bed, and worried that someday she would go over the edge and let loose with all that pent up rage of hers. As my mind spun out its worst case scenario, I imagined visiting Callie at Sing Sing, holding her cold, indignant hands in mine.

"I had to do it," she would confess. "Somebody had to put an end to all of that. How was the funeral? Was MollieO relieved?" Even in my dream she showed no remorse.

I lay in bed until my radio alarm clock played an old Doris Day tune, "Que Será, Será," then jumped out of bed and brushed my teeth like the actress did in the Ipana toothpaste commercial so that I, too, was a good girl.

It was 8:00 A.M. on Sunday, and Father's fingers were already smudged from the *New York Times.* Smoggy sunlight filled our canary yellow kitchen. Callie had the blender out and was squeezing orange halves in our new juicer. I climbed onto a step stool and peered into the bright, pulpy liquid.

"Is it in there already?" I whispered.

"Not yet. It has to be just the right moment." Callie looked at her junior Cartier watch, took a breath, and said, "NOW!"

Into the blender she poured the juice, accompanied by the cloudy, acidic, lemony liquid. She covered the mixture and pressed a button, and the blender whipped the juice into a frothy smoothie. Callie took off the top and sniffed. "Here," she said, tipping the blender in my direction. But I refrained. It was just too gross.

"Girls!" MollieO shouted, "Where's Father's juice?"

When there was no immediate response, she twirled through the kitchen door like Loretta Young. She was decked out in a hot pink negligee with ostrich feathers lining the V-neck. She flitted around the kitchen hyper as hell, the way she usually was in the beginning stage of a migraine.

"C'mon girls, get the glasses! Chop! Chop!" Her voice was filled with tension. A breakfast delayed two minutes could prove to be devastating for everyone involved.

Lupe increased her pace as she whipped up pecan waffles and eggs scrambled with heavy cream. Callie carried the crystal pitcher of juice into the dining room where silver bowls of fresh strawberries and blueberries, maple syrup and peach preserves glistened on the mahogany table. The fragrance of thick sliced bacon hung in the air. MollieO, Callie and I waited patiently like three good girls while Martin sat fortressed behind the newspaper. My heart was beating out of my chest.

Finally, Callie said, "Well, I'll pour Father's orange juice." She picked up the pitcher and filled his silver goblet.

I watched, transfixed, as Father took a good long drink. Then, prepared to flinch at the sound of his six-foot frame hitting the rug, I waited for his face to contort. I closed my eyes, but there was no thud from the floor. My eyes popped open again at the sound of his voice.

"Terrific, Callie!" Martin smiled approvingly. "Mmm, wonderful. Pour me some more."

I was speechless.

"Darlin'," MollieO gleefully joined in, lifting a long thin arm in Callie's direction, "If it's that good, pour me some, too. I'll take it with my Phenobarbital."

Callie looked over at me, and I looked at the floor. "Mother, I don't think orange juice is a good thing to take for migraines."

"Nonsense. My immune system can always use a boost. I don't have allergies like you girls do."

Her delight in her revenge suddenly deflated, Callie poured the concoction and MollieO swigged it down. She was taken with the flavor as well. Breakfast was declared a success.

Callie got up to leave the table but Martin reached out to take her arm. "It looks like I got a little carried away with the scissors, Callie," he said in a surprisingly vulnerable voice. "I'm sorry. You're becoming quite a pretty young girl. I know that how you look is very important to a person your age. Mother," he said, cutting into a runny egg, "Callie needs a little cleaning up. Take her into the Salon Fantastique. They'll know what to do with her."

By this time the Phenobarbital had kicked in, and MollieO could hardly hear Father. She nodded, smiled and excused herself from the table. We heard her instructing Lupe to draw the velvet curtains shut and pull down the velvet spread. And that was the end of the entire incident.

But Father's benevolent mood continued through the rest of the morning. He was like that, enraged one moment and then ashamed the next. It would have been so much easier to hate him if he had been a one-dimensional psychopath, but of course, no one is. After a scene Martin often tried to patch things up with expensive gifts, trips abroad or some such startling act of generosity. He'd turned tail on me plenty of times. Once in a while, after a particularly ravaging late night visit, he would unexpectedly enter my room during homework time and ask with genuine interest how I was doing. He would offer suggestions and let me know that if I graduated with good grades I would secure the education to create any career I wanted. That nothing could stop me, I was destined for great things. Part of me listened and was grateful for the encouragement and the attention. Another part was resistant to every syllable he spoke. After all, this was the same man who entered my room at other times, for other reasons.

MollieO, on the other hand, was remarkably consistent in her malaise. Almost every day of our lives she reclined in the cool silk sheets for hours, her face twisted by the pain of a horrible migraine. I would sit at her side before and after school and hold her hand. There wasn't much else I could do. I worried, and I felt helpless to make her suffering go away.

As I got older, when my mother's moaning got unbearable, I would go through the marble-topped bathroom cabinets looking for a miracle drug in the stacks of prescription bottles. My mother's personal stash rivaled any pharmacy in town, an attribute that stayed with her pretty much all her life. Years after the hysterectomy that abruptly ended her thirty-year bout with migraines, Mother came to stay with me for a weekend and brought two big Louis Vuitton suitcases with her. She hung up her pastel Dior skirts and Chanel suits while I opened the other bag. It was lined with sixty or seventy plastic pill bottles.

"What's all this?" I said, unable to conceal my panic. The number of pills was appalling.

"Well, you know very well what 'this' is. This is my arsenal against illness."

"But there's stuff in here for arthritis. Do you have arthritis?"

"No, darlin', I don't," she said cheerfully.

"And there are six bottles of tranquilizers. Why do you have all of these brochures on cancer, Mother?" I made myself take a deep breath. "Is there something you're not telling me? Do you have cancer? Are you in pain?"

"No, Billie," she replied, tossing some of the bottles in the air, catching them perfectly in her outstretched hands. "And with all of these I never will."

5

AROUND MIDNIGHT, 1957

I hated the darkness of my room around midnight when I felt helpless and totally alone. My bedroom was at the far end of our apartment, a perfect setup for Father's clandestine activities. I never knew when he would appear, so there was no such thing as relaxing into sleep. No matter what time it was, I was always half awake. I would lie crunched up in a ball, part of me envisioning fighting him off the way Callie might have if she had been the chosen one. Another part of me, more like MollieO, would just give in, surrendering to the event.

One night after Father had finished and quietly shut my door, a miracle happened. "Mama," I cried to myself, "Mama, please help me." The door opened, and I looked up to see a figure walking toward me. I shuddered, thinking it was Father again. But when the person turned to close the door, I noticed the faintest scent of blossoms like those pale pink flowers woven into the lei Father had brought me from Maui. Sweet and welcoming.

At first, as the body moved toward me it seemed different, somewhat translucent, like a piece of silk billowing in the wind. Royal purple silk. Shimmering.

As she moved closer, but still halfway in the shadows, I began to make out the face of our housekeeper, Lupe Martinez.

MollieO had changed Lupe's schedule a few days before, and now this gentle woman cast her protective presence on our darkened house.

"Oh, my poor baby," Lupe whispered, climbing into bed next to me. "Come here." She opened her warm, brown arms to me, arms that were soft as doeskin. I was still scared and somewhat removed from reality. I let her arms encircle me. I let her strong hands stroke my hair.

"I know what's going on. I seen him coming in here. I follow him down the hall. I hear his sounds. Poor baby."

Lupe began to rock me and I gave in and sobbed. "Going to be okay," she told me. "He's no going to hurt you no more. I know he hurt your Mother too, but she don't want no help."

We stayed like this and I felt myself slowly returning to my body. But along with my recovery came anxiety.

"What are you going to do, Lupe?" I asked, troubled. I was scared that she would tell Father, and MollieO and I would have to pay.

"Don't worry, little one. I know what to do. You rest now while I clean you up."

Lupe let go of me slowly and went into my bathroom, returning with several washcloths. She delicately removed a necklace from around her neck and opened a little jade bottle that had hung there like an amulet. Then she opened the bottle and poured some liquid onto the cloths. Pulling the covers back, she placed one cloth across my forehead, another over my chest and a third on my belly. Gently she dabbed my cheeks and lips with another warm cloth. She paused to pour out a bit more liquid, then passed the cloth over my neck and down my tiny shoulders. Softly she patted my bony, little girl ribs as I inhaled the scent of ambrosia, honey, lemon blossoms and nectar.

"Do you hurt down there, baby?"

I nodded.

"Would you like a warm cloth down there, too?"

I nodded again. This time she handed it to me.

"You do this one," she said protectively. I took a hold of the towel and opened my legs. I let the healing warmth sink in. Lupe continued to stroke my cheek, reassuring me that my father would never hurt me again. Her confident voice guided me into sleep.

A few days later Lupe was dismissed from her position. I had seen her go into father's library and close the door. There were no loud words. I guess Lupe threatened to call the authorities if he didn't stop, so he fired her. We were later told that Lupe had stolen one of MollieO's ruby rings, but that out of the kindness of his heart Martin had decided not to prosecute.

Lupe had done her job well. Martin never approached me sexually again. He looked a lot, though. Shortly after, MollieO complained about the music that Callie played all day long, and my sister's bedroom was switched to the little den next to mine. I could breathe again.

6

A DAY AT THE RACES, 1958

If only I could have settled for just plain hating my father, I might have gotten by with some semblance of trust intact. But it wasn't that simple. The same man who trampled my spirit on those dark nights and terrorized the whole family on his worst afternoons, could also put a light in his little girl's eyes when he turned on the charm.

When I was very little, Martin was my man of the hour who taught me to smile like an angel, fly courageously through the air on our terrace swing and jump from the high dive twenty feet down into the sky-blue pool. Even as I grew older he could still charm me. One of the happiest times ever was the day he gave me my first camera, a Brownie. It was a rare golden moment when he was also able to give me something I actually needed.

After I took the little dark brown camera out of its elaborate wrappings, Martin suggested that we all go out to the racetrack, that he had another surprise for us. Going anywhere public was always a mixed bag for me, because Father would often say and do inappropriate things to "his little thoroughbred" in front of his society friends. Then again, sometimes he would treat me like I was the most precious commodity on earth. So that day, as usual, my emotions were churning around in my belly like they had been loaded into our brand new Maytag washing machine.

"Sit up straight," Father commanded in the car. I tried to gain confidence as I pulled my shoulders back. My hands were perspiring on the camera. Finally I told him I wasn't sure I could take a good picture. "Nonsense," he told me. "You are beautiful and smart and you're a Bartholomew. And, you're *my* little girl. You can do *anything*. Do you understand me?"

As we sped through the city, the scenery changed drastically. Gone were the skyscrapers and prestigious high-rise apartment buildings, and in their place came burned-out looking housing structures—"tenements," Martin called them.

"You see," he told us, pointing out the window, "you give these burrheads a nice place to live and they destroy it. A new refrigerator . . . a stove . . . within weeks they've ruined it. Poor ignorant sons-of-bitches! Girls, you've sure got it good, don't you?"

Father continued on but I no longer heard what he was saying. Our limo had slowed down as it crossed the bridge, and I focused in on two small children sitting alone on a tenement building fire escape some one hundred feet away. Their skin was shining purple black against the white of their diapers. One of the baby's plump legs dangled through an open slat. They looked so joyful playing in their dismal surroundings. I positioned my Brownie to capture that feeling, but the car picked up speed and moved on before I heard the shutter open.

When we arrived at the track, Father was excited as hell. He loved the track and, in turn, everybody there loved him back. "Come on, come on! Get out of the car!" he said with growing impatience. "We haven't got all day!"

So MollieO and Callie and I ducked our heads so we wouldn't flatten our bobbypin curls on the roof of the limo, and Geoffrey's grey silk driving gloves gallantly pulled us from the car. "I'll be right here, waiting for you," he assured us.

Father was way ahead, trading tips and shaking the hands of other big time gamblers. Then he stopped and, tapping on his watch, looked back at us with disdain.

"Looks like a great day for a winner like you, Mr. Bartholomew!" an older man said with a wink as he passed Father the *Racing Form*. I saw Martin hand the gent a one-hundred-dollar tip.

"C'mon girls! We're going down below to the paddock area. I have someone very important for you to meet."

A light rain had turned the sawdust-covered walkway into a soggy path. "My Lord!" MollieO squealed as her red high heel pumps sank down into the wet brown earth. Callie and I were much better off in our shit brown loafers. The air was ripe with hay and horse droppings as we sloshed our way into a little clubhouse area. Martin opened the door and suddenly we were immersed in a room full of pint-sized guys.

"These fellows are world-class jockeys, girls. Men of discipline, courage. Men of grit and dignity."

Men of my eight-year-old stature, I thought.

"This is Jocko Juarez. Over here, Tommy Flannigan," Father continued in a delighted manner. All in all, seventeen miniature riders were introduced and each one dutifully put his callused hands into ours. The only really cute one of the group put his arm too tightly around my shoulders, which visibly upset Martin. Apparently only he was allowed to touch us. Somewhere a splintered feeling was registered in me; I realized that I felt far more at ease with the jockey. Father quickly ushered us away.

"Now we're going some place very different, where you have to be very quiet. So I don't want to hear any bitching or whining from any of you!"

We walked outside again, and felt the warm sun breaking through the clouds and the nervous energy of the horses waiting to race. Their coats looked so shiny and clean. A big black thoroughbred with massive sexual apparatus reared up as we walked by. "My Lord," MollieO shrieked again.

We continued to follow Martin, past the stadium, down the road to the stable area. He asked us to wait outside while he went on ahead. A moment later he reappeared and motioned us in. The four of us crouched against the wall and watched Father's thoroughbred, Moulin Noir, cleaning up her brand new foal. I had never seen anything so vulnerable, so new.

"Take a snapshot of her standing up," Martin said to me. "There's good light coming through the window over there. You need the light so the picture will pick up the innocence of the moment. Go on, Billie, you can do it."

I tiptoed around the stall until I found what I guessed was the proper lighting. I squatted and pressed the little brown button down. It clicked. "Now turn the little dial so you can take another," Father instructed me. "And this time you decide what would make a good picture, what kind of pose would tell the story. With your 'Bartholomew eye' and your new camera, you can tell a great story."

I straightened my shoulders and stood a little taller as I snapped one picture, then another and another. Martin watched, smiling, encouraging, and something way down inside of me started to breathe.

And besides, Martin was right about this photography thing. There was definitely something to it. In the years that passed I became a student of great photography, devouring books by Steiglitz and Cartier-Bresson and, later, Annie Leibowitz and experimental West Coast artists. At first, photography was merely a device to fill time while Callie was away at school. But somewhere in my late teens, I began to relax and enjoy my own artistic eye and the silent statement that accompanied it. In my senior year I actually won first place at the Art League for my study on uppity-looking, East Side women hailing cabs. I called it, "Risky Business." Martin was pleased indeed.

7

A CHARMED LIFE, 1960

"What's this?" I asked nonchalantly. I was rummaging through my mother's top dresser drawer, looking for lingerie to go with her pale mauve silk blouse. "What's this beautiful thing with feathers doing mixed in with your panties?"

With an ice bag propped up against her head and another under her neck, MollieO was in serious pain. Cucumber slices covered her eyes. I had heard that sometimes with migraines you can't even talk. That was never the case with MollieO.

"Put that down!" she hollered, investing her voice with plenty of authority. "Just take out my undergarments and get out of my business!"

"Yes, MollieO," I responded in my good girl tone. I carefully placed the leather feathered thing at the very bottom of her undies so it wouldn't break, knowing that later when she was getting her daily massage I would sneak a closer look.

Weeks passed. It was late December and the prospect of another Christmas hung over us like a spider's web. MollieO distracted herself by indulging the canine portion of the family. She marched me through the Prestigious Puppy Pet Store, tossing various gourmet stocking gifts for her precious ones into the cart. The bill came to well over five hundred dollars, which, back in the 'sixties, was a whole lot of chewies.

Later we wrapped each toy in purple and gold (the Bartholomew Christmas motif) and stuffed each stocking to the top. It turned out we were short on gifts for Roskolnikov, until MollieO remembered that she had bought herself a tiny golden heart at Tiffany's. Now it seemed perfect as another gift for her four-legged boy. She directed me to one of six jewelry boxes.

"Not the Harry Winston, Billie. Monsieur Poodle's not about to get my diamonds!" she said in an oddly giddy voice. "Bring me my Tiffany box. You know, the one that's got my charm bracelets."

I picked up the silk box, felt the weight of the charms, and slid it over to MollieO who was lying back against her monogrammed pillows.

"Come here, darlin'. Sit down next to me and I'll show you the treasures of my early life." Slowly she fingered the intertwined bracelets, methodically freeing them from each other. "I'm so glad I bought these charms in my later years. They make my childhood seem so much more . . . uplifting."

"Here it is!" she began excitedly. "My high school megaphone. Isn't it adorable? And right next to it, look, my cat, Sinner. All of these are mementos of my senior year. Here's a miniature fan—it was dreadfully hot—and this is a diploma! Oh Billie, what fun this is! Look, here's my baby bracelet. And what have we got here?"

I listened as MollieO did her "Show & Tell" for me. My mother was utterly fascinated by her own life.

"Now, this little bitty charm is a miniature mansion like I always dreamed about when I was your age. We were poor, Lord knows, but we did dream! You know, you set an intention of what you want and draw it back like an arrow and shoot—well, look what you get." MollieO opened her arms to embrace her lavish life. "Who'd a thought I'd end up with all this?" She placed the bracelet back in the box and I returned it to the drawer.

"You forgot this, Mother. The circle with the feathers." I lifted it up.

"Oh, it's just a silly thing, really. Doesn't mean anything. I suppose Grandma Liz Beth wanted me to feel light as a feather. I don't really know. Never thought about it much."

She continued to search for the tiny heart charm that was meant to grace Roskolnikov's stocking, but her demeanor was suddenly different—closed, like her Tiffany box.

8

GET IT ANY WAY YOU CAN, 1963

Gwennie Stonington, Missy Beard and Georgina Jones-Wood waited for me by the seventh grade classroom clothes closet. Ever since the private school boys had voted me "Most Popular Teenage Girl," these three ladies had been showering me with attention.

"You think you're so smart, don't you?" Missy said while the three of them pushed me into the closet. "Well, you're not. You're not smart at all and you don't belong here. You're not pretty, either. Your legs are chunky and your hairstyle is gross."

Gwennie pushed my face back further into the coat hangers. "But the worst thing," she said, lowering her whining voice, "is that my mom says your father is a Jew. Is that true, Miss Popularity? Are you a stinky old Jew?"

Georgina looked appalled. "I never saw a Jew before." She paused and smiled a demonic grin. "Is it true? Do you really have a tail? Show us your tail, Billie!"

They all started laughing. I kept my head immersed in the coats and jackets.

"That makes a lot of sense," Missy continued. "I've heard that Jews are cheap and cheat on their friends to get what they want the way you cheated on us by trying to steal our boyfriends. Cheap and greedy."

"Cheap and greedy, cheap and greedy!" they chanted.

"If you ever look at my boyfriend again," Missie threatened, "I'll knock your stupid teeth out."

"Me, too," Gwennie said. "And we'll see how your fancy-pants mother likes that, *Darlin'*!"

The bell rang and they walked off to French class smug and satisfied. I climbed out of the closet and into the number one position of Manhattan's Most Popular Girl for one more year. Apparently nothing or no one could stop a greedy, uptown, white trash Jewish-American princess.

9

A WORLD WITHOUT CHAOS, 1964

There are very few things I'm sure of, but one of them is this: If there is such a thing as reincarnation, I'm coming back as a jazz singer. A sexy, soft-skinned chanteuse who can sing the hell out of Antonio Carlos Jobim, Cole Porter, Nina Simone. A passionate, deep-souled goddess draped in a sparkling midnight blue gown. A throaty ambassadress of things that matter, like new love, old love, abandoned love, imagined love, everything that has to do with the experience and thrill of connection.

As for this lifetime, I decided I wouldn't be a singer because that was Callie's domain, and I wouldn't do anything to mess that up. Besides, she was so damn good. When the director of her choral group wrote MollieO about Callie's "astonishing talent and range," MollieO got right on the phone to Manhattan's most celebrated voice teacher and signed her up for summer school. Nothing was too good for a Bartholomew.

Self-effacing as always, I watched it all unfold with my stomach churning. Of course I was happy that Callie could go after her dream, considering all she had been through. But I hated the thought of spending the summer pretty much without her. When you come from a family where insanity reigns day and night, you learn to live in the future, where things are bound to be better. Callie was my ally, and I had already planned a ton of activities to keep us out of the house and away from our father.

Late that spring, before the voice lessons started and Callie began easing into a world that didn't include me, we took a walk one afternoon to the Museum of Modern Art to gaze at the Gauguin girls.

"Aren't they exquisite?" she commented after a long silence. "Can you imagine what it would be like to live there? God, what would it be like to walk around bare breasted without being afraid of verbal attacks on your 'tiny titties'?"

I cringed, remembering how Martin never missed an opportunity to draw attention to our developing breasts whenever, wherever the mood struck him. Whether we were seated at the dinner table or standing around the pool on vacation, it didn't matter. It was always enough to make us squirm and blush until our faces turned hot. MollieO always giggled as if it was all in good fun, but we knew Martin got a real kick out of humiliating us.

"What must it be like to live in such a simple world? A world without chaos." Callie's eyes got that dreamy look.

I said the first words that came into my head. "A safe world."

She took my hand and squeezed it tightly. "It seems so far away, doesn't it, Billie? But remember we will always have each other. You can count on me to be there for you."

I wanted to believe her, but I knew her singing was going to deliver her from Bartholomew hell, leaving me to my job as MollieO's full-time nurse. I fantasized about spending summer nights with Callie at Birdland or the Village Vanguard jazz club, but I knew my parents would never let that happen. Besides, I was too young to get into any of those hangouts anyway. In my heart, I realized that Callie would soon be off taking lessons and singing her heart out, but it would be a solo act with no part for a kid sister.

That summer played out the way I thought it would. I was probably the only fourteen-year-old in Manhattan who would choose Nina Simone singing "Strange Fruit" over the warblings of Paul McCartney. Callie had taught me well.

The down side was that Martin hated my taste in music and made one big scene after another over my selections. I'd be lying on my bed petting Bijou, MollieO's newest Pekingese, lost in some Ella or Sarah or Billie H., when Martin would burst into my room and scratch the needle over the vinyl, then rip the record off the spindle and hurl it against the wall.

"No daughter of mine is going to listen to some colored girl singing a song like that," he'd roar, his face twisted into a scary caricature of rage, the veins in his neck bulging. "I don't spend thousands of dollars a year on that lousy finishing school so you can undo everything you've learned listening to this crap!"

And I'd been so sure that this was going to be my summer. I'm sure if I had begged Callie not to be gone all of the time she would have given up her dream. She loved me that much. But I never asked. Not asking was safer. If you didn't ask, you couldn't get shot down, humiliated or disappointed. Besides, I'd already seen what expressing one's wishes and desires had gotten my mother.

I guess MollieO understood Callie fairly well in some ways, even though she never spent any time with her. Or maybe she simply knew when to give up. Championing her children was not MollieO's strong suit. That would have taken time, empathy and a display of unselfish love that wasn't part of her makeup. She had a bottom line of sorts, a way she established her priorities. Basically, she wasn't interested in any activity or cause unless it brought her immediate prestige or comfort.

Meanwhile, Callie stole a thousand dollars out of Martin's money clip without a second's hesitation and bought a top of the line tape recorder to practice on. And did she practice! I've never known anyone who wanted anything as much. Day and night her scatting, strutting, whining and purring seeped through the wall of our adjoining bedrooms. My sister was obsessed with jazz—steaming stuff that filled your soul and wrenched something out of your guts every time you heard it. Now and again she would surprise me by doing a really good Doris Day imitation. But no matter what the genre, all of the lyrics had one common theme—sadness. Even when they weren't really meant to be sad, that's how the words came out of her, as if transformed by their journey from her heart to her throat. Callie sang her pain. For her, every song was the blues.

That summer my sister stayed out of Martin's way, but she kept at her dream. And I hung on every word of every song she sang. I had no dreams of my own; hers filled up a few of my empty spaces.

By summer's end, Callie had mastered dozens of jazz classics. Her plan was to finish her senior year of prep school the following June and be in Greenwich Village by July, singing her heart out. She was driven, and there was something else that I had never seen before. She was happy. Even her bedroom reflected her new mood. Every item of clothing was put away, stacked or hung up in perfect symmetry. For the first time even the drapes were drawn back and sunlight was streaming in through her windows.

While she was away at summer school, I often sat in her room, remembering our Gauguin era of cherry cokes and hot, greasy fries at Stearn's and afternoons spent watching one movie after another. We had thoroughly enjoyed *Tom Jones* no less than twenty-three times. Callie wasn't much into white American men, but she had a real thing for Albert Finney. And José Feliciano. And Smokey Robinson.

I looked up at the poster hanging on the wall of Callie's bedroom and stared into Miles Davis' eyes. I saw the artist's fear and perseverance, his rebellion and his pain. I could guess why Callie was so drawn to Miles. He was a genius who defied the times and said and did exactly what his heart told him he was meant to do.

My sister and I had spent hours discussing the mistreatment of minorities while the "housekeeper of the week" served us petit fours and jasmine tea. We fantasized about how someday we were going to speak up and work to change things. Somehow those talks helped stem the tide of oppression and injustice in our own crazy lives.

10

UPTOWN HOMELESS, 1964

As we sashayed arm in arm down Fifth Avenue in our silky flower print dresses, Callie was scatting her head off. My sister had just returned from her first trip to Europe and her feet were fifteen thousand miles off the pavement.

"One of these days I'm going to move there, Billie," she told me. I felt my heart dive into my calfskin pumps. What could I tell her about my plea, the one that immediately welled up in my soul? *Please don't leave! You're all I have! Take me with you, okay?* Being far away at boarding school was bad enough, but now she would be traveling abroad for long periods of time.

Instead I nodded. "Yes," I said confidently. "Of course. You gotta do what you gotta do."

Callie was right in the middle of describing how Paris devoured jazz, when she stopped and looked away from me.

"What's wrong?" I asked, tuned in to her every move.

"In Europe you'd never see this," she muttered, gazing at a man lying on the ground in a department store entryway. "Over there they take care of their own. Here nobody gives a shit. We just keep assuming it could never happen to us."

"What's someone like that doing way up here?" I asked. "He belongs in the Bowery, or in one of those shelters MollieO gets so upset about."

I looked at the man's rubbery face smeared with the city. It was strange to see poverty in our neighborhood; we were not used to stepping over the poor. The East Sixties mostly offered up degenerates and felons, none of whom looked the least bit hungry.

Take Peter the Pencil Penis Pervert, who used to greet us on the corner just down the block from our apartment building on our way home from school.

"Hey, whatcha doin'? Whatcha doin', girls?" he would ask in a super friendly voice. Then he would pull out his cigarette-sized penis and say, "Ever see one of these? Did ya?"

Even after the tenth time, I still registered panic, but Callie stayed calm. I think she was enjoying herself. One day she went on the attack.

"As a matter of fact, I have, on my four-year-old cousin, Ralphie," she told him, waving her little finger in the air. "His is *teeny* like yours. TEENY!"

"O-o-o-o-h!" Peter wailed, running down the block. "O-o-o-o-h!!!!"

"Where do you think he's going?" I asked. Despite my fear and distaste, my budding caretaker self was already worrying that we had irreparably hurt the flasher's feelings.

"What do you care?" Callie said, setting up the joke. "You're not secretly attracted to him are you?" And then, waving her little finger once more, she teased, "I mean, you don't want to suck on it do you?"

"O-o-o-o-h, ick!" We shrieked with laughter and ran toward our lobby's revolving door.

Our neighborhood also had its share of construction workers who barked out obscenities like wild dogs. "Hey, prrreetty dolly!" they jeered. "Want to come home with me?"

Always wanting to please everybody (even schmucks and nut cases), I smiled meekly while trying to get out of their range. In my naiveté I tended to group together all people with inappropriate behavior. But there was one character in particular out of the legions of untouchables that Manhattan spawned. She got inside me and destroyed my sleep for more nights than I ever would have guessed.

Every Tuesday after school I took the bus to visit my Aunt Lillian and rode past the New York City Library on the way. I don't know why, but that building always made me feel safe. Perhaps it was the two massive lions who flanked the front doors. I loved seeing them stand guard as the bus passed by, and always favored them with a nod.

It was on one of those Tuesday afternoons, when I was excited about hanging out with MollieO's eccentric sister, that I first encountered the red-haired girl. I had chosen a seat alone and was hoping as hard as I could that no one would sit next to me. It irritated me the way some people sat down and touched my elbows and stared at my camel hair coat. They breathed close to my ear as if to say, "Can I have a piece of you? Can I?" It gave me the shivers.

I was lucky that day and had the torn, lumpy seat all to myself as we approached those giant stone cats. As the bus edged closer and the exit door moaned open, my eyes caught a remarkable scene. There, propped against the female lion, sat a beautiful young woman with firey red hair streaked with gold. Her head was tilted back, resting against the lion's torso, her face taking in the sun. Her skin was light brown, and I wondered if she was from Rio or some other country far away. What a beautiful girl! So exotic. My eyes traveled down her giraffe-like neck. She must be a ballet dancer, I thought. Or an actress. She seemed so . . . dramatic. My eyes moved down to her tee-shirt, with its sleeves rolled all the way up to her shoulders, and her bright red skirt billowing in the winter wind.

As I continued my inventory, suddenly I felt my stomach fill with acid. *It can't be!* I thought my eyes must be fooling me. Surely this beautiful girl could not intentionally be exposing herself to all of Manhattan! I looked, and then looked again. My eyes were riveted on her thighs spread-eagle before me, and her dark mons veneris exposed like the entrance to the Holland Tunnel. I could not tear my gaze away.

The bus began to move and picked up speed as my mind raced for an explanation. *It must have been syphilis that's made her mad,* I fantasized. *Or maybe her parents died in a plane crash. I wonder if she had a bad love affair that took her over the edge of sanity. Or maybe one of her parents molested her.*

I walked slowly from the bus stop and sat for a while on the front stoop of Aunt Lillian's apartment house, ignoring the cold seeping in between the folds of my coat. The vivid image of the red-haired girl still floated in my mind, disturbing a sense of order that meant more to me than I'd realized. It had never occurred to me before that someone young and beautiful could end up like the girl in front of the library. All at once I felt a frightening and reluctant kinship with people I'd always dismissed as "unfortunate." If it could happen to her. . . . *Oh God,* I prayed as I sat on the cold concrete. *Don't let that happen to me.*

Lillian's hair was pulled into a tight braid that rested in the center of her back. Her dark hair was so thick that the braid never seemed to move; it just rested there in a peaceful way. I liked to hold it in my hand, but after awhile it reminded me of the rope we had to climb in gym class. If I let myself go there, I could actually feel the burn as I awkwardly slid down the rope. Nobody liked that damn thing except Senator Nichol's daughter KiKi, and she was a freak. Mostly all the girls in my gym class were proud of their petite, feminine hands. Strong hands and arms would not be attractive to the smallish prep school or private school boys that eagerly waited to be our partners at the cotillion dances. But KiKi practiced on the ropes every chance she could. Uncomfortable with her upper body strength, we snubbed her and wrote her off as a major lesbian.

I was always surprised when MollieO allowed me to visit "The Kook," "No Million Lillian," "Auntie No Brainer," "She who reeks of incense and myrrh." And on and on. For as long as I could remember, MollieO had let us know that she was ashamed of her sister. Calling Lillian a kook was as absurd as calling MollieO a spiritual leader. They were more like twins who embodied opposite qualities. I imagined them as children playing in the cool forests of Tennessee. "You be the light and I'll be the dark," Lillian would say. "Later, you can be the moon and I'll be the sun." Many years later when MollieO started to get her headaches, Lillian dutifully traveled uptown to bring her Chinese herbs.

"Tastes like swamp juice," MollieO would wail. "You don't expect me to drink this swill, do you? Really, Lil." But Lillian showed up anyway.

Lillian was way ahead of her time. She had been married at an early age to a poet who moonlighted as a magician, who had died suddenly of cancer. During the late stages of his illness, Aunt Lillian had discovered occult philosophy and metaphysics. The handmade shelf in her minuscule red bathroom was crammed with titles like *Zen and Cancer, The Art of Metaphysics, American Indian Spirit Guides, A Layman's Guide to Homeopathy, Land of Lemuria* and book after book about Edgar Cayce. My aunt's living room was wall-to-wall books on meditation, psychic surgery, and Eastern religions—subjects that made MollieO shriek with sardonic delight. MollieO said Lillian was too far out for the rest of the planet. A born nut. In my desperate need to trust my mother in some area of my life, I chose to believe her. So I peeked at the illustrations and tried to ignore the text in all those books. That way I wasn't lying when I told MollieO that I didn't really pay any attention to all that "nonsense."

During this particular visit, Lillian was busy canning peach preserves, my absolute favorite, so I decided to forego the literature in favor of the warm, happy kitchen. "Here, honey," she said, passing me a piece of nine-grain toast topped with a thin layer of cream cheese and a mound of the warm, sweet preserves. Wonder Bread was absent from her household, along with Velveeta cheese, Hellman's mayonnaise, Peter Pan peanut butter, and gherkin pickles. I was secretly hoping that Lillian had layered a super gooey eggplant casserole and that it was waiting in her tiny oven ready to drip all over everything.

"How's things at home?" Lillian asked.

You mean, "How are things at home," I thought. MollieO may have sometimes sounded like a hick with her southern drawl, but she never made a grammatical error. Why was I so proud of that? I shook the question out of my head.

"Things?" I said, shrugging. "Pretty much the same, I guess. Got any peanut butter?"

Her stainless steel knife dipped into healthy almond butter, and I began to forget the woman at the library. Nothing helped me stamp out unpleasant thoughts like good food, especially the greasy, salty kind like gooey casseroles, crisp roast beef fat, fried chicken skin, or mashed potatoes with butter and sour cream. Unfortunately, those foods never graced either Lillian's table or ours. But at least Lillian's food was simple and edible.

"Want another sandwich, Billie? You seem starved."

"Yes," I admitted. "May I have two?"

"MollieO still feeding you that highfalutin stuff she calls food?" Lillian asked playfully. "Like that *rat*-a-pa-too-ey?" She laughed over her intentional mispronunciation. "Makes me wanna retch! That's not food for a child. You need nurturing. Lower middle class, healthy soul food, and honey, this is it."

I loved Lillian's unpolished face. She was three years older than MollieO, but looked a century younger.

"No makeup and plenty of cold cream." She had shown me her regimen during one of our overnights. "Just keep plastering it on daily." At the time, she looked as if she had been hit squarely in the face with a key lime pie, which made it hard to take her advice seriously.

"Well, lovey, it works," she said, reading the embarrassment on my face. "Now don't be like your Mother," she said, folding her lips into an exaggerated pout until I broke out laughing.

"There's my girl!"

I'd headed for Aunt Lillian's that Tuesday with an agenda. I was pretty sure she could answer my questions about the strange item hidden in Mother's dresser drawer—if only I dared ask. I cleared my throat several times. The questions I had for her were important to me, but I couldn't help feeling guilty, as if I was somehow betraying MollieO. Besides, the image of the red-haired girl on display in front of the library was stuck in my mind, scattering my thoughts like a wind-blown pile of leaves. I had no idea where to begin.

"So what is it?" Lillian intuited my pent up questions before I'd even begun. "You've been fidgety ever since you walked through that door. You know you can ask me just anything at all, honey. Don't you?"

"I suppose so," I said and then paused. I decided to work up to the MollieO questions by asking Lillian first about something a little less close to home. "Today, on the bus coming here, I saw this girl sitting in front of the library. She was so beautiful! When the bus stopped I saw that she was doing this terrible thing." I paused again. "She had her legs open and didn't have any underpants on. Lillian, why would a girl do that? What happened to her?"

"I can see how shook up you are," Lillian said, taking a hold of my trembling hand. "That must have been a terrible thing to see. It breaks my heart to see some women on the street. I wouldn't pretend to tell you that I have any answers, neither. But just 'cause she's pretty or smart doesn't mean she's gonna turn out okay. You just can't account for what goes on in somebody's family, inside their home.

"Take my family when I was growing up. Our Mama was sweet as the day is long. Kind. But she spent her life tending to

Grampa George who was always sickly. Mama just plain had no ambition. Now, MollieO hated that. Hated it! She scolded Mama and made her feel bad. But Mama just wanted to love people and make them feel better. She didn't care about money or society or none of that. You'd have thought that some of that kindness would've rubbed off on MollieO. But you see? You never know how somebody's gonna turn out.

"And don't think I don't worry about you. I know it's got to be hell living with that demonic father of yours! If he ever touches you or Callie or MollieO, you come and tell me, okay?"

I looked out the window.

"You hear me, Billie?"

"Yes, Lillian, I hear you." *I hear you and I want to tell you everything, but I can't. I can't because I'm afraid to even think about the things Father does to Mother and Callie and me, let alone hear myself say the words out loud. I'm afraid of what it would feel like if I even started to talk about it.* At that point I wasn't even conscious of the worst of what Martin had done to me. There was no chance I could let Aunt Lillian help me.

"I may worry, but I also know a child can come from terrible, awful circumstances and turn out just fine—like you. I'm so proud of you, honey. I know you've seen some hard times in your fourteen years."

"I suppose so," I answered quietly.

Finally I got down to it. "Aunt Lillian, I want to ask you something," I said, changing the subject. "I want to know about something that MollieO hides in her drawer. It's a beautiful round leather thing with feathers hanging from it. She acts all weird when I ask her about it." I felt pangs of guilt squeezing my chest.

Lillian capped the last jar of preserves and set it on the crowded shelf. Then she turned fully toward me and sighed.

"It's high time you knew some things about our past. Lord knows my sister isn't ever gonna tell you. But I think it's your right to know. Girl, this family is who you are. Your roots! Come in here with me."

We walked down the short hallway into Lillian's little bedroom. The walls were bare. The only decoration was a small pitcher of yellow tulips sitting on the nightstand. Lillian reached down and pulled a weather-beaten suitcase out from under the terry cloth covered bed. To my surprise, the suitcase was filled with handmade objects that I recognized as American Indian.

She pulled one out. "This is a fan that was used to heal people. The Indians burned sage and used this fan to move the smoke around all over their bodies. They did it to keep them healthy and to ward off negative spirits. Too bad they didn't use it on MollieO," she said, her smile softening the words. "These feathers were part of a headpiece that a warrior wore."

Lillian held up another object—a leather circle with thin pieces of leather cord strung across it in the pattern of a spider web. From the circlet dangled bits of minerals and feathers. "This is a 'dream catcher.' It's supposed to be hung above where you sleep to catch your sweet dreams."

"That's what Mother has at the bottom of her drawer."

"That figures." She reached over and placed the beautiful piece in my hand. "I want you to have this one. I want my Billie's dreams to come true."

Reluctantly I took it. "But where will I put it? Mother will make me put it away."

"My Lord. Can't you do any little thing without letting her know? That just isn't healthy. Keep it in a secret place, then, and later when you have your own home you can hang it anywhere you want. You can still make your wishes now. But you know, for your dreams to come true, you got to believe." The room went silent. "Do you believe, Billie?"

"Maybe," I said. I was already well into a full-blown guilt trip for betraying MollieO's wishes.

Aunt Lillian shrugged her shoulders. "These are turkey feathers."

I looked into the suitcase. "Why do you have a rattle?"

"That's very special," she smiled, sighing. "This was Grandmother's rattle."

"Whose grandmother?" I asked.

"*My* grandmother and *your* great-grandmother, that's who! Where do you think you came from? Our family has a history, even if MollieO acts as if she sprung full grown from a pumpkin patch."

I felt my face flush with embarrassment. Why hadn't I ever quizzed MollieO more closely? Was I really so afraid of my family secrets? Aunt Lillian must have sensed my dismay. She pushed the suitcase aside and motioned for me to sit down beside her on the bed.

"I don't know if you're ready to hear this, but I'm gonna tell you anyway. Your great-grandmother was a powerful healer, Billie, a full-blooded Cherokee." She paused a moment to let this new and startling fact sink in.

All my preconceived notions and upper-class pretensions fought with a sudden burst of excitement over being an Indian. The pretentious impulse won. "That was three generations ago, Aunt Lillian. I don't see how it matters to me, or to MollieO."

"It matters to her. Your mama has always been scared to death that you and your sister might find out about your Indian heritage. She thinks it's a stain on the family history. Can you believe that? I guess she was afraid you all would be run out of the country club. Some people think it's bad enough she married a half Jew."

I winced, knowing full well that she was right. I was young, but not that young. I'd already learned about the social chasms that not even money could bridge.

"Let me tell you, Billie, the Cherokee people are a beautiful people. Ever read about them in school? Probably not. Or if you did, it was probably written by white folks who couldn't begin to understand. The Cherokee are a nation of strong spirits to contend with, whether historians like it or not."

Lillian picked up the rattle and shook it sharply. I jumped, startled by the sound, but I was drawn to the strange object. I stared at it.

"Here, honey, you try it." She nodded as she placed it in my hand.

"I don't know what to do with it," I said, fumbling with the gourd. "You show me, Lillian!"

Instead of taking back the rattle, she looked me in the eye. "Grandmother taught me when I was just about your age. She told me to close my eyes and let the energy move through me. You know, the energy of Spirit. Comes from above. You know it, baby, and you can do it. This thing doesn't come with instructions, because your own spirit knows exactly what to do. Just use your imagination. Imagine you can sense the energy around me and use the rattle to release any negative energy or dark spirits."

I closed my eyes. I was like a toddler taking her first steps. I pictured my great-grandmother watching me from above.

"Do you remember when you were just a little thing and you used to talk to your make-believe friends? One time I was baby-sitting for you girls, and you were out on the balcony all alone babbling your head off with no one but the sun and the trees to hear you. All of a sudden you started laughing for no reason that I could see. I said, 'What the heck's going on out there?' And you told me how you were just talking with your friends."

"I did not!" I exclaimed, thoroughly embarrassed at the idea of such childish behavior. "You're making this up, aren't you?"

"No, Billie." She looked wistful. "Why would I tell a fib like that? Don't you remember any of this? I swear to God, MollieO's brainwashed all the important stuff right out of you!"

Lillian's face turned serious. "Another time MollieO and Martin were out of town and I was staying at the house. I guess you were about three years old. Cutest baby around. Anyway, I'd gone downstairs for something and before I got back you started shrieking your head off, talking about how a witch had come into your bedroom. Do you remember that, honey?"

"No," I said. Yet I felt my body recoil, which probably should have sent me some sort of message that there was truth all around me . . . and in me.

"I came up the stairs and heard you screaming, 'Mommy! Mommy! Help!' You were pushing against the door so hard I couldn't get in. Finally you decided to trust me enough to let me come in and sit on the bed with you. You were scared out of your mind. You said this witch had gotten in bed with you. You were terrified because the *thing* told you that you were bad and would never have one happy day, that you deserved to die. That you had caused the family's unhappiness. Don't you remember this, Billie? You said the only thing that saved you was the Indian woman, that she scared the thing off. You slept in my arms that night, waking up at the slightest sound. I always thought you were talking about your great-grandmother. I always thought she must be your guardian spirit watching out for you from the other side."

Aunt Lillian reached out to hug me, but I stood up abruptly and dropped the rattle on the bed. "Gosh, I didn't realize how late it was. I'd better be on my way." I couldn't get out of Lillian's apartment fast enough. All of this talk about witches and medicine women. No wonder the family thought Aunt Lillian was crazy.

For a moment I felt guilty. *No,* I told myself. *I'm not going to feel bad just because my aunt is nuts and believes in spirits. It isn't my fault if I'm too mentally balanced to believe in all this crap.* I tried not to break into a run as I headed for the hall closet where my sweater hung. My aunt didn't follow me, she just let me go without a word. "Bye," I flung over my shoulder as I opened the door. "Thanks for the peaches."

Ten minutes later I settled into my seat on the bus, humming a tuneless tune while my mind settled itself. *I don't remember MollieO and Father going away and leaving us with Lillian. She's making all of that up!* And with that, I promptly locked away the day's revelations where I hid all my other big secrets.

11

COBRAS IN MY AURA, 1966

But Lillian's simple truths and mystical worlds drew me to her again and again, much to MollieO's chagrin. I guess Mother let me continue those visits because it gave her more time for her meticulous makeovers. After all, it takes a lot of time and energy to look fabulous when you're besieged by alcohol, migraines and tranquilizers.

It was an Aunt Lillian summer afternoon, complete with homemade apricot pie and mint tea. As usual, Lillian and I had talked at length about a few of the important issues of life—like how to survive.

"You always were special," Lillian said, pulling her hair up into a ponytail. "From the minute I saw you I knew you were different."

"How so?" I was sixteen then, with zero self-esteem and badly in need of some positive strokes. Lillian was giving me what MollieO didn't have time for, and I was beginning to trust her down home philosophies. More than anything, though, it was great to get some attention, to feel recognized for being alive.

"The first time I saw you in MollieO's arms I knew in my bones that you were a born healer. It was your energy, the colors in your aura." She hesitated, sensing my nervousness at hearing her talk about "that woo-woo stuff."

"Grandmother taught me how to relax and tune in to what she called 'the non-ordinary worlds.' You know, other worlds just beyond this one?" She stopped. No doubt she saw a wave of confusion pass across my face. "Why, Billie, you didn't think that this is all there is, did you? Oh, honey, you got a lot to learn."

I looked down at my finger nails, and Lillian touched my arm. "Stay with me now, honey," she said. "If I didn't think you could handle it I wouldn't tell you. Besides, if you get really quiet, you'll notice a part of you that isn't scared about anything I'm telling you. That's your spirit. Your spirit understands what I'm saying.

"Well, anyway, I saw purple and turquoise light around your body when you were *this big,* and those colors told me you were here to live a life of service, to help folks. The turquoise told me that you were gonna be a good communicator. But what really clued me in was the animal you had protecting you."

"What kind of animal? You mean like one of Mother's dogs?"

"In a way, but not really. What I'm talking about is a spirit animal, an animal that hangs out in the energy field around your body and brings a special kind of medicine to heal you. And because the animal is 'other-worldly' it can do the most amazing things. For instance, it can shape-shift its body into anything it wants—a human, a tree, a particular kind of energy like laughter—anything at all. A spirit animal might try and strike up a conversation with us, but most of the time we don't listen. It can move energy around a room, knock over things trying to get our attention. But it's almost always benevolent, and comes to heal us and protect us. That's why the Indians call them medicine animals.

"Grandmother taught me how to communicate with these animals, and I feel honored to be able to tune in to them. I used to have a spirit dog around me that I named Cheyenne. If I closed my eyes and got real quiet, she would come real close and talk to me about life, about what was gonna happen. She even talked to me about my crazy neighbors and told me how to deal with them. And it worked! She's not around anymore, though.

"If you think about it, maybe that's why MollieO has so many dogs and Martin goes to the racetrack all the time—you know how they both just adore their animals. Maybe that's their way of connecting with Spirit. But of course, they don't know it."

"So? So, what was mine?"

"So, yours wasn't exactly a dog or a horse. When you were born there was a snake coiled around your leg." I shuddered and squealed. "A white cobra." I squealed again. "Oh, hush now," Lillian said with a nudge.

She went on, "I remember trying to look up what the cobra meant in a book about American Indian beliefs, but there was nothing written about cobra medicine that I could find. So I checked around a little more and found some fascinating stories taken from Eastern philosophy. Now don't go getting your head all swollen, but they say that only a chosen few will experience the soul-expanding power of the cobra. In other words you oughta be honored to have a white cobra as your protector. This one came to help you move through different stages of your life. Different passages. He came to help you survive your karma, your spiritual lessons." I began to calm down. "He's your ally."

"Is it, he, still here?" I said, looking down at my skinny ankles.

Lillian closed her eyes. "Yes, Billie, he is. I'm guessing this animal will be with you for a long time. Perhaps your whole life, although you never know. They come and go according to the agreement you made with them before you were born into this lifetime."

She stopped and was quiet for a moment. "And there's someone else, too. There's a big cat out there—looks like a tiger, but he's way out on the edge of your aura." She stopped and kind of shivered. "Now, that's one powerful animal. Lord, I wouldn't want to mess with him."

We lay on our sides on her floral rug and inhaled the essence of sage drifting through the air. Lillian's "seasoned" air conditioner hummed along with the simple American Indian flute melody playing in the background.

As we both floated through the images of Lillian's stories, MollieO called to tell me that she would be home late from the beauty parlor and instructed me to take a taxi home.

"Now that I told you there are spirit animals watching over you, how about trying something wild and dangerous for a change?" My aunt's eyes were fiery and playful. "How about taking a subway home? Now that could be risky!" When she saw the grey shadow of fear pass over me, Lillian laughed out loud.

"MollieO would freak out!" I said passionately. "She has made it really clear—'No subways ever. Filled with de-generates!'" I looked up to see if Lillian would goad me further.

"What does she think is gonna happen to Baby Billie anyway? Does she think New Yorkers are gonna up and eat you alive right there on the uptown train? Not this time of day. It's too crowded for a barbecue! C'mon, where's your spirit of adventure, girl? Imagine yourself as a subway warrior ready to take on the rush hour masses!"

I was feeling scared and exhilarated. And naughty.

"C'mon, precious. There's only one way to act in life. You gotta walk right up to your fear and march right through it!" Lillian continued to suit me up for battle until I gave her a look of total surrender and yelled, "All right! All right! I'll do it! Stop already!"

As I was leaving, she handed me her umbrella. "It's not raining," I said. "Why do I need this old thing?"

"Just in case," she said with a dramatic tone, pointing the umbrella, then slashing the air with it like it was one of Zorro's swords.

She hugged me really tight, and off to the underworld I went.

Inside the subway station I asked the woman in front of me how to get change for the train, and she looked at me like I was a foreign particle that had hurled its way here, north, from Uranus. I could tell she hated my little private school blue tam and blazer.

Downstairs in the jungle it was dark and muggy. As it turned out, there was quite an array of cannibals waiting for me. Actually, everybody appeared pretty normal, somewhat subdued, until the guys with handkerchiefs wrapped around their foreheads arrived. Eight shirtless young men who were probably not named Lance or Morris. One of the guys, who I heard someone call Jorge, wore a shark tooth necklace around his well developed neck. He must have liked me, because he kept puckering his lips and shooting me an artillery of kisses. I kept my eyes to the ground.

The door of the train flew open and all sixty of my fellow travelers and I poured into the subway car. Jorge was right behind me. Through nervous eyes I saw a nun sitting alone and I raced and sat down on the seat next to her. She had her eyes closed and was fingering her rosary beads with her right hand. I could feel the energy of the gang members moving through the car. Soon they would be standing next to me. I glanced up at the big wall map that showed how many stops the train would make between here and home, and wondered if I would still be alive and kicking when we got there.

Jorge was whispering all kinds of sweet nothings next to my ear. I started to shake, and then the weirdest thing happened. The Sister turned toward me and smiled. Then she took a hold of my arm and held it close to her body. I wondered if she was really one of my spirit animals that had shape-shifted into this sweet, middle-aged Sister. Whoever she was, Jorge picked up some kind of signal and moved back a bit.

Four stops left, and my savior, the nun, needed to leave. When she stepped onto the subway platform and disappeared into the crowds, I closed my eyes and pictured my sleek white cobra ally slithering down the aisle of the subway car and wrapping himself around Jorge's sweaty torso. The big snake turned face to face with the guy and lunged forward with his terrible fangs and cobra breath. When I opened my eyes I could hardly believe it—Jorge was getting jumpy, and made his way back to the rear of the car.

Only three more stops. You can do it.

Beneath the map of the subway route sat an elegantly dressed black man who must have been in his late eighties. He wore a brown bowler hat that had pictures of children tucked into the brim. *Must be his grandkids,* I thought. It was his eyes that got to me, though. Eyes that were time-worn, filled with love. His eyes, I was sure, had seen it all. He noticed I was staring and tipped his hat, so I smiled and shifted my gaze out the window next to the door. I could just make out the graffiti spray painted across the passing subway wall. It said, "KILL THE GODDESS."

I closed my eyes and imagined an island where it was safe, like Gauguin's paradise. I wondered if that was what it was like in those other dimensions Lillian talked about—that is, if they really existed at all. Abruptly the doors opened and closed again and a dozen more commuters pushed their way in. Everyone grabbed for the finger-marked pole except for one person, a girl with red hair, who obviously wanted to surf the subway. And she had brought her transistor radio, with the volume turned up full blast, to accompany her ride. James Brown was singing "This Is a Man's World" while she tried to steady her drugged-out self. She must have felt me staring because she whipped around and looked right at me with a blend of intuition and fragile arrogance.

It's that girl! I told myself. It was the one I'd seen a couple years before in front of the public library. I was absolutely mesmerized. So were the gang members who had, thank goodness, shifted their hungry gaze in her direction.

Her stare was challenging mine, and she was smiling in this out-of-control, inebriated kind of way. She looked me up and down and broke out laughing with her head thrown back, surrendering to her own private joke, the way you do when you're slam-dunk stoned. Drunk on bliss.

She was thinner than I remembered. Every time she turned away I stared harder. God, she was beautiful. Flaming Medusa-like hair to her waist, strong, high breasts, long sinewy limbs and raucous hips. A tattoo of pink roses made a bracelet on her right wrist. There was a large purple bruise behind her ear on her upper neck. I watched as her eyes circled to the right and then to the left. She was weaving, going into some kind of trance.

"Whoa! Be careful!" a man in a grey leisure suit shouted as she fell into him. And then he kind of propped her up on the pole. Her head kept jerking as she went in and out of consciousness. Her jeans were torn and her tee shirt screamed out *Caliente!* Her left knee was bandaged and she was favoring it. She was, maybe, twenty. From where I sat she was the most stunning young woman I had ever seen. Heart-shaped lips, full as inner tubes, and big white teeth. Hot cocoa-colored skin. No makeup. No jewelry. No purse. No little tam or blazer. And her bare feet had walked a lot of pavements in this dirty city, making her look even more primitive. Free-spirited. Mentally ill.

Her eyes flashed open and in her foggy funk she appeared to recognize me. She started to heave toward me but the train was coming to my stop, and I stood up in the crowd and forced my way out the back door. I turned around and she was watching me leave. As the train pulled away I caught an image of her laughing beyond the dingy subway window. I figured she had already forgotten me, and some other actor was starring in the movie that was premiering in her head.

12

THE QUEEN OF KISSERS, 1967

I have always been a connoisseur of kisses. I'll take a long, deep, meaningful kiss over intercourse any day. You can tell a lot about a person by the way he kisses. For instance, men who kiss with pursed lips don't want to face their feelings. Men who open wide, *Jaws*-style, are out to control you. A man who forgets about kissing you while you're making love has issues with his mother. Think about it. You can get to the truth with a kiss. Personally, I like a man who starts very slowly. First he engages you with searching eyes, with sweet breath and available petal-soft lips, encouraging surrender without uttering a word. Lips that tango and samba to their own tender melody. Lips that answer your call again and again.

In my teenage years, my criterion for choosing a boy was simple: My guy had to be a great kisser. While my mother checked out the *Social Register* for the pedigree of each prospective candidate, I auditioned his lips.

"Billie," MollieO asked while I was massaging her shoulders, "why do you like that Simpson boy so much? Everybody knows his family is New Money." And then I heard the Bartholomew credo for the ten thousandth time. "As I have told you before, darlin', there are two kinds of men: those who read the *Wall Street Journal* and those who are great in the sackarooni. They don't come in the same package. Which is it gonna be?" Then she turned her tormented face toward mine and whispered in a weary voice, "Haven't I taught you anything? Anything at all?"

Most of my time as a teenager was spent taking care of my mother and escaping my father. On my time off I busied myself with a new boyfriend every week and continued my reign as the private school boys' choice for Most Popular Girl. The girls at Miss Jenkins School hated me for this, but I didn't care. I needed the attention to feel alive. Despite my social butterfly status, however, it wasn't at the Friday night cotillion dances that I found my first love. It was in the service elevator of my apartment building after school where I stood shoulder to shoulder with John Castellucci, the world's greatest kisser. I was seventeen and he was twenty-one.

There was absolutely nothing about our secret relationship that my mother would have condoned. I was a socialite's daughter, he was an elevator boy. I smoked Players cigarettes, he smoked Salems. While John rebuilt his robin's egg blue VW engine and took the cross-town bus to work, most of the time I relied on the family limo. He smelled like Sicily and the Bronx, prosciutto and eggplant. I was all Monaco, Bonwit Teller and 21.

"What's that dreadful stench coming from you?" MollieO questioned after my first encounter with Mr. Right. She wrinkled up her nose and added with a laugh, "You been dating a sailor?"

"No, Mother," I lied. "He's a really nice boy. You'll like him. All the girls at my school are wearing Navy Spice, that's the fragrance you're smelling. I like it. NeeNee Van Bursin wears it." That bold-faced lie settled the matter in MollieO's mind. If the daughter of the president of Manhattan Bank reeked of five-and-dime store cologne, it must be acceptable.

Months passed, and my kisses with John Castellucci deepened. They butterflied, swan dived and jackknifed their way toward intense petting. In the darkened elevator, poised between the thirtieth and thirty-first floors, we plotted a night together that would lead us to total intimacy, to doing *it*. I was so anxious my knees were sweating. We talked about it as if it was going to be our first real date, not twelve hours of unbridled sex.

He outlined the plan, counting off each step on his fingers. "First we'll go to Greenwich Village and listen to jazz. Miles is in town." Miles Davis! That would cost a small fortune. Could he afford it? That clinched it for me. John Castellucci was the right one. "Then we'll go to Asbury Park and ride the roller coaster all night. It'll be a blast." I trusted his every word. I was rendered brain dead by a poor boy's kiss.

When Friday, June 16, arrived I packed a carton of European cigarettes, four pairs of super clean white bikini panties and my toothbrush into my alligator overnight bag under the pretext of spending the night at a classmate's house. "I'll be at Pooh Steuben's house," I told MollieO. "They're the Steuben Construction family. They built half of Manhattan." MollieO smiled warmly at the thought, and off I went without any restrictions to my rendezvous with Kisser Man at the back elevator.

Maybe it was my imagination, but Miles looked pretty ripped on stage and spent most of the first hour with his back to the audience. The vibe between John and me was so hot that Miles suddenly put his trumpet down in the middle of "My Funny Valentine," turned around and smiled at us. I was on my fourth rum & Coke, totally immersed in the music. John was clearly drunk. Later, when Miles passed our table, I wondered if he was going to the bathroom to shoot up. He leaned close to me and whispered in his raspy way, "Lady, you got big ears." This was the first time in my life that I recall not feeling ashamed of being special.

Around 2:00 A.M. John and I entered the gates to Asbury Park. By 2:10 we were kissing big time on the Ferris wheel. John's ID bracelet was cold against my chest, and I let my head fall back as I watched the stars roll by above us. Then the wheel stopped, and in seconds I was bare chested. "Just until the wheel starts up again," he said with a grin. "Stay like this until then."

A lot of time went by in the top car and, although I was enjoying every second of his mouth on my nipples, I was getting fidgety. I wanted to go somewhere else, someplace private.

He quickly buttoned my shirt as the wheel began to move again. Then he said the last thing on earth I expected to hear. "I don't want to do it tonight, Billie."

I was devastated. I was sure I wasn't good enough. I wasn't exciting enough, mature enough, pretty enough. I fought back the tears. He saw all of that on my face and said in the most tender way, "I love you too much to go all the way. I like it the way it is. Let's not ruin it."

Ruin it? The idea had never occurred to me. I wanted to say, *No! I want to do it with you. . . . Right now.* But I didn't know how.

"Okay," I said suddenly. The attendant opened the safety gate of our car and we stepped out. "I guess I'll just go home."

It was almost morning when John drove me back into the city. He parked his car and hailed a cab for me. When I opened the taxi door, he leaned over and kissed me so lovingly I nearly passed out. We made plans to meet the following day at the end of his shift.

When the cab pulled up to my familiar awning, there must have been a hundred state troopers and city cops in the lobby of the building. I could hear Martin yelling, and MollieO was collapsed like a bean bag chair in one corner of the reception area. Her head was in her hands and her perfect "do" had come frantically undone.

"Billie!" my father shouted. "Where have you been?" The state troopers put down their coffee cups damn near in unison. "We've had police from three states looking for you. We thought that wop killed you!"

"Hey, watch it, Sir!"

"Who the hell are you?" my father demanded.

The young officer touched his badge. "Officer Fortunato, Sir. Angelo Fortunato."

I stood there trembling with a strange combination of fear and anger. How dare they do this to me! Humiliate me in front of total strangers. But I kept my voice under control. "I wasn't doing anything wrong, Father. . . ," I started off lamely, but he wasn't in the mood to hear anything.

"I don't want to hear what you have or have not been doing. You're a disgrace to this family! Now you get upstairs right now!" When I started to speak again, he took another step closer. I was sure he was going to knock me across the lobby. Officer Fortunato moved toward Martin as though he was preparing to restrain him.

My father's fists, face and teeth were clenched as he repeated himself. "Upstairs, now!"

MollieO roused herself from the couch as if her bones hurt, walked over and put her arms around me. "Your father is furious," she said vacantly. Then she leaned closer and whispered, "Do whatever he says or he'll kill us both. I mean it, Billie." She took me by the arm and led me to the elevator. I could hear my father behind us, apologizing to the men. I turned to face the front and saw them all shaking hands. The Chief of Police was patting Martin on the back. Officer Fortunato was standing off to one side with his arms folded over his chest like the King of Siam. He shot me a concerned look just as the elevator doors closed between us.

Back upstairs, Mother positioned me on a stool across from Father's massive red leather chair.

"Remember, do anything, agree with everything he asks of you or it will be hell around here," she warned.

I waited there, afraid to move, furious that I didn't have the guts to storm into my room, slam the door and tell him to go to hell. But I couldn't. And it wasn't just my own safety I was considering. I couldn't shake the image of MollieO's eyes full of terrible anticipation. Her words echoed in my ears, ". . . it will be hell around here." Like it hadn't been hell already.

The front door slammed and I heard Father clear his throat several times out in the foyer. MollieO went over to him. I couldn't hear the words, but I knew she was making excuses, trying to buy time, hoping to somehow placate him. Whether it was for me, or for herself, or for both of us I didn't really know. But I did know that she'd suffered enough. If there was any way to keep from causing her any more pain, I'd do it.

I heard him say, "Stay out of it." Then he was in the den with me. Martin sat down with a vengeance and began rhythmically slapping his leg with a rolled up morning newspaper.

"Why would you do such a thing to your mother and me? Have you no shame whatsoever? Acting like a tramp!" He stood up and advanced on me. "You are a Bartholomew! Do you have any idea how the newspapers will portray your shenanigans? Do you? Do you know what this will cost me? How this will affect my reputation?"

I took a deep breath and kept my tone as respectful as possible. "Father," I began quietly, "I don't think I'm so important that the newspaper will want to write—"

"*Don't* contradict me! You are Billie Ann Bartholomew, daughter of Martin Bartholomew, soon to be Senator Bartholomew. Whether you like it or not, you *are* somebody."

He leaned into my face, daring me to disagree. I could see the veins in his nose about to explode. I didn't dare look him in the eye, and that made it worse.

"You pay attention to me. Look at me when I talk to you!"

Then I looked into his bloodshot eyes and tried to let my mind go somewhere else. I didn't want anything in my expression to send him into the velvet boudoir to vent on Mother.

"I put up with enough crap from your mother. So don't think I'm going to put up with any from you." He stepped back and dropped the newspaper. I closed my eyes, sure that at any moment I would be slammed against the wall like one of MollieO's overcooked lamb chops. But instead, Martin reached for the tiny Venetian glass sculptures that MollieO had collected while vacationing in Italy. Glass sprayed thirty feet from his first try.

"You stupid, stupid bitch," he said, his voice a low, vicious snarl. He hurled a blue dolphin into the wall. "Stupid little bitch! You and your sister would do anything to humiliate me, wouldn't you? You're a couple of stupid fucking cunts."

In one movement he had me by the throat and slammed me against the glass door to the outside terrace. I could see MollieO watching from the hallway. Her arms were wrapped around her torso, and her whole body was shaking. I could see that she was crying. It occurred to me that, if I were going to die, at least I'd seen actual evidence that my mother cared about me. Of course, there might have been easier ways to find out.

Just then through the haze of dread and disgust I heard the front door open and close. But Martin jerked my attention back to him.

"What did you do with that piece of shit, anyway?" He was so close, all I could focus on were his yellow false teeth. "What did you let him do, you little tramp? Handle those pathetic little tits of yours?"

Even though Father had my face clamped between his hands, I could see out of my right eye that the cop from downstairs— the one who had objected to my father's put-down of Italian-Americans—had entered the room. The officer forcefully cleared his throat.

"Mr. Bartholomew," he said, "your limo is parked illegally downstairs and your driver doesn't seem to be anywhere around. I know you are in the middle of a family, uh, situation, but I thought I'd come upstairs and save you a ticket."

Martin moved back. He froze as if in another time frame.

"Can you hear me, Sir?" the officer continued, taking a solid hold of Father's arm. "Looks like this is just the right time for you to come downstairs with me to take care of that automobile. Let's go, Sir."

Martin's breathing slowed down, but my pounding heart didn't. I looked down to gather myself and I saw a bulge under his zipper. Finally Martin gave in and turned to follow Officer Fortunato out of the room. But before he was out the door, the young cop turned and looked intensely into my eyes. He nodded his head as if to assure me that everything was going to be all right. For a moment I believed him. Then I ran and blockaded myself in my bedroom.

"Callie," I cried, as if she weren't hundreds of miles away at college and could actually hear me. "Please help me, Callie. Come home now, please."

I cried for a long time that day, mostly from helpless rage at Martin. But there was also a part of me that wept for John, the man who'd taken me to the peak of sexual desire and then decided he cared more about loving me than just "doing it." And now he never would. The boy who had fulfilled my fantasies, given me kisses I had only dreamed of, was forever out of reach.

"Billie," MollieO whispered at the door, interrupting my mourning. "Let me in." I pushed the furniture aside and my mother eased herself down next to me on the bed. Her ancient Pekingese was licking my feet.

"Billie, everything is gonna be okay. I talked your father into you going to see a therapist twice a week as a punishment. Rory Rittenauer—you know, the chairman of the ballet?—sees a famous Freudian psychoanalyst, Dr. Janowitz. Martin agreed that would be okay. It's a good move, don't you think? Then everything will calm down. It's better that way."

"As compared to what?" I said, raising myself up on one arm, ready to pour out my anger and frustration. But I could see

MollieO was doing the only thing she knew how to do—to patch things up, make compromises, keep herself from getting "torn up" anymore. So I said, "Yes, Mother."

"I got your father to drop the charges on the elevator boy. But you must promise you will never see him again. Not that you're likely to see him again anyway. Obviously, he won't be working here anymore." She looked as if she might say something more. In her eyes I thought I caught just a glimpse of understanding, of compassion, almost as if she knew how I felt about John. But then it was gone and her vacant expression was back, along with her glamorous pout.

"Aren't you proud of me, Billie?" Mother asked. "Of how I took care of everything?" She snuggled in close and thrust her arms around me. "Darlin', could you push right here? My temples are killing me. That mean old Mr. Migraine's back in town." I sighed, knowing that the trauma of this morning was now expected to be over and done . . . and forgotten about. So I rubbed and pressed and shifted the stress away from her face. We heard Father greet our neighbor with a pleasant voice, and the front door solidly closed.

The following Monday afternoon I squeezed through the revolving doors at 54th Street and Madison Avenue for my first session with Dr. Leonard Janowitz. Little did he know that one day his young patient would become a therapist herself. I quickly learned both the power and limitations of psychotherapy. At the time, I thought the whole process fairly absurd. Leonard would sit there pretending to know what to do, whispering occasionally, "And Billie, how did you feel about that?"

He was a good man. I'm sure a part of him wished he could reach over and do the one thing that might have helped me actually know what I was feeling. If only he could have climbed out of his perfect brown leather chair and embraced my poor starving soul, held me in a protective way. Maybe if he could have connected with my fern green eyes a little longer, dared to venture in a little closer, something major might have transpired. As it was, a typical session went like this:

"Tell me how you feel about being punished for lying to your parents."

"Fine."

"Do you think you deserve to be here?"

"Sure."

"Are you mad at your parents?"

"Not really."

"Tell me about your relationship with your father."

"It's fine."

"In what way is it fine?"

"Okay. Okay. You know, *okay.*"

Every Monday and Thursday it was the same. I wandered in, plopped down and stayed as distant as possible. I'm not positive, but I don't think that Leonard ever got a glimpse of who I was. Not once. And that was really too bad, because I had some secrets going on that needed extrication. Aside from the obvious, I could have let him in on my addiction to caffeinated aspirin, or told him how my morning didn't begin until I had popped four 65 mg. capsules before breakfast. Or I could have filled him in on the frenzy of cleaning my room ten times, doing two weeks worth of homework and having lots of energy left to feed my equally obsessive attraction to boys, all in one day.

As it was, I never did touch on any true feelings while I was in therapy. Instead, I merely compensated for denying my feelings by staying busy all the time. I was an underachiever who was coping by becoming an overachiever. I wasn't conscious of being one, but I acted like one.

I realize now that Leonard Janowitz did the best he could, gave the most he was capable of giving. A person needs a certain inner strength to be able to reach beyond his perfect façade and create the space for another to feel safe and ultimately be able to grow. That just wasn't Leonard's way. If I'd known enough to ask him for that kind of support at the time, I don't think he would have had any idea what I meant.

But what was important was that week after week I sat in that toasty warm womb of an office and created a vision of what real therapy could be like. After my sessions I would imagine that I was Leonard, asking the appropriate questions, being witty and direct and, of course, compassionate.

I noticed how wonderful it felt to orchestrate the flow of conversation—to feel connected, but not too connected. Fifty minutes was just the right amount of time to probe around and let go. I fantasized how I would help my patients release their pain and discover their true motivations and desires. Then I would open my heavy office door and they would leave, drunk on enlightenment. "Thank you so much, Dr. Bartholomew," they would say with gratitude. "No, thank *you,* I would say." And I would be reborn a heroine at the beginning of each new hour.

13

NO MATTER WHAT YOU THINK, GUYS ARE NOT THE ANSWER, 1970–80

Unconsciously, MollieO set me up for a lifetime of desperation. She really didn't care whether I went to college to learn anything. What she cared about was who I met there, how much social position their families had achieved, and who was ultimately going to take care of me. That was the only way she knew how to evaluate life and the people in it.

I was anxious about finding stability, too, in part to get away from her—so much so that my ability to retain information was practically zilch. Nowadays we therapists call it Attention Deficit Disorder; I called it Bartholomew's Overwhelm. I rolled through classes in a fog until finals week, when I took something called Black Bombers—amphetamines—once every two hours during exams, and lost my hearing for three weeks. I guess the pharmaceuticals made me a genius, because all of my professors gave me A+ and wrote notes on my exams like, "Simply outstanding. You have connected so deeply and correctly to Sartre. You sound like his mother or his mistress, you understand him so well." No, merely a first-rate caretaker.

I should thank MollieO. After all, it was her migrained advice that enabled me to pull my grades up at the last minute. "The world is run by men, darlin'. Get as close to them as you can if you want some of that power. Always think like a first class hooker." That brief, "this is life at ground level" philosophy lesson enabled me to ace my finals and saved my life in academia.

My personal life with men was a very different story. My self-esteem was so underdeveloped that I constantly worried that no one would want me. Besides, there was a large part of me that was quite happy to be unwanted. I was a mixed bag—a pretty young thing whose jealous girlfriends sulked when guys stared and whistled at me on the street or pelted me with popcorn at the movies. They frowned when strangers dedicated pizzas to my beauty at the 86th Street pizza parlor.

On Saturday nights, my girlfriends and I would wedge our way into the crowded scene at our favorite Eastside bar and wait until one of a thousand guys would notice my waist length wavy hair shining in the dark, or mistake my shyness as a "hard to get" come-on. Drinks would be forthcoming. As were lots of immature offers. It was typical for a guy to act like he was trying to be my friend, then later act like a horny moron. Once in a while it felt like a real betrayal. For instance, I wasn't surprised when a brother-like protector, Jake, the main bartender at our drinking establishment, poured me a series of shots one evening and then told me they were on the house. He was always taking care of me. But as I swiveled down off the stool, he came out from behind the bar and whispered in my ear, "I'd love to look down at your beautiful face on my waterbed. Your hair would look great against my pillow." I was so let down I never talked to him again.

I did venture out with a couple of guys I met at that bar, but they didn't stick around, thank God, because they could sense that I wasn't going to put out like all the other females in their black fishnet stockings, leather skirts and knee-high boots. I was unique. I was a virgin.

I had a hard time seeing that I was attractive. The truth was I didn't want to. Being pretty and pure made me feel like there was something wrong with me. Everybody else was sleeping around, why wasn't I? So with all of the different messages I was putting out, the guys I hung out with were a pretty sorry lot, and if my choices in men were indeed an outer reflection of my inner world, I was in deep shit. Not that I noticed at the time. Realizing what my choice of boyfriends said about me took a lot of perspective.

No matter what their personal hang-ups were, about fifty percent of the guys were bad kissers and another twenty-five percent were emotionally unavailable. The remaining twenty-five percent were in love with Mommy. At least that's what I made myself believe, and it gave me a great excuse to avoid getting involved in any way, shape or form.

Somewhere in my twenty-second year I decided I had to *do it*. I had to bite the bullet and have sex. I couldn't enter my mid-twenties and still be a virgin. Everyone would think I was a pervert when I was really just plain terrified.

I auditioned several okay men but nothing happened. I finally realized that it wasn't the fine qualities of the guys that was going to relax me enough to give in, it was the volume of booze I could put away. So every evening when I ventured out I carried a silver flask filled with Jack Daniels in the bottom of my purse.

MollieO somehow picked up my quest to be normal, and cornered some young son of one her cronies at a Saturday night dinner party. "This one's a looker," she told me in the kitchen later that evening, pouring herself a drink. "He's unbearably handsome, financially blessed and charming. I'd take him myself if I wasn't already spoken for." She paused and took another long sip.

"He's comin' by to meet you tomorrow evening. You better fast so your tummy'll be flat."

His name was Michael Berry III and he was gorgeous. So gorgeous, in fact, that I damn near passed out when I met him face to face. Monsieur the Third was a dead ringer for Al Pacino. *Oy vey zhmeer.*

We started seeing each other every night. There were two important components to our romantic rendezvous: kissing and marijuana. Michael was a fantastic kisser, warm, sensual, gentle. His night job was drug dealing and his bedroom was stashed with the greatest marijuana in the history of Manhattan. Nickel bags, dime bags, coffee cans and bricks—he sold it all.

When the Day of Deflowering arrived, I lay in his arms and inhaled incredible quantities of sensimilla and hashish. Finally, I could relax. As his tongue progressed slowly down my neck I let go and flowed into a stupor. I have no idea where I went and I don't care, because I felt fabulous—no images of my misused childhood sexuality, no fears at all. Euphorically, I prepared myself for the big moment.

Michael had always orchestrated our romance with great dope, provocative food and inspiring music. We liked to make out to José Feliciano. But tonight was a departure from that scene. As Michael lay down on top of my naked body, the needle of his record player lay down on a hard rock tune, a song that for some reason he had cranked all the way up for our enjoyment.

"*Squeeze my fruit,*" the singer moaned and wailed as Michael entered me, "*until the juice runs down the sheet.*"

Michael's movements were harsh, but the lyrics hurt worse. The whole "intercourse experience" lasted the length of the song. Michael's face was dripping with sweat. Triumphantly, he looked at me, lit a huge joint, and turned over the album. Without checking out how I was feeling, he lifted my legs and tilted them backward, over my head against the wall. I felt totally exposed and started to cry.

"Hey, babe," he asked me with a husky voice, "what's the big deal? You're acting like a scared little virgin, not the sophisticated woman I know you are. Turn over." When I didn't comply he got up to go to the bathroom, and I quickly zipped up my miniskirt and sneaked out the front door. Unfortunately, Michael's parents were coming out of the elevator at the same time. "You're the Bartholomew girl, aren't you?" Mrs. II asked me, checking out my stoned eyeballs and wild hair. I didn't feel like anybody's girl. I had nothing to say.

Descending the sixty-some floors by elevator, I was a peculiar blend of drugged-out disappointment, sore thighs and major relief. I had done it and I felt alone. But this time, unlike my childhood experiences, I was not a prisoner. I was free to leave, an option that became a source of power in my later years—one I had a hard time relinquishing.

14

MOTHER AND I COME OF AGE
IN MANHATTAN, 1971

I had just turned twenty-one, and had come home to visit. It was October, and MollieO had recently done the living room in a garish orange motif. I remember feeling simultaneously relieved and disappointed that no one had remembered my birthday. That occasion, like most others in my family, always had the potential for disaster.

"Mother, I'm here," I called from the bottom of the staircase. "Where are you? Are you up there?"

I walked to the doorway of my parents' bedroom and guessed that the darkness signaled one of my mother's migraines. There had been many dark afternoons in 33J when I was growing up. Rather than risk waking her, I walked quietly down the hallway to my room. I was unpacking my jeans when I felt her presence behind me. I turned as she slumped against the door and began to slide down toward the floor.

"Oh, my God, Mother! Oh, my God," I said, not wanting to believe what I saw. I propped her up on my four-poster bed. Her right eye looked like a prime cut of filet mignon and her entire neck was black and blue. Her delicate hands were trembling and cold. She was barely conscious. My heart was going like a triphammer. I grabbed a quilt off the bed and wrapped it around her.

"It's all right, I'm here. Just don't move . . . oh God, oh God, what has he done to you?"

Tears streamed down my face as I tried to keep her steady with one hand and reach for the phone by my bed with the other.

This was the first time she didn't fight me when I called for an ambulance. I guess she knew she might die. We both knew.

"Oh, Mrs. Williams," the emergency room nurse said, meeting us at the door with a wheelchair. "Not again. Oh, you poor thing."

I looked at her, then I looked at my mother and something inside me broke apart and let the truth spill over. "Her name is Bartholomew," I said softly, but very firmly. "MollieO Bartholomew. I'm her daughter, Billie."

I'll give the nurse credit. She didn't bat an eyelash. She simply nodded. She took my hand in both of hers. "Hello, Billie," she said. "Let's get your mother to an exam room right away." The police arrived for questioning shortly after.

Hours later, I lay catty-cornered on MollieO's hospital bed. In the evening light I could barely make out her features. Her breathing was labored yet steady, and she held on to my hand with a grip that periodically tightened as if to make sure I was still there. When I looked down at her wrist, I noticed she wasn't wearing her charm bracelet. It must have been torn off in her struggle with Martin. There was an irony there, but I was too tired to give it much thought.

Well into the evening, Mother's eyes finally opened, but her lips and face were so swollen she couldn't form the words. Her silence told me enough of the story. And, being a survivor of Bartholomew hell, I could fill in the details for myself.

Finally I said, "I won't leave you, Mother. We'll make it through this." I let a washcloth absorb cold water in the sink and folded it over MollieO's eyes. "So don't you leave me."

When I took her hand again she tightened her grip, and I began to weep tears that wouldn't stop, as if gushing from a bottomless well of grief. She squeezed my hand harder still. For the first time in our lives we had made a connection, and I was terrified my mother was going to die.

I stayed in the hospital room with MollieO for a week until I could bring her home. I didn't dare call Callie, who was out of town almost all the time now playing in jazz clubs across the country. There was no telling how she would have responded. The depth of her anger was so real, and its ignition point so close to the surface, it frightened me—not for Martin's sake, but for hers.

The first morning after we arrived at the hospital Ms. Jacobs, the ER nurse, brought in the police photographer who would document the beating. A man sensitive to the horrors he had witnessed through the lens of his camera, he was extremely gentle with MollieO. Very delicately he opened her tunic to expose the bruises. He apologized for the indignity of being photographed, murmuring that it would be done as quickly as possible. I watched him shake his head at what he saw.

"Good Lord," he cursed under his breath. "What kind of a monster would do this?"

This was particularly devastating for MollieO. She had made it her life's goal to be the center of attention, but not this way, not with her weakness and pain exposed to the eyes of strangers.

"What will happen to me, Billie?" she asked on the morning we were checking out, almost like a frightened little girl. "I'm going to lose everything."

"Mother," I countered, patting her hand, "you're a wealthy woman. You're young and gorgeous and you can make it without him. You're going to find this out. You're going to have to take it day by day. Once you start really feeling better, you'll see. You won't have the answers all at once."

"They're all going to shun me, you know. All of the men and their wives, all of Marty's friends, they're all going to hate me. I'll have to start all over."

I had a momentary urge to snap at her, but she looked like a fragile animal caught in one of those hideous steel traps. Even her voice seemed pale.

"Will you help me, Billie? I can't make it without you."

"Stop worrying, MollieO," I said in my most adult voice.

"Look who's talking now," she said, in a teasing voice. She sounded like she almost knew me.

My father was picked up on the seventeenth hole at his country club and taken downtown by a couple of cops who didn't care who the hell he was. They'd seen the pictures and the hospital records and talked to the nurses. Martin was booked immediately, denied bail by a judge who apparently thought that using your wife as a punching bag for twenty years was inexcusable. Despite excellent legal representation, Martin received a one-year sentence at a "white collar" prison. I imagined him complaining about the food and throwing it against the wall. He'd finally found a place where his behavior was normal.

In the meantime, I spent lots of time gearing Mother up for the divorce, making sure it would come through before Martin got out. And it was only then that I truly began to understand how dependent she had been on Martin, a state of affairs which I knew suited him just fine. The woman could not write a check or pay a bill. She had no idea how much money they really had or what to ask for in the divorce. Together we went through his office, spoke with an attorney, pieced everything together. There was an enormous amount of money. MollieO was destined to be one wealthy woman. Happily, the more we uncovered, the faster MollieO recovered.

"You know, I think I'm gonna be okay," I heard her tell her housekeeper while she was making a pasta dinner. "Half of fifty million clams makes a lot of linguine."

15

MERCY, MERCY ME, 1971

The door flew open and Callie jumped onto my bed with a pretend microphone in her hand, singing some soul song. She was bopping around the room all dressed up and raring to go.

"Come on, girl! It's time to party!"

Before I could say anything she had me by the arm and was dragging me out of bed.

"You're twenty-one, not sixty-one! And have I got a birthday surprise for you! It's going to knock you out! I'm sorry I couldn't make it on your day—I was giggin'—but I'm here now, right?"

Callie grabbed something sleek and sexy from my closet, zipped me up, and we tiptoed out the back through the maid's quarters and down the service elevator. For a brief moment, John Castelluci's beautiful face appeared before me in fantasy form. We kissed slowly and then Callie snapped her fingers in my face and brought me back to the present moment. Was John the only great kisser I was destined to experience in my lonely life?

"125th Street," Callie smugly announced to the driver.

"Nyet! Too late for dat!" Mikhail Romanov told us in the taxicab mirror. "Two chix get in plenty trowble uptown Harlem now."

125th Street, that's Harlem!

My mind finally registered what they were both saying. "Yeah, I don't think that sounds like a smart thing to do," I said, starting to perspire. "He's a cab driver, he knows what's safe. And besides, even I know that Harlem's not safe for us late at night."

"How would you know? You've never been above 92nd Street. It's time to see the world! Besides," she told the driver as she turned toward me, "it's time to celebrate my sister Billie's burgeoning womanhood. This is the perfect ritual to call in your life as a sexual female."

The driver shook his head, "Go to muzeeum tomorrow. See Peecasso. Go to Zoo. I weel not take you."

"There's an extra fifty in it for you," Callie said, waving a crisp bill in the air.

Mikhail put his foot on the gas.

"Look up!" We had stopped at a red light, and Callie deftly applied mascara to my tender lashes and underlined my lower lids. "Now, pucker!" She dipped and re-dipped her lip brush into a gooey pink gloss and spread it over my pooched out lips, just as the taxi lurched forward again. "Oh, right," she said, remembering the finishing touch just in time. She dotted the mole by my lip with an eyebrow pencil. "Tonight my sister is earning her beauty mark," she announced proudly to the driver.

The taxi moved quickly until we left the posh side of town, then everything slowed down to a crawl . . . 99th, 100th, 101st, 102nd, 103rd, . . . Harlem! I was perspiring like crazy. I looked in the cars on either side of us but there were no white faces anywhere. Callie picked up on my growing paranoia.

"Now you know how people of color feel every day of their lives," she told me, taking a hold of my hand. "It'll be all right," she said laughing in a gentle way. "You'll see. Pretty soon you'll forget all about it."

Even though I thought of myself as a forward-thinking person who would do anything to stop racism, sexism and the like, I was incredibly naive.

"You're kind of agoraphobic, aren't you? It's like you have an invisible blueprint of the 'acceptable' part of the city etched in your mind, and those are the boundaries that you stay behind. You better be careful, all those years with MollieO's snobbery and paranoia are making you afraid of living. Pretty soon you won't feel safe leaving the block where we live.

"Don't worry," she went on. "I will *never* let you turn into one of those soulless Fifth Avenue intellectuals who talks as if she understands what life is all about, but doesn't have the heart or the time to find out."

Callie was quite the opposite. "I feel more at home here than anywhere else in the world, because I have a feeling that people aren't judging me. When I'm in the Apollo, I feel like I'm part of a family."

"Mm-hm, mm-hm," I kept saying.

As the cab pulled up in front of the theater, my heart was running wild. Mikhail took the extra fifty and told us to watch our *ahses*. The streets were packed and almost everybody turned around when they noticed us walking up to the ticket line.

"I don't know why I'm feeling so scared," I whispered to Callie.

"Do you trust me? Have I ever done anything to hurt you or mess you up?"

"Well, there was the 'orange juice incident of '54!'"

We broke out laughing.

Then Callie said, "Scared is a word that fits with your childhood. Tonight we are waving good-bye to your younger years and awakening your womanhood!"

As the line inched ahead and we neared the theater entrance, I looked up at the brightly lit marquee. It read:

THE APOLLO THEATER WELCOMES
THE VOICE

"I hate to be totally ignorant," I said, "but, who's 'The Voice?'"

"You'll see. It's part of your puberty ritual. We're gonna bring a little sexuality into your life, girl. We're gonna make you sweat!"

If I sweat anymore, I'll slide out of my seat.

The two women behind us, listening to Callie's comments, shook their heads in total agreement, and said only, "Mmm, Mmm, Mmm."

"Must be some kind of man," I said, turning around.

"Girl," the woman with the brightest eyes said, "you better get ready to cross your legs!" Callie laughed a knowing laugh along with them.

The crowds started moving and soon we were inside the Apollo. We were near the end of the line, and almost every seat appeared to be taken. All of a sudden Callie cried out, "Oh, my God, two people in the front row are leaving! We can sit right in front of The Voice." And we did.

The room was an ocean of exultation, with waves of ecstasy crashing over us. Everyone, and I mean people of all different ages, was ready to explode. Comments and cheers echoed from all over the room.

"Good evening, ladies and gentlemen. . . ."

"Mm-hm."

"The Apollo Theater is proud to present. . . ."

"oooooOh yes!"

"The greatest artist of our time. . . ."

"Hallelujah!"

"We're gonna jump, we're gonna jive . . . we're gonna feel soulful and alive!"

"Tell it to me!"

"Are you *ready?*"

"Well, come on!" shouted a woman in the balcony. She was dancing and waving her arms.

"I didn't hear you. I said, 'Are you ready?'"

"Ready, ready, ready!" we screamed in a semi-fervor, and the audience went nuts clapping.

"Well, then, let's give an Apollo warm welcome for the one, the only . . . The Voice, Mr. Marvin Gaye!"

A tsunami of animal passion swept over us. The curtains opened and the most handsome man I had ever seen walked toward the microphone. He was only twenty feet away from us. Silenced, we waited for his cue.

Apparently, Callie couldn't hold back. "Oh, my God," she cried out.

Marvin looked down and whispered into the mike, "Hey, young thing! What's goin' on?" He grinned and blew her a mouth-watering kiss. My sister began to shake and quake. Seated beside her, a large woman with huge bosoms, wearing a canary yellow cloche hat, put her arms around her to comfort her. I mean, she didn't even think about it, she just did what she had to do to help the sister survive.

Marvin's band started grooving, and finally we were going to hear The Voice. Women of every size and hairdo started swooning, growling, licking their lips, digging their nails into the backs of the chairs in front of them. Even the curtains were dripping.

"Sing it to me pretty, Marvin!"

"Oh baby, I'm yours, now and forever!"

"Uh-huh. Give me some!"

Marvin sang several upbeat numbers and then the music slowed down. *Uh-oh,* I thought, *here it comes.* Marvin was perspiring so much that the woman to my right, who had gotten all fired up, offered him the fan she had been using to cool herself down.

"Oooh, you make me so hot," he teased, waving the fan back and forth.

"Better stop that or I'm comin' up there," she told him. "Better stop, hear me?"

"Okay," he said, in a super playful voice. "I'll be good."

"Miss," he said, looking straight at me. I pointed to myself in disbelief.

"Yes, you. Could I have this dance? I want to dance with you. You won't let me down, will you?"

I looked at Callie. "You have to," she declared. "This is the best birthday gift the universe is ever going to give you. Get up there now!" She and the woman next to me lifted me out of my seat. My legs were shaking so hard I could hardly make it up the steps.

Marvin opened his arms and, hardly moving, we embraced. Ever so gently the band began to offer up the first sultry notes of a ballad. The stage lights were brutal and soon we were soaked, rib to rib, stuck together like two lovers, in the late hour, all alone. The audience was stunned, watching every move we made; silence hung thick and juicy in the air, sprinkled only with an occasional jealous comment. I looked down at my sister to make sure everything was okay. She was grinning and sobbing like the rest of the crowd.

"You okay, honey?" Marvin asked protectively, looking down into my face.

"Yes, Mr. Gaye," I told him, and he bent his head forward much closer.

"Oh my Lord, he's not gonna do it, is he?" I heard a woman say. "Marvin, Marvin!" she yelled. "The woman you need is over here!"

"No, she isn't!" another woman yelled. "I'm the one you want, honey! Look over here!"

Females were wildly gesticulating, sobbing, shaking their fists in the heated air. House keys, limp bunched carnations and single roses, a wadded up one-hundred-dollar bill, paper-wrapped toffees, a torn black brassiere, love poems, a dime bag and perfume-drenched bikini panties of all different colors sailed through the air and landed all around us on the stage floor.

I felt Marvin's eyelashes on my cheek and his mouth traveling down. His lips were warm and smooth and buttery like caramel.

He rested them gently on mine and they delivered the most innocent kiss I would ever know. It was as if he was paying tribute to the feminine, kissing every woman in the audience through me.

This was the first time in my life that I was absolutely sure there was a God.

16

BEFORE AND AFTER, 1976

It was Thanksgiving time again, and this one was going to be a corker—even Callie was coming home. And MollieO seemed more and more lost as time went on without Martin around.

My sister had been *killin' 'em* in the Catskills, and her first album was heading up the charts. She only agreed to come because I had shamed her into it over the phone. "Oh, okay!" she told me. "But I'll be late!"

I had talked MollieO into letting me prepare the turkey out of a sense of guilt, pure and simple, because I'd been keeping my distance for a month or so. Actually, I was feeling totally empty and didn't want to have to share the experience with my mother. I guess writing my dissertation, "The Resurrection of the Innocence of Childhood," had something to do with it. After six weeks of effort, I hadn't been able to write more than the introduction.

It was early afternoon, and I was trying to break out of a thick funk, with little success. I sat on the toilet seat, looking at the floor in the room where I had suffered for so many years. I knew that a part of me was dead. And the rest was scared. I reached for the phone.

"Callie, come home now," I said in a vapid voice. That was all.

I just sat there and held my face in my hands.

"Come home now," I repeated. *Come home now.*

Hours later, Callie knocked on the bathroom door, but I couldn't find the energy to respond.

"Billie, can I come in? What the hell is going on in there?" She opened the door.

"What are you doing? Dinner is set for five o'clock and nothing's started. That's not like Billie The Dutiful," she said, winking at me. I couldn't speak.

My sister edged over slowly and sat at my feet. She put her November cold hands on my warm legs, and I started to cry.

"Sweet sister, what's all this about? I haven't ever seen you cry like this before. What's happening with you?"

"I'm dying," I finally admitted. "Every day a little piece of me is dying away."

There was a long silence.

"The truth is I've been worried about you for a long time—but I'm feeling it's a good sign that you're crying."

Then I really began to wail. "I can't do this anymore! I can't pretend I love myself and that everything's all right when it isn't. I know you don't understand because you seem to be sailing through life. But I'm not you. I'm exhausted. I don't have an idea in hell who I am."

"And you think I do? You think I've got it all sewn up? Do you think I haven't had days where I couldn't be alone or when all I wanted to do was sleep? Well, I'm here to tell you, Sister mine, that I used to have plenty of those. That is, until Sweet Mama Jefferson set me straight. We were performing together in Newark. After the gig she sat back and watched me get messed up on gin for four hours straight, then put her arms around me and brought me to bed. Mama said, 'Honey, how come you ain't got the picture yet? Life ain't perfect and nobody's gonna give you nothin' 'cept yourself.'"

Callie took me by the hand and we stood in front of my bathroom mirror. She turned on the switch so that all twenty-five white bulbs flashed on, adding drama to the moment.

"This is the secret," Callie said in a wise, comforting voice. "Until you get your life in order you've got to *act* like you already do. You've got to wake up and stand in front of this mirror and say, 'I love you, Billie.'"

Callie waited for me to respond, and when I didn't she patiently tried again. She stood in back of me and wound her arms around my waist to give me support and looked straight in the mirror and repeated, "I love you, Billie. Go on now, you say it."

Finally I couldn't contain it any longer and I yelled, "What are you, fucking nuts? I can't say that. It's a goddamned lie."

"Then lie!" my sister commanded. "Lie and then lie some more until you begin to believe it. And you're going to have to be vigilant. You're going to have to drag your sorry upper-class ass to the mirror and say, '*I love you, Billie. I love you, Billie!*' Come on! Be Liz Taylor, for Christ's sake. Go for an Oscar!"

I liked that. I thought of Simone Signoret's sensual lips forming the words, and I said, in a self-mocking, pouty French accent, "I loave you, Beelee."

As both of our faces searched in the mirror, my sister was silent. Then suddenly she kissed me on the cheek. "It's a beginning," she said, "but I meant what I said. You have to pick yourself up and look into the mirror until that little person inside of you starts to get big. Until your power kicks in. And Billie, give up that dissertation on innocence. No wonder you feel dead. Pick something fun like 'Adolph Hitler's Sex Life' or the power of kissing. You love kissing!"

Yeah, as long as it stops there.

"Here's another idea: Write the story of your life and describe how you want the rest of your life to be. This story is only for you, so tell the truth and don't feel guilty for asking for what you want, because nobody else is ever going to know—except for your beautiful sister. . . . In fact, let's start now. Get that pad of paper. Wait a minute, hold on. . . .'"

Callie left the room and returned with Martin's marble desk lighter and the dissertation. "And for God's sake," she said, as the flame caught the first page, "Cut this shit out! Stop depressing yourself."

We watched as the pages burned in the sink. I looked back up in the mirror and saw more of my outline filling in. My sister placed her arms around me again. "I love you, kiddo. You're the best thing that ever happened to me."

We stood in the silence while my soul drank in the incredible safety and comfort of the moment. Callie was hugging life back into me. For a moment I thought about telling her about the early years with Martin, but quickly I reasoned with myself that I should have been over it by then. After all, Callie wanted me to be excited about my future, not caught up in the past. I put on my "rising to the occasion" face but I felt unbalanced.

Then she passed me the pad.

"I'll do it later," I told her with resistance surging up. "I gotta get dressed. I gotta stuff the bird. I gotta—"

"You gotta make a life," she interrupted, placing the pen in my hand. *"Create the life you want. Write with intention. Say it out loud. I want to hear you!"*

"Okay," I said, doing it for her. It was the only way I was going to get her off my case. But also, as much as I hated to admit it, I could feel something was beginning to shift in my emotions, too. "I want to live in a swanky brownstone far away from here," I blurted out, totally surprising myself.

"Yes!" Callie affirmed.

"I want to be a goddamned great psychologist, give my soul to my patients. Really help them. . . ."

"Well, okay, as long as it's healing and fun for you. I don't know about giving away your soul, though. Sounds suspicious. More fun, please."

"I want a sports car. Black, I think. Or is that too morose?"

"I think it's sexy. Go, girl!"

"I want to stop taking care of MollieO. I don't want to totally let go but I want some SPACE!" Predictably, my stomach knotted up. "God, do I feel guilty about that one," I said, grasping on to Callie.

"Yeah, well, every time you feel guilty think about how hard it's been for you to love yourself, and what role Mother has played in that."

"Okay, okay!" I snapped back.

Callie took me by the hand and together we created a fabulous feast. As luck would have it, MollieO had a migraine and did not attend. We stuffed ourselves and drank several bottles of Dom Perignon. I vaguely remember my sister lugging me off to the bedroom, where I passed out.

When I opened the front door to leave for grad school the next day, I found a perfect red velvet journal propped up next to the elevator. There, scrolled across the opening page, I read:

In Which Billie Discovers Her Boundaries
And Learns To Fly
Scene One

17

"BLACK MAGIC WOMAN," 1980

While having a "senior moment," MollieO slipped in the shower and went to bed for what would turn out to be a four-month retreat. Even though she had two twenty-four-hour nurses, along with her other live-in staff, she called me to her bedside the first evening and made me promise that I would come by on my lunch hour every day and walk her precious animals. Nobody else would know how to tend to their needs the way I would.

Dutifully, I arrived the next day around noon to corral the troops: Prince Pei, the Pekingese; Beckett, the Irish wolfhound; Mirabella, the poodle; Rothschild, the cocker spaniel (and elder of the group); Marilyn, a blonde Afghan; and a long-haired dachshund who was incredibly hyper, named The Senator. They jumped and flirted and pulled at my coat, ready to cut loose in the Big City.

In my naiveté I decided to walk them over to Central Park and let them experience the provocative sights and smells of twenty thousand canines. Needless to say, they were beside themselves, sniffing and leaving their mark on practically every inch of at least two acres of the Park.

We all collided on a park bench and sat to take a breather. Scarlet red coats and pastel ski jackets paraded before us, announcing the coming winter season. In the distance I noticed a man and a woman emerge from under a small bridge. Both were wearing torn, floor length trench coats that dragged along the ground. The man carried a large boom box and the woman a Bloomingdale's bag. They sat down at the other end of the park bench, a safe enough distance from me. They were speaking Spanish in a low voice, murmuring in a seductive, playful way. I heard the spray of beer cans opening.

I watched them out of the corner of my eye. The woman bent forward and her red hair spilled out of her hat over her shoulders. The man was lost in every move she made. He had his arm around her and was curling her hair with his fingers. He stroked her hand, caressed her face. She was laughing from a very private place.

They started kissing long sweptaway kisses, and he stood up and grabbed her by the shoulders and pulled her to him. She was eagerly drowning in his desire and moaning like crazy. Then they lay down on the bench. It was all so lusty I felt like I was going to pass out. *Oh, my God, they're going to do it right here!* I thought, outraged, and yet carried away along with them.

But the man made the bench move and it groaned too loud, and The Senator freaked out. He jerked the leash out of my hand and nipped the woman in the leg. She yelled out "Ay!" and reached down to push the dog away.

"I'm so sorry. Are you okay?" I said as I grabbed the end of The Senator's leash and pulled him back to me. It was then that I saw that the woman's wrist was encircled with a tattoo of pink roses. The woman from the street had entered my world again. But this time she was in love.

I looked into her face to see if she recognized me, but she looked away and abruptly got up and took her man friend's arm. They walked over to the fading green grass, placed their raincoats on the ground under a neighboring oak tree and lay down. Santana sang about a "Black Magic Woman" as I watched the man lick a path between her neck and breasts. I turned away; they were too alive.

The rawness of their lovemaking pulled me in again and I let go of my literal way of seeing and watched with a photographer's eye as the enigmatic sunlight drifted in and out of clouds, shifting the perspective of their bodies blending on their trench coats in the autumn afternoon.

18

KARMIC FAMILY, 1980–90s

Every client I have spent time with was, most likely, a part of my karmic past, part of the Big Picture. Each one in a different way helped me uncover parts of myself that I needed to integrate. My patients weren't sick. They were just trying to get well.

I was the only psychologist in a sea of psychiatrists on the tenth floor of the Bentley Building. While the others prescribed "the meds" of the hour to stave off their patients' depression and suffering, I gently coaxed my tribe into integrating those feelings with hypnotherapy, guided imagery, even hands-on healing. I encouraged them to focus on their intuition and tried to teach them to quiet their coyote minds through meditation.

Portraits of Freud and Jung did not appear anywhere, although like any good therapist I utilized what they had to offer now and then. Instead, drawings of American Indian healers graced my walls as well as portraits of Gandhi, Buddha, Martin Luther King, Vietnamese Zen master Thich Nhat Hanh, Indian philosopher Ramana Maharshi, Audrey Hepburn in her last years holding children on her lap in Africa, and my hero, the Dalai Lama. Ancient healing tools sat like sculptures on my coffee table, and I had a stellar collection of rattles from many different tribes stacked one above the other on top of the book shelves. Once in a while jasmine incense would filter out into the hallway.

Neighboring colleagues would walk by my office, tap on the half-opened door and ask me a little bit about my work. What exactly was I practicing? I think there may have been some interest there, but all in all I was treated like a kooky "New Ager." A blonde wild card in a strictly black and white deck.

All of these eccentricities drove MollieO nuts. On the rare occasions when she'd stop by my office, she'd wander around grimacing as she picked up one after another of the various relics and implements I'd collected from different cultures and belief systems. "For the life of me," she would say, "I don't know where I went wrong. This feels like Lillian's work! I should've known better than to let you spend so much time with her when you were young. She's turned you into an absolute weirdo!"

Long Live Lillian!

I have to admit that I did enjoy watching my mother's face fill with confusion as she stared at the portraits of great spirits hanging on my walls, all of whom—except Audrey, of course—she considered heathens. "What will your colleagues think?" she exclaimed one afternoon as she picked up a Peruvian clay pot used for mixing herbs. She quickly put it down because her hand had gotten a particle of dust on it. "Have you lost your mind? If you don't remove all of this *stuff* you'll scare your patients away, and then where will you be?"

Despite my mother's admonitions, new and long-term patients came in droves to my office, with its sweeping views of Fifth Avenue. They breathed deeply and told me of their daughters' promiscuity, a second bout of uterine cancer, fantasies of self-mutilation, their secret racism or obsessions. . . . On and on the fears mounted: fear of flying, the color red, getting stuck in an airplane bathroom, traveling into cities alone, dying alone, dying of a broken heart, dying surrounded by people they didn't like, driving in the suburbs, eating alone, dancing in public, drowning, anal sex, lisping, running injuries, sleeping alone, being raped, being beautiful, being married, being old, being abandoned, being disrespected, being used for money, being too short, lacking courage, being too sexy, too greedy, too understated, too open, too withdrawn. Too unlovable. That was the big one. No matter what dark secret each confided, underneath it lurked the same terrible fear: being unlovable. I could relate.

Together I and my karmic family created a relationship supported by warm, freshly baked oatmeal cookies and strongly brewed teas. I was adamant about placing fresh vases of daffodils and freesia and Hawaiian orchids in constant view. Peach colored curtains draped from the big windows that faced the Avenue cast a soft, loving hue. It was a healing space.

I had become a seasoned champ at this, and I was loving it. In only a few years I had made my practice my life—each patient was a fresh novel to dive into, an ever-expanding journey into the unknown, away from the city's noise and grit. A sedative to remedy my own loneliness. Each client's small breakthrough became a new glint of color woven into the flimsy tapestry of my self-worth.

My credentials covered the wall behind my desk. My monthly calendar was over the top with appointments. It appeared to be a full life. The story I was creating about myself had begun to take root. I thanked my sister Callie again and again in mirrors and department store windows. "I love you, I love you," I would tell her, hoping the message would reach her across the oceans wherever she was singing. She had taught me well. It felt good to know I would survive.

19

CLOSE-UPS AND PIN-UPS, 1980s & ON

My private life was a whole other story. I guess all of my unresolved emotion molded me into a magnet for bad men. I told myself all the good men were already taken or gay, but the truth is I did meet some good men along the way. I just couldn't understand why they would choose me. The weird guys were different. They swarmed around me like killer bees. I guess they picked up my true scent, "Ambivalence." I swear, I could have sold my musk to Calvin Klein.

Michael was a three-piece-suited financial analyst speed freak. Oh, so vain. Vernon was leather, leather, and more leather. Greg was an up and coming SoHo artist going nowhere. Miguel was uncomfortable being gay but comfortable with me. *What a surprise.* Ralph was your basic marketing guy, with big ideas and no substance. Skip was a closet alcoholic airplane pilot. Gino twalked like dis.

Dutch always wore grocery bag brown. Tad was in love with someone else. Herbert hated animals. Len met me for our first (and only) rendezvous at a very swank nightclub with his slithery boa, Hillary, wrapped around his neck. Skip was a salesman who was gone a lot of the time, which could have been a great arrangement if I had been attracted to the guy even a particle.

At the door, after having quite a subdued, sophisticated evening, Brian inquired boldly, "So, babe, wanna fuck?" *Next!*

Cliff brought his radio to dinner and listened to the ball game while we got to know each other. *I don't think so.* Glenn carried a little gun next to his heart. In the first four seconds of our date, Walter confessed to me how little his penis was. *Ewww!* Greg worked on Harley Davidson motorcycle engines, so you know what his fingernails looked like. And his tattoos.

Garth was built like a massive flabby baby. Billy loved country music and only country music. Tig was a colleague of my father's who had taken EST and had just "gotten" that he was God. George worked for one of those "rooter" companies, and stared too much at my plumbing. Brent was *so* white.

Akli had the gall to stroke my leg at dinner telling me it was a Moroccan custom. Frank drank. And Tom was his A.A. sponsor, the only man in the group who was a real threat to figure out why I hid from men. The poor guy made the mistake of gently alluding to my Houdini-like disappearing act, so I dumped him before he got me into the sack. Actually I dumped all of them before they even saw my living room.

Men were meaning less and less to me even though there were more and more of them. How did I get these men to hang out with me on my terms without doing the deed? By being the world's best listener, earth mother, baker and shrink. Of course, this way I was in no danger of sharing too much of myself. Happily, they were all so self-absorbed they didn't notice. All were perfect opportunities to practice my philosophy that I would not sleep with a man until I felt he really knew me. Fat chance with these guys. I went out of my way to make sure none of them could get me to open up. Many moonlit evenings I would raise a chilled Stolichnaya in a crystal gimlet glass and toast Della, my big female marmalade kitty, once my boyfriend of the hour had disappeared.

20

HUNGRY GHOST, 1985

Most lunch times you could find me at Zoe's Deli, a block from my office. I was sitting at the counter waiting for my tuna on rye one afternoon on one of those rare occasions when a patient didn't show up. When I looked out the window, my heart turned over. The woman with the red hair had wandered uptown and had once again entered my world.

She arrived like a hungry ghost staring from outside into the Deli. I met her stare, and motioned to the chair next to me. She turned away.

"Not this time," I heard myself say, and walked through the Deli doors right out of my safe little existence.

"Hey," I said in a soft but not too friendly voice. She didn't look or answer. I tried again. "Hey, are you hungry? Can I get you something to eat?" She was leaning against the deli wall for support. She looked into my face blankly and shook her head.

"It's cold out here. How about some coffee?"

Her nose was running, and she started to cough. I went back into the deli and got several napkins and handed them to her. Her hands were shaking.

"Come inside. It's warm in there."

"No," she said, coughing again. "Sick." Her skin had a hepatitis yellow tint and she was too thin. Her body slumped forward, and I caught her arm and helped her steady herself against the restaurant wall.

"My name's Billie. I've seen you before . . . around . . . the city. You've got that pretty flower tattoo, right?" I pointed to my wrist. "Las flores?" She looked at me directly, trying to figure out how I could know that. I had finally gotten her attention.

"What's your name? Cómo se llama?"

"Maria Milflores," she said, holding her belly. She put her hand over her mouth like she was going to be sick.

"Can I give you a ride to the doctor? Do you have a place to stay? I have a—" but then I stopped, not knowing if I should offer anymore. The truth is, I had scared myself. What if I offered her a place to stay and she accepted? What if she wanted to stay for good? She picked up on the uncertainty in my words, and I felt her energy shift. I was rapidly becoming a typical half-hearted, well-meaning annoyance.

She walked away from me, one hand balancing herself against the buildings.

"Can I drive you to the hospital? Please," I yelled, "let me help you!"

I had gone too far, been in her face, and then backed off. Maybe I sounded condescending or too much like a social worker. P. I. Bartholomew. It was hard to know how far to go with her or how much I could handle. We both had strange, jaggedy boundaries. I followed her for a couple of blocks but she didn't look back. We were deep into rush hour, and soon she was just another junkie untouchable, swallowed up by the Christmas shoppers flooding Fifth Avenue.

21

YOGA, BIRKENSTOCKS AND
A YOUNG MAN'S SWEETNESS, 1992

Except for the occasional flirtation or romance turned friend-ship, I had given up the idea of ever experiencing a "real" rela-tionship, which I loosely defined as hanging out with someone special without much happening and, of course, trying to stay in my body. There might be a little trust involved too, a concept quite foreign to me where men were concerned.

In my forty-second year I organized a therapy group that met one evening a week, and worked at a battered women's shelter until a terrible exhaustion overtook me and I had to quit both. So I created a full-on fitness program and actually stuck to my goals. I stretched, I ran, I ate alkaline, non-fatty foods, I swam, and Aunt Lillian talked me into taking a yoga class with her twice a week in the East Village. Lillian was nearly seventy but moved like a twenty-year-old. I was a mere child, and as rigid as the diving board at the east side Armory.

Lillian raved about the "Wise Old Soul" who was to be our teacher. As we placed our bare feet on the warm, wooden floor of the yoga studio, I pictured our teacher as a dark, sinewy, sixty-ish yogi who had come from India to educate the ignorant and the portly. I was quite surprised when a man who looked to be in his early thirties showed up.

Sean O'Rourke had the face of a sunflower: radiant, gentle, at ease. When he bent over to help me adjust my posture, he touched me ever so lightly. *This guy must not have a mean bone in his body,* I thought to myself in the beginning. *I can tell that he likes women.* These were high marks coming from a cynic like me.

After class one evening Sean asked me out for tea, and we ended up spending the evening together. We talked for hours, and then he asked me if I would like to meditate at his apartment down the street. I agreed. I didn't have the vaguest idea how to meditate, but I admired people who did. I closed my eyes and tried to quiet down. My mind was outraged that I would try such a thing, and it fought me like the enemy. When the meditation was over, Sean O'Rourke turned and kissed me in the nicest way.

"I'm totally attracted to you, Billie," he said. "I have been from the first time you came to class. There's something so soft about you."

What?

"I feel energized when I'm with you. Can I see you again?"

I figured I'd better say yes, because I didn't have anything else to do. Besides, I had to try to be in a real relationship sometime.

And so began a three-year relationship that started as sweetly as a precious haiku, but ended more like a nineteenth century death dirge. It wasn't Sean's fault. He tried everything to help me open up, but it seemed the deeper we got into it the more distanced I became.

Our first year went pretty well. I thought Sean was adorable in all the right ways. He was a gentle lover who knew enough to take his time. In other words, he spent about twenty hours kissing my lips, another fifteen on my neck, and a couple of months on my breasts. By the time we got to the oral sex part, I felt trusting, and yet excited. And believe me, that was some surprise.

For a man twenty years younger than most of the other men who had been in my life, Sean was light years ahead in the "sensitivity to your lover" department. He was an interesting blend of masculinity and femininity, not macho but not a woosy either—kind of like the Dalai Lama, one of the sexiest men in the world in my humble opinion.

After a year we were spending almost every day together. He had his own drawer in my dresser, and we were getting pretty serious. Or, let's say Sean was pretty serious and I was trying to go there. After two years things started to change, and I got very restless. Downright moody. I told myself he was too young, but that was a lie. He was the most mature man I had ever known. I began to look for things I didn't like.

Funny how one day you can think your lover is the most beautiful being on the planet. You watch him in the shower and feel completely turned on. Then maybe you have a little talk a week or so later, and he says something that feels threatening, like, "I think Mary in my nine o'clock class is pretty." Or, "What would you think about living together?" and you go absolutely wild. Suddenly that cute ass you've been ogling isn't as perfect as it was yesterday. In fact, there might be some cellulite forming, and is that dandruff on the shoulder of the new navy blue silk shirt you just bought him?

By year three I was bonkers. On the inside I was an insecure, jealous infant who was waiting to be betrayed somehow, or left. On the outside I was a perfectionist, resistant to everything Sean tried to do and be for me. For instance, he would bring me red roses and I'd thank him, but mention how I really loved purple ones. When he wanted to hold me through the night, I projected that he was weird and needy. Why else would he want to be close to me all the time? The closer he wanted to become, the more my mind tortured me with fantasies that it was my father, not Sean, lying in bed with me.

I'd say nasty stuff that would push him out of my space and pretend that I was a strong adult woman totally in the right. I caused dramas and emotional outbursts while he created stability and a nurturing, peaceful environment—something I found nearly impossible to accept. My distancing manifested in the most transparent ways. I found myself exhibiting the same kind of fear-filled behavior that my patients reported. Soon, with all of this craziness, there was no sex to be found or energy to be ignited.

"It has nothing to do with you," I told him as he packed his belongings in the bedroom on our last night. "It's me. I'm no good at this. I don't know how to love anybody. And you're an easy one to love. You're wonderful."

Sean's bewhiskered face was filled with sadness.

"You gave me everything," I went on, "and I just couldn't take it. I've been in and out of therapy for years, but nothing seems to change. At least with you I gave it a shot. We did great for a while didn't we? Maybe that's all one can ask."

"Do me a favor," he said, loading up the last of his things in his backpack. "Don't come to yoga for awhile. I need some healing time. And Billie, you're a magnificent woman, no matter what happened to you. I wouldn't have missed one moment of this."

I didn't feel much of a reaction to our breakup except that I pigged out on a pint of ice cream every night for a month. When I stopped, the feelings started coming. I was sure that if you looked in the dictionary under spinster you would find my picture. I was destined to stay shut down and die alone, like MollieO, absolutely doomed.

22

WOMAN OF A THOUSAND FLOWERS, 1993

"There she is!"

Lillian and I had gone to a matinee and were on our way to a late lunch when I saw the street woman, Maria, sitting on the curb across the street.

"There's the woman I told you about—the one I wanted to bring home. The one I wanted to help, but couldn't. Remember how I beat myself up about that?"

Lillian nodded. "She looks pretty bad. If you're gonna try and help her you better do it now. You know what's been happening in this city, don't you? As soon as they find her the authorities will force her off the streets into a hospital or rehab or something. By tomorrow, she could disappear completely, lost in the system. I'll translate for you right now if you want. Come on."

We crossed the street and sat down next to Maria. She was talking to herself and making grand gestures with her hands. She was definitely schized out, picking imaginary things off her clothing.

"Maria? Maria Milflores, right? How are you doing?"

Lillian repeated the words in Spanish. "She says, 'Ándale'— Go away."

"Tell her I want to help her. Tell her I want to get her some food. I want to find her a place to rest away from the street."

Lillian shook her head "No. She says the street is her home. She felt safe until you came. She says, 'Get away from me. People like you make me crazy. Let me live in peace.'"

Lillian pulled me up from the curb. As we walked away I felt my heart turn over in my chest.

"You know, Billie, not everyone thinks and feels the way you do. Maybe she thinks she's doing okay. We don't have an idea in hell what she's lived through. Living in a shelter has its rules and regulations. For some it's like being in jail, while living on the street is a form of freedom. At least you get to call your own shots. You learn a different kind of trust. You're in a different kind of community. Just because we don't understand it, doesn't mean it isn't right. Maybe it's the only home she knows. You know?"

I knew Lillian was right. Still, I didn't want to let it go. "But it's obvious she's even sicker than the poor people I saw when I worked at that shelter for battered women. Can't we try to help her? Isn't that the humane thing to do when people can't take care of themselves? Shouldn't we take control of the situation and make some choices for her? We could call an ambulance. . . . If she stays here too long the cops are going to pick her up anyway. Do you think she's well enough to know that?"

"She already told you she wants to live in peace," said Lillian. "My intuition tells me we should respect what she said and leave her some dignity. Who are we to take her freedom? She's not harming anyone. She may be sick but she's well enough to tell you to leave her be. Can't we accept that?"

I looked back at Maria and thought about what Lillian was saying, but I was still upset.

"Besides," said Lillian, "who is it you're really trying to save from all that suffering?"

23

FATHER–DAUGHTER DAYS, 1995

After spending years in relationships and different kinds of therapies that went absolutely nowhere, I realized I still needed to heal. And in order to heal, I needed to go to the source. I got the big idea to confront my father about my childhood molestation. I believed that this singular act would release my outrage and suffering and bring my power back. Then, healed, I could miraculously trust again and create a relationship.

I made a dozen phone calls to my father's apartment but always got his housekeeper. "Mr. Bartholomew no home," she would say. "Out of town."

The truth is I was so nervous about confronting him that I was relieved when he didn't call back. I wrote numerous letters outlining the various abuses he perpetuated, demanding an apology. Of course, I never sent them.

I had fantasies of how the confrontation would go down. About half of the fantasies had happy endings. "I'm so sorry," he would say, wiping his eyes. "What can I do to make it up to you?" In another fantasy, I was thrown off the balcony and landed on the street fifty-six floors down. My hands would shake just thinking about the randomness of his rage, and the high-voltage scenario I was stepping into was anything but random.

Even so, I had gotten to the point where I couldn't stand my lonely life any longer. I asked MollieO for the address of his apartment.

"He's living quite a life, you know, dating around. Never remarried. He's rebuilt his practice like nobody's business. I swear that man can charm anyone! Who would guess he's a convict! I hear he's on a radio talk show once a month and he's made another fortune in real estate. Judge Van Denberg's widow sees him at the racetrack quite often. And I know he hangs out with those bankers, playing poker. I told you he had another small stroke, didn't I? Well, anyway, he did. But I guess he's doing fine. That man is so resilient, isn't he? If you've got a message for your father, why don't you just give it to me."

Not this time.

One evening after work I gathered my nerve and headed to Father's apartment, passing St. Luke's Church on the way. I always got a kick out of the titles of their sermons, so I stopped in front of the kiosk to see what was planned for that Sunday. It said, "Live And Let Live."

Just as I was turning away to head toward the corner, I saw the woman again. Maria. She was walking down the front stairs of the church holding a little boy's hand, and a cop was holding her arm. As they got closer I recognized the city-worn face of that officer who had spoken back to my father in our old lobby years ago, the day I was forced to say good-bye to the world's greatest kisser, John Castelucci. The officer nodded and looked me straight in the eye. Strangely, I began to sense a feeling of confidence wafting through me. Then the three of them turned and walked in the opposite direction, so I continued on to father's building.

I raced past the doorman, who yelled at me for my name and destination. "Bartholomew, 56C," I shouted back as the elevator door closed. "I'm his daughter." I knew I would be turned away if he contacted my father. After all, it had been some fifteen years since he'd had the pleasure of my company.

I pressed the doorbell once. I pressed it twice and a bunch of dogs barked excitedly. Someone on the other side looked through the little peephole in the door.

"I'm Mr. Bartholomew's daughter. Can I come in?"

"He no expecting you. Come back later," I was told.

"No, you don't understand. It's an emergency!" I said in an exaggerated voice. "I must talk with my father, now!"

The door opened. Four white standard poodles charged toward me in semi-attack mode.

"Come in! Come in!" the servant yelled at me. "No let them out! No good!"

I pushed myself past the dogs and they followed us down the long corridor nipping at my heels, jumping up in the air to the side of me.

The apartment was massive, even more palatial than the apartment of my childhood. Everywhere I looked were paintings by modern masters and pictures of celebrity well-wishers. There were massive pieces of Louis XIV furniture grouped together and huge vases of white carnations in each room. I was surprised to find family portraits scattered amidst pictures of his beloved thoroughbreds.

"Wait here," the servant said and disappeared. Minutes later he came back. I was so anxious I was having a hard time breathing.

"You father say okay. Go in, please."

I walked into a mammoth bedroom that was thick with shower steam and cigar smoke. The smell was nauseating. I could vaguely make out my father's form standing in the adjoining bathroom.

My heart was beating fast, and it occurred to me that this was probably a bad idea. I started to turn around when Father said, "You've come this far, you might as well come in, Billie."

"I don't want to intrude. I'll wait in the other room until you're dressed."

"This is a busy night for me," he said, continuing to shave. "If you want to talk, it will have to be now."

His voice was even more intimidating than I had remembered. I walked further into the room, but there was no place to sit down except on the bed. I quickly looked around for a phone. With Martin, you had to know that there was a phone nearby so you could call for help. Luckily, there was a white phone next to the carnations on the table. Not that I could have actually picked it up, dialed it and put it to any good use before he'd knock it out of my hand and into the next county. But somehow knowing one was within reach made my knees shake a little less.

As the steam lifted, I could see that Father was bare-chested with a towel wrapped around his waist.

"Sit down," he said, looking into the mirror. My legs folded.

"So, what's the big emergency?" he asked, sliding a razor up his sudsy neck. I was getting really scared.

I could not remember any of the speeches I had prepared for this moment, but I managed to say, "I'm here because I'm having a tough time in my life. I'm not happy and I thought—"

"Who the hell is happy?" His voice was definitely picking up energy. "You know, I haven't heard a thing from you or your sister after you cut me out of your lives." He turned around and looked directly at me. "What is this all about? Do you need money? Is that why you're here?" I started to feel paralyzed. There was no safe place for me in that room.

I've got to get out of here!

"Look, Father," I went on, "I'm not here for money. I'm here because there's something that I need to say." My voice felt weak.

Sensing my fear, he took full advantage and said, "Well, what the hell is it? Speak!"

I felt like I was going to pass out.

Martin changed direction.

"How's MollieO?" he asked. "Do you go to see her or do you treat her the way you treat me?"

"Yes, I do," I said, collecting myself. "I see her quite often. But I'm here to talk to you about something that's been bothering me for a long time."

"For Christ's sake, Billie!" he yelled in my direction. "Just say it! It's my poker night."

That was it. My guts let go.

"I know what you did," I said standing up. "I remember what happened."

"What the hell are you talking about? Get to the point."

The tears started rolling down my face. I was not forty-five years old. I was five.

"I remember you coming into my bedroom when I was very little, when I was asleep. You whispered things to me like 'You better take those panties off by the time I come back or I'm going to take them off you myself.' You said that!"

He came out of the bathroom with the razor in his hand. "Is this some kind of joke? Have you lost your mind?"

"You came in my bedroom and touched me, you touched me," and then I started sobbing, "in very inappropriate places. You did bad things—to me." I was getting semi-hysterical. "You ruined my childhood! My life's falling apart because I can't trust anybody!"

The air was dense with Martin's unspoken emotions. When I could find it in me to look up, I watched his face flush with indignation. He started to move closer toward me.

"You're not going to try to get me to believe this shit, are you? You enjoyed it as much as I did! I remember how you used to seduce me with those sexy eyes of yours. Even when you were a very little girl you lured me into your bed. *You* tempted *me*! Don't you remember how you moaned and made those sexy little girl sounds? You were asking for it. You loved it! So I don't want to hear any more about this terrible thing that *I* did to *you*. Grow up for once and face the truth. You did it to yourself!"

"Listen, you bastard." I heard the rage welling up inside of me, growling with vengeance. "I'm only going to say this once." I stepped closer, into his energy. "You took my innocence away from me. You took my joy. You devastated my life!" I felt as though a dam was bursting in my heart, with all the years of horror crashing through. There was no holding back. "You will never be happy until you face what you did to me. Never!" I shouted. "Do you hear me?"

My father took a step toward me, his razor clenched close to his chest.

"You're a soulless devil who feeds on the death of the human spirit!" I screamed. "You deserve to live and die in hell!"

Suddenly Martin cut through the air toward my face, but I ducked, and my right hand fisted and slugged him hard in the groin. He backed up and collapsed on the bed in shock, writhing in agony. I ran from the room, grabbed my coat off the living room chair and raced out the front door. I was sobbing hysterically when the elevator door opened on a group of men with dark hats and coats. They were all smoking cigars under their black umbrellas. A couple of them glanced my way with a look of disdain as they headed toward my father's apartment.

The night was boldly blue and I had so much adrenaline moving through me that I ran all the way home. At the corner of my street I stopped and leaned against a parking meter and laughed. I laughed so hard I thought my rib cage would collapse. I laughed until my lungs hurt, then I went inside.

Once I got myself centered a bit, I built a fire. The power in me kept building, and as I paced back and forth I pictured hitting him again and again, bombing his apartment building, going to the police and filing charges. I saw myself in a courtroom defending all the children who have been shamed, while their fathers and brothers and aberrant uncles and neighbors lowered their heads. The more dramatic the scenario, the greater the healing my heart felt.

Finally I began to calm down. I sat before the fire, sipping on a Scotch and replaying the real scene. "I want you out of my life!" I shouted. Della jumped off the couch and bolted into the other room. I followed her and pulled out a scrapbook of pictures from my childhood that Aunt Lillian had made up for me. I whipped through the book, tearing out every picture of Martin that I could find. I sat close to the fire and looked at the different scenarios, the ungodly situation of our lives.

"From now on, you are dead to me," I announced quietly, with venom.

Then I flung one picture at a time into the fire and watched the images curl up and shrivel in the flames.

24

CHEZ CALLIE, 1997

The years rolled on, and Callie and I managed to talk every couple of months, but we hadn't seen each other for almost five years. Predictably, it was I who was always there for her spontaneous phone calls. "Hi, it's me!" she would exclaim from Paris or Berlin or Moscow. I can't describe the grin on my face when I received her phone call from a hundred blocks away.

"Oh, my God! Oh, my God! Where are you? What are you doing here? When can I see you?"

"Here's the deal. We're only here for a couple days. Actually this is our last day. We're on our way to L. A.," she said half apologetically.

"Oh," I said, letting her timetable sink in. "Who's we?"

"Me and Philippe. I told you I met this amazing percussionist on the Côte D'Azur, remember? He's playing with my group. You've got to come down to the club tonight, Billie. It's our only chance to be together. We're taking a real late night red-eye. You *will* come, Billie. . . ?"

"Of course I will. Anything to see you. It's just so short a visit, I wish—"

She interrupted me mid-sentence. "Let's not go there. Let's work with what we have. At least we have tonight. Come for dinner and bring Mother. I have a surprise."

She gave me the directions and I hung up realizing I only had an hour to get ready. There never was any planning to be done when it came to Callie.

To say the least, I was a little surprised that Callie would want to see MollieO, especially when she and I had such little time together. I was racing around, trying to find something vaguely hip to wear when the phone rang again.

"Darlin'," MollieO said, "you're there. I'm so glad you're there! I'm so lonely. I need to see you. Come for dinner. I can't be alone another night, I'm going crazy. Say you will, Billie, please!"

"I'm sorry you're feeling lonely, but I've got great news. Callie's in town and she's invited us both down to see her. She says she has a surprise for us."

"I know she's in town because the *Times* printed those raunchy reviews about her."

"Really? She made the *New York Times*! What did they say?"

MollieO let out one of her super frustrated sighs. "They said she's a turn-on. A real tease. They said she was carrying on with some African gentleman on stage. Why does she always have to embarrass me? Who taught her to act like a . . . a . . . ?" Mother held her tongue because she didn't want to lose me. She was desperate for company.

"Oh, c'mon, Mother. It can't be that bad. She's always been a bit risqué. That's her style."

"Well, I refuse to be a part of it. I'm not going to some filthy little club all the way downtown to hear her cuss and sing dirty songs. Forget it. This is not the Callie I reared!"

There was a long pause because I had no idea what to say. That is, besides the truth, and I wasn't about to walk that road with MollieO. That would take a decade of dialogue.

"So, are you coming by?" she said in her depressed, repressed, suppressed voice.

"I told you. I can't stay with you tonight. I'm going to be with Callie. She's never in town, you know that. This may be my one chance for a long time. Your chance—"

MollieO hung up.

I held my new cat, Ellington, close to my chest as I paced back and forth, trying to feel good about not saving my mother. I envisioned Callie and I sitting close and talking about our lives, laughing and forging our relationship. I pictured her new boyfriend opening his arms to me, welcoming me in. I would like him, and hug him back. We would make plans for the holidays when they would stay in my home. We would toast the New Year in front of the fire. Sometime before they departed we would call MollieO and invite her to breakfast on New Year's Day. She would say no, but that would be okay because Callie would change plans and leave on an earlier flight anyway. And then the inevitable: I would be left alone with MollieO once again. Yeah, but tonight I have Callie all to myself.

I grabbed the nearest black outfit in the closet and hailed a cab.

There was a line two blocks long leading to the jazz club. I stepped out and walked to the front door.

"I'm Callie's sister," I said to the guy at the door, and he grabbed my arm and pulled me through the crowded entryway. I checked my coat and was lead to a tiny, oval ringside table. A beautiful young woman poured me a glass of Mumm's while I inhaled the scent of a perfect yellow rose. I looked around the room and recognized the animated faces of a couple of jazz greats standing at the bar. What a turnout! I noticed a certain legendary songstress receiving a grand amount of attention as she took off her coat and revealed her décolletage. *There's only one reason that woman's here,* I told myself smugly. *She's checking the "new girl" out.*

Callie's group began to assemble their instruments on stage, and the sound check got underway. I loved the attitude that prevailed on stage—not quite smug, but close. The smoke from European cigarettes and pot made its way to the front row, to my usually uptight nose, but in this little jazz joint it smelled good. It felt right. A hip-looking young woman softly cleaned off the drums and the keys of her piano. Another gentleman prepared the vibes and accompanying percussion. I loved the sweet tinkling of the bells and high-pitched tone of the triangles. Soon my sister's lover would enter into my life. In my mind I saw him walk on stage like an ambassador of cool, stunning in his double-breasted dark suit. A super elegant dude. Smoother than smooth.

The lights cast turquoise and indigo rays across the stage, and slowly the musicians materialized.

"Ladies and gentleman, put your hands together to welcome Mitch Crocker on drums, William Blainey on bass, Ron Markowitz on guitar. . . ."

They took their places and then we waited some more.

"Direct from an award-winning engagement in Africa, please welcome, Philippe Durant on percussion." Out he came in a white tux—no shirt—and what seemed like a thousand waist-long dreadlocks. His skin was walnut. His black sunglasses impenetrable. He reeked of elegant rebellion.

The mike made a terrible high-pitched screech. "Mood Indigo is honored to introduce Capital recording artist, Callie Durant!" Wild applause brought my sister on stage, and as she passed the vibesman he grabbed her hand and kissed it.

Durant? Oh yeah? Why am I always the last to know? This was indeed going to be an evening of surprises.

Ultramarine lighting streaked across the stage and *Ms. Durant's* bassist created an awesome intro for her to begin. I sat sipping my champagne, merging with the whole scene. Callie had her eyes closed. Slowly her body began to sway to the guitar, and she began to sing.

"I never knew a love like this before. The touch of your hand, . . ."

And then I watched Callie walk over to her percussionist, breathe in his essence and sing, *"The smell of your skin."*

Remembering when love felt alive like that, everyone smiled.

At the end of her first song, she turned to her group and whispered some directions, then she turned back to the audience and said, "Ladies, I wonder if you've ever felt like this. If you have, then this one's for you. . . ."

"I want a little cream in my bowl," she growled.

"I want a warm sausage in my roll.

Baby, please, can't you see

I'm as randy as can be?"

"We'll be back in a few," Callie whispered in a throaty voice into the mike. "Stay with us." Philippe joined her and they exited the stage hand-in-hand and walked to my table. We hugged and then she whispered, "I want to introduce you to someone." Then, looking at both of us, she said, "Here you are, my two favorite people on the planet."

"Hello," I said and held out my hand. "Non, non," he said and grabbed me and hugged me tight. He smelled like lemons and coconut and brown sugar. Callie was right. The man was one great-smelling sexpot. Totally edible.

Philippe brought some chairs from the back of the room and we all crowded together. "We got married in Paris and we're going to Africa for our honeymoon," Callie told me. "Isn't that the best?"

"I'm so very happy for you," I told my sister. Then, looking at both of them, I repeated in a desolate tone, "For both of you."

"Where's MollieO?"

"She couldn't come. She isn't feeling well."

"It's okay, I was expecting it," Callie said. Phillippe shook his head and all of those dreadlocks caught the light, "Such a shame," he remarked.

"It doesn't matter," Callie told him, taking a hold of his hands in hers, "I won't miss her, she's never been anything but trouble anyway."

"She's had a few good moments," I said in a semi-protective manner.

"With you she has. And I suspect you'll have more. I gave up a long time ago."

Philippe picked up on her sadness and buried his head into her chest. He started kissing her neck like crazy, and Callie began to giggle like we did in the old days.

They played the last set, we hugged some more and then Philippe went to get their bags and call a cab.

"I'm always so happy and so sad when I see you," I said. "There's so much I want to tell you. First of all, I like him a lot."

"Secondly," Callie said, taking my hand, "we're going to adopt a child from Africa."

"Wow! Two surprises in one! I wish Mother was here, too."

"Mother has never been here."

"Actually I'm glad we have this time alone. I'm really worried about her. She's getting much worse. She's afraid to be alone. She's constantly calling me, crying on the phone. It's impossible for me to have a regular life."

Callie's posture got defensive. "So why don't you stop trying to fix her life? She's never going to change. She's always going to manipulate you, that's the only way she knows how to be in life. Stop answering her calls and let her grow up."

"Maybe so. But I need your help. Couldn't you call her on the phone once in a while? Drop her a postcard from Madrid or Beijing or some damn place?"

"Now you sound hostile."

"I'm not hostile, Callie. It's just that I'm worried that my worst fear is about to come true. I'm scared that in the end it will be me hanging up MollieO's fancy dresses, pouring her vodkas, brushing her thick silver hair and applying her face cream as she passes out. It will be me who will be left without a husband, childless, to take care of a pathetic, drunken, solipsistic southern belle. . . . *Our* mother."

Philippe arrived and Callie got up from her chair.

"*Your* mother," she told me in a matter-of-fact voice. "I stopped playing into all that eons ago."

And then it was the long, sad hug good-bye and the promise of another visit that wouldn't happen for years.

Callie was annoyingly right. Unless I got vigilant, learned to say, "No!" and hired a nurse in the form of a Billie Bartholomew clone, it would, most assuredly, always be me.

25

LATE NIGHT STREET LIFE, 1999

The first Saturday of every month I treated myself to an off-off-off Broadway play in Greenwich Village. Unlike their celebrated cousins uptown, those plays were unpolished and risky, and it was this uncensored energy that reawakened a passion in me. It made me remember why I lived in Manhattan.

Walking through the semi-lit streets after the show looking for a cab made me remember why I wanted to leave. New York streets at night are wickedly detached. The stuff of nightmares.

It was one of those nights when the dampness chills your bones, and I walked and waited, but even the busy streets were empty of cabs. I picked up my pace when I noticed smoke pouring out of an alley way. The air was thick with burning rubber. Concerned that there had been an accident and a car was on fire, I reached the corner and peered into the alley. There were several people hovering around a burning trash can.

"Come here," someone said in a flat voice. I started to walk away.

"Could you help us out?" I turned around just as the flames jumped up, illuminating the faces of five men. I backed up a bit when I saw the body of a woman lying in a blanket next to the can. The flames jumped again and I could see it was Maria, curled in a fetal position. There was a bunch of drug para-phernalia and broken glass by the can.

"What's the matter with Maria? Is she okay?" I asked.

"Lady, you know her?" asked a man walking toward me. "She's real sick, needs money for food. Probably needs a doctor. Can you help her out?" He moved in closer.

"Yes, I can help . . . her"

"You can trust me," a teenage kid toned in. "I won't take her money. I'm not like everybody else. I look out for her. You can trust me. Come on."

"Shut up, Radio," an older man said. "Do your rappin' some-where else."

I walked over and bent down and felt Maria's forehead. She was burning up. "You okay?" I said softly. Her eyes were half open, but there wasn't enough will in her to respond.

"She's very sick," I said, standing up and turning around. "You need to get her to a hospital. Do you want me to call an ambulance?"

The big guys had formed a circle around me and I could feel desperation and insistence breathing against me, so I dug into my purse and pulled out a bunch of bills and handed it to the kid. "You *will* take her to a hospital, right?"

"Sure thing," he told me, fingering through the paper. "How do you know a chick like this, anyway? You so clean!" They all laughed.

"If you don't take care of her," I said emphatically, pushing my way through the circle, "she'll die." I kept walking.

When I got home I called the Emergency Room at Manhat-tan General and explained the situation, and they put me on hold. "We will notify the police," the night receptionist ex-plained when she came back on the line. "It's tricky because of the drugs."

"She's very sick. She needs attention immediately!"

"There's a certain protocol we have to follow because she's homeless."

"I don't know," I lied. "She might have a family somewhere. I saw her with a man once, it could be her husband. I think we should give her the benefit of the doubt."

"We'll do whatever we can," she told me and hung up. I felt a terrible helplessness descending over me.

26

THE MAKING OF A SPIRITUAL PATH, 2000

The astrology column of the *New York Times* claims that Scorpios are pretty hot numbers, super sexy, ready to go and all that. Not so. Actually, more Scorpios are born nuns and priests, and we have more sexual problems than any other sign. All this sounds like a great excuse to prospective suitors, anyway.

Most likely it was my Scorpio sun, moon and rising sign that drove me to the edge of reason. Maybe it was the stark reality of my birthday or maybe I had finally cracked up. But for the first time ever I scheduled an encounter with a psychic—Manhattan's most popular, no less, one Madame Courvoisier. Maybe she would bring some clarity to my nutty little life. Several of my patients had gone to her for past life readings and raved about her. I just wanted to check my future out, and get some information about my questionable destiny.

"Par-don me?" I could still hear the incredulity in MollieO's voice. "You're what? I must be hearing things. My daughter, who graduated from Columbia University, *summa cum laude,* would never be stupid enough to see a fortune teller!"

My first appointment cost me a mere one hundred and twenty-five dollars—exactly what I charge for a session. In that fifty-minute reading I learned more about myself than in all of my years in therapy, and my ego was shaken to its foundation.

How could it be that this stranger could see me, feel me, understand me at such a deep level, in so little time? How did one get
such a gift? I was completely enthralled while totally leveled.
And believe me, control freaks don't like this kind of thing. It's
way out of our comfort zone.

"It's all of that Scorpio, dear," she told me, positioning her
black designer glasses in her silky white hair. Steel-blue eyes
gazed out at me from a gentle, kind face. I had the fleeting
thought that she could have been Paul Newman's sister. Looking
up from her yellow-lined tablet with its scribbled notes, she
heaved a massive sigh.

"With five planets in Scorpio, it's exhausting and exhilarating
all at the same time. Many little deaths and rebirths happen constantly. Lots of anger and resentment to be gotten rid of. You
feel you can't trust yourself. You go to others to find answers.
Don't do that too often, it's disempowering. Return to yourself
for those answers. You've been out of touch with your feelings,
yet you feel everything so deeply, don't you, dear?"

"I try not to," I said defensively. How did she know about my
daily ego deaths? The fact that I occasionally felt reborn. *It probably happens to everyone,* I told myself. *Yeah, right, Billie.*

"It looks like I have lost you again, Ms. Bartholomew," she
reminded me gently. "Come back into your body! Relax, and
try not to get so caught up in your mind. Two hundred fifty
thousand thoughts a day—none of them very important—and
you're holding on to every one of them!"

Madame Courvoisier pulled out her tarot cards and asked me
to cut the deck three times to the left. *Why to the left?* I thought.
This was silly. I looked up and checked her out again. I had to
admit, she looked a lot more motherly than menacing. So I
complied with her instructions and cut the cards, then drew one
out of the deck. She turned it over.

"Hmm . . . ," she said. "You have drawn the Tower card.
Soon everything will fall apart. But it needs to before it can

change." She handed me the card. I didn't like what I saw. Two people jumping from a burning tower into the flames of what looked like hell.

"What do you mean, soon? How soon?"

"It has already begun. You know that, dear. The process will speed up and your life as you have known it will change dramatically. Nothing will remain stable. Not your work, your home, your relationships. . . ."

"My sanity?" I asked, only half joking. "I sometimes feel my mind is unraveling. Is my mind going to make it? I mean, I like to know what's going to happen day to day. I don't do well with chaos."

"Billie," she offered, "if you look back at your life, you will see that you do very well in chaos. In fact, you flourish. That's part of the problem. Getting you to be quiet and open and take care of yourself is the real challenge. Getting you to see who you really are. A teacher. A healer. Now, please draw another card."

Again I cut the cards three times and chose from the bottom of the deck.

"The Sun!" she announced with apparent delight. "This is fabulous!" She handed me the card. "It's the card of innocence, of starting over, of being happy. Of course, this might be a hard one for you to absorb, right, dear?"

"Happy, huh?" I sat back in the white cane chair and studied the card. She was right. This card was more difficult to accept than the Tower.

"Even your spiritual path will change," she added with a smile.

Spiritual path? What spiritual path? This is where she's trying to hook me, I thought. *Of course my spiritual path will change, I'm going to be paying thousands to her. Madame Courvoisier is going to own me! That's why everyone's afraid to go to a psychic. They're afraid they'll end up on Poverty Row.*

"Well, thank you, Madame. This was fascinating," I told her, opening up my wallet, pulling out a couple of fresh one hundred dollar bills. "How long should I wait before I come back? A week? What would you suggest?"

"I suggest that you follow your own intuition, Billie. Your fiftieth year is going to be fabulous! After you finish the life lessons of the next few weeks, perhaps I should come have a reading with *you.*" Madame Courvoisier winked kindly. "By the way, with a chart like this, you'd make an excellent psychologist. Did I mention that before?"

As I was leaving she asked for a hug, and when my arms encircled her I inhaled a familiar fragrance: MollieO's *Joy* perfume. It smelled like honey on her, warm and resonating.

"Billie," she said, placing her hands squarely on both of my shoulders, "take care of yourself. Don't look for answers out here, it will only confuse you more. The world is just the world. Beautiful. Mean. Seductive. Ridiculous. It's never going to change. Do your inner work. Go inside into the stillness to where *you* really are. That's where you'll find your answers."

Spiritual path, I thought, walking out into the beautiful and ridiculous world, *what is that?* Did having lunch with Bishop John O'Reilly count as a spiritual path? I didn't think so. I remembered Martin suddenly demanding we attend church every Sunday morning, but what he really wanted was for the Bishop to introduce him to his glamorous socialite parishioners and movie star friends.

In college I had enjoyed courses in Eastern Religion, but faced with the concept of "embracing my suffering," I had left the lecture early. I preferred to erase my suffering with the aid of a martini or two. Or five. A few lectures did not a spiritual path make. Even I could figure that out. There was an ex-boyfriend who had taken courses in Tantra. He couldn't wait to walk me down that path. But as far as I could tell, he was just another horny guy with a new excuse to have sex all the time. I was not impressed.

Of course, throughout my childhood Aunt Lillian had opened me to many different facets of spiritual philosophy. Her visions of protective "medicine animals" and of my great-grandmother watching over me had brought me some solace. Was that my spiritual path?

Some years later, while vacationing in Santa Fe, I had found myself genuinely moved by the art and culture of the Zuni and Navajo people. Without quite understanding why, I'd spent a lot of time privately weeping in museums and galleries that featured their jewelry and paintings and sculpture. I'd gone on to buy a painting and eventually ended up redoing my townhouse in the Southwestern style.

In one corner of my bedroom stood a hand-hewn ladder of bleached piñon, the sort of ladder used to descend into the underground kivas, the sacred Hopi places of worship. On its rungs were two small Navajo rugs and one from the Ortega family of weavers in Chimayo. Another bright rug adorned the floor near the window. Several large kachina dolls protected my front door. Smack dab in the center of my living room hung a massive dream catcher, bound in doeskin, embroidered with tiny seashells and horse's hair. It was absolutely exquisite. I liked the interweaving of the masculine and the feminine, the earth and the water, the idea that I could weave a dream and it might happen. My palomino sculpture stood on the table beneath the dream catcher. Her name was "Night Wind Rider." I loved the tiny periwinkle blue reindeer painted on her side and the fact that she was a big, strong female. She reminded me of Lillian.

Did all of these moments add up to a spiritual path?

Madame Courvoisier was right. My spiritual path had no name and no form; it was unique to me. It was born from unexpected moments of peace transmitted through the paws of my cat, Ellington. And through the sudden smile of one of my heartbroken patients. Planting fiery red begonias in the midday sun. Reclining naked on a cushy divan, drinking in Gershwin, Rachelle Ferrell, Tuck & Patti, Stevie Wonder and, of course, Joni. Ultra violet blue and the open-hearted hue of turquoise, these calmed my soul. And moussaka. Cedarwood sputtering in an open hearth. The hot-blooded tempo of Latin American poetry. Long, steamy, lavender-scented showers. Pale pink roses and a Helen Frankenthaler watercolor print. Silky green grass and swaying palms. Opaque Lalique stemware dripping with Veuve Clicquot champagne. Candelabras set against a window of Manhattan sky. Cashmere, and Caribbean breezes. Dew-soaked lilacs. Drifting in a canoe on a celadon lake in the Adirondack Mountains. The rough soft skin of necks. Chagall. Biting into a caramel cinnamon roll with butter oozing down its sides. French tulips and Baryshnikov. These were my meditations. Unknowingly I had been collecting them as stepping stones on the slippery path to inner peace.

Part Two

MY SUBLIME UNDOING

*"I have come to rebuild what has been shattered.
To rebuild love."*

—Thich Nhat Hanh

27

ANOTHER MONDAY MORNING,
MANHATTAN, 2000

The rain blew into my third floor brownstone window, hurling the cactus-colored curtains way out into the room. I was lost in contemplation of my favorite painting, "Twilight Woman." There, poised on the desert mesa, an American Indian woman sits in the purples of the night. I wanted to live like that. Connected to the sacred energies of the land, the woman was alone, but not lonely. She appeared content in her quietude. It was no accident I'd placed her directly across from my bed, like a mirror.

Until this morning I thought I had loved my desert oasis in the center of the city. But today the rain poured in, and I was relieved. A good inch of water must have been soaked up by the Navajo rug before I got up to shut the window.

"It feels so dry in here," I whispered to myself. "No, *I* feel so dry. My inner tributaries are too low!"

I looked in the bathroom mirror and was horrified. My face seemed sunken.

"I've got no goddamned elasticity!" I wailed, pinching the skin on my left arm, stretching it down like a bat wing.

Who the hell was I? By someone's standards, relatively pretty. Not by *Vogue* magazine's maybe, but I was attractive, wasn't I?

Looking back at me from my bathroom mirror were Charlotte Rampling eyes. Green and sexy. Eyes that had a problem focusing on my life.

When I cupped my hands around my breasts, they felt tired. Deflated. My friend, Barbara Billingham, M.A., had hers lifted, but after the surgery the nipples wouldn't reconnect. Talk about a nightmare. I could imagine my nipples falling off and floating away—that's the kind of neurotic mind I possessed. No surgeon was going to touch these babies. They're kind of, how you say, *à la goddesse.*

Looking further down: all right, honestly, they were fabulous legs, long like my palomino sculpture. Sweet knees. Lovely ankles. A striking beauty mark on my inner right calf. I definitely felt good about that. Two autumns ago Mark Levin, a psychiatrist on my floor, had kissed that very spot when we were lovers for a short time. He liked to slip off my blue Joan & David pumps and lick his way all the way up these gorgeous gams until I about passed out. Still, when we finally got around to the real thing, I was always terrified. That happened every time. All of that *closeness.* I always wanted to exit my body until it was over.

For a woman who was a psychologist and an expert in psychological problems, I had avoided some of the most important issues of my life. During my own therapy I was only able to touch on my sexual behavior for a moment here and there. It felt as if I was trying to work it through, but then a moment later I couldn't remember what I had been talking about.

It obviously had a lot to do with my relationship with my father. That's what my training had taught me: bonding with Mommy first, Daddy later. No bonding or too much bonding with Daddy in adolescent and pubescent years meant intimacy issues galore, and you can be sure I had them. I had found some comfort in knowing I had the rest of my life to learn how to stay in my body. Someday I would learn to trust that a man might want me, and to be able to stay present enough to feel like I deserved it.

No matter what I did, stress was always with me. It crept into my shoulders and neck and congealed like papier-maché. Some days my chest was so tight I could hardly breathe. I knew it was because I held a lot of my patients' problems too closely. I worried for them. That way I thought I could re-create their existence, talk them into getting well.

Gin had given me a lot of help through the years, but recently I had cut way back, taking an occasional glass of Merlot with dinner or a martini at lunch with a friend. In my forties, wine had warmed me and helped me stay in touch with my feelings— sometimes too much so. At fifty, wine left me abandoned and exhausted, and martinis produced my worst fear—MollieO's migraines. Couple that with those wonderful palpitations that I used to get every other day, where your heart somehow flip-flops in your chest. That was plenty of reason for me to get off the sauce. When the headaches started, I went to see my internist who diagnosed it as hypoglycemia moving toward chronic fatigue syndrome. I immediately began to clean up my act.

I was quite sure that what was really causing those symptoms was my sadness about not making a family. Lots of other single women I knew felt as exhausted as I did, and they stuffed their pain, too. It was easy. We were an attractive, accomplished group of females, polished and prosperous, who had worked hard to rise in our careers and had mastered the art of letting go of relationships that didn't work. But on the outside we were looking a bit tight; on the inside it was downright messy. At home, sitting alone in the midnight hour, we hurt. We'd reached a point where we were only able to sip tiny brandies in front of our elegant fireplaces, because we were afraid that one apéritif too many would take us over the edge and into the abyss of childless despair.

To counter my immense gloom, I told people that my patients were my family and my cat was the love of my life. Some of that was true, but I was succumbing to that drifting off kind of staring that sad people do—and my focus was on mothers and daughters sharing their love.

I was a voyeur for mother-daughter love. Silently I sat, looking out my bedroom window at the street below. I watched beautiful, vibrant women holding on ever so cautiously to their daughters' red-mittened hands. I studied them gabbing joyfully in front of me on Bloomingdale's escalators. I wondered if I would've taken my daughter—I would've named her Brigitte—to pee in the big stall in the Ladies Room for the first time. I asked myself whether I would let her sit by herself and feel the majesty of the moment or have her sit in front of me while her red Capezios tapped happily against the bowl? I wept at the prospect.

No one understood how I could have never gotten pregnant. In my thirty years of lovemaking I had never used birth control. Something in me knew it was never going to happen. My gynecologist hypothesized that my body was broken down there, that my tipped uterus had ruined my chances. Each time my hormones overtook me and I cried out to the sweet doctor, she tried to come up with some bit of information to make me feel better. "You know," Dr. Beatrice Cohen would tell me after our yearly pap, "you have the prettiest vagina I've ever seen. It's perfect. Be grateful for what you have." I love my gynecologist.

Maybe it was all the times I had crossed my legs too tightly in the presence of prospective suitors. Or that my territory down there just wasn't used enough. That was the ticket. Secretly, I feared it was some kind of curse that had been put on me after Martin had been down there that had rendered me childless. It was as if I had made a silent pact not to bring more Bartholomews into the world. *To stop those genes right now!* Whatever the cause, I moved in and out of a pseudo depression over having no man or child to love me. All the while, I was trying to help my patients move ahead.

Monday meant overwhelm. I looked at my calendar to see how I had mapped out the day. Monday, 9:00 A.M., Mary MacArthur. Oh God, how could I have done that to myself? Mary MacArthur had a strange thing going on. Mitsy, her beagle-poodle mix and primary relationship, terrorized her. Mary maintained a simple life in Scarsdale, making the world's best sour cream potato salad laced with capers. Twice she'd brought me casseroles, and I had devoured them alone in my kitchen. But no matter how generous and tender hearted she was, every day at exactly 3:15 P.M., Mitsy ran to whatever room Mary was hiding out in and bit her. Hard. Tranced out, all Mary could manage to do was watch and wait, hoping Mitsy would experience some kind of epiphany.

This bizarre dance had gone on for a month. My perverse mind framed family snapshots: 2:00 P.M.—Mary offering her pup a late lunch of tuna salad with a side of mayo served on a china plate; 2:30 P.M.—Mary gently brushing her little lamb's long, fleecy ears; then, 3:00 P.M.—Mitsy is ready to roll, poised to pounce off Mary's deceased husband's favorite grey Barcalounger.

Nothing we tried seemed to help. Mary felt immobilized, convinced she was doomed. I just kept showing up for her, hoping that would work. There wasn't much else I could do.

This was what my practice had come to. I wondered what had happened to me since the early days when I'd felt passionate about every one of my clients. I was fresh then. Optimistic. Now, in my twentieth year of practice and deep into major burnout, I was tired of the old intellectual ways I related to people.

I wanted more physical closeness in every area of my life. The last time I had let someone hug me was last New Year's Eve, and it was one of those very detached "I'm not really here" hugs.

You know the kind I mean—cheeks are touching, but chest and genitals are miles apart. It had been a long time since I had taken a chance on love. The last time out I had noticed a neediness in me that freaked me out. This nice guy had come into my life and had let me know that he wanted me, that he wanted to belong to me. According to the Story Board of Billie's Life, I had waited my whole life for this moment. To be chosen. For someone wonderful to say, "You're the one. No one else." And then this salt-and-pepper-haired, lovely, poetic man showed up and said exactly that, and my insides fell apart. Fear leaked into my cells and my colon shut down. I got the dreaded feeling of doom and started radiating insecurity, emitting stupid statements like thousands of interconnected bubbles. So long, grey-haired man.

Somewhere in the desert dryness of empty love, I had lost my compassion and patience. But I also knew that the same hug that would bring my waters back might save the soul of any one of my patients. And yet I could not do it. Why was it all so difficult?

It was my Aunt Lillian who noticed how stressed I looked. "You need to protect yourself. Strengthen up your boundaries! You *have* to be vigilant about not taking on your patients' stuff."

But that's my job!

I couldn't escape the hard fact that Overwhelm Monday had to be dealt with, so I broke up some fresh rosemary needles between my fingers to throw in my bath to release my impurities, and wondered what would bring the great waters back. Maybe if I chanted hard enough I would rain inside. I conjured a floating picture of my great-grandmother, the medicine woman. I envisioned her with her gourd rattle, clearing the energy close to the medicine wheel of life.

"This is you, Great-Granddaughter," she said, pointing to the hard, cracked land. Great-Grandmother raised her rattle to the sky and chanted long and hard for Billie Bartholomew's soul, for love to enter through the center of my heart. She rattled all of my fears away from the circle and walked into the scorching day.

I went through my bathroom shelf and grabbed several flower essences: Mustard for gloom, Star of Bethlehem for sorrow, and Daffodil for every possible emotional disaster. I dabbed them above my eyebrows, over my heart, and let ten drops fall under my tongue. I took a long swig.

I looked at the clock on the bathroom wall. It was 8:00 A.M. I wanted to pick up a plant on the way to my office, something strong that could suck up the sorrow, drink down the disappointment, root up the rage. Perhaps a Venus flytrap would do. Probably too delicate.

And so it was that I, Dr. Billie Bartholomew, was journeying out of my native digs that morning, walking down Fifth Avenue in a pensive mood. I felt a few raindrops hit my cheek and I looked up at the slate grey sky. Ahead on the Avenue I could see a cluster of umbrellas hovering over something. I walked toward what at first seemed like just a garbage bag, but as I looked more closely I could see that the plastic was wrapped around a woman's body huddled against the curb.

"Oh, God," I muttered. "Oh, God." Instantly I was mentally running through a list of clinical descriptions of the woman lying in the street. But listening to the sound of my inner professional voice upset me. Why was it so easy to feel so removed? Yet that inner voice was sweet compared to the reactions of the people around me.

"Someone should turn a hose on her, clean her up," an older tweedy gentleman grunted, running too slowly to make the bus.

"Right here on Fifth Avenue, for Christ's sake," a hip-looking young man with black wire-rimmed sunglasses observed. "Someone call the cops."

"She's paying off a karmic debt," an auburn-haired woman stated matter-of-factly. "It's the India thing," she shrugged, cinching in the snakeskin belt that secured her elegant raincoat.

The woman in the drenched garbage bag poked her head out, and her dark eyes stared into mine. The gate to my heart swung open. It was Maria, the woman I had come to know from a distance for some thirty years—the woman who had told me to leave her alone and let her die on the street. And I could *hear* her.

"Help me die."

I looked around to gauge the reactions of the other onlookers, but they didn't change expression. They stood as if in a frozen tableau while the woman spoke to me, and to me alone.

"Please . . . help me die."

My stomach was clenched like a fist.

"Hey, Dark Meat, ain't you dead yet?" came a demonic voice from a laundry truck that had momentarily slowed down at the corner.

A homeless gentleman to my right declared, "She probably makes an income ten times yours," he said looking at me. "Check inside the bag and you'll see."

I knew it was going to be like this all day long. New Yorkers and out-of-towners alike wouldn't know what to do with her, and they would hate her for the discomfort she made them feel on the most fabulous avenue in the greatest city in the world. But no matter, the authorities would have her removed from the streets before the day was out.

Part of me wanted to go closer. I wanted to lift Maria up in my arms and take her in a cab to my office. I'd revive her with a good strong cup of Earl Grey tea. A chicken salad sandwich on a Kaiser roll. An unfaltering hug.

But the fantasy of lifting this dying woman faded as my fears brought me back into the real world. The thought of the woman's vulnerability wrapped around mine made me cringe. I imagined her juicy madness seeping through my skin. My once compassionate feeling was becoming a sloppy boundary issue.

God, I felt depressed. Why couldn't I just help her? The truth was that I didn't know what I would say if she began to sob. How would I counter her bottomless despair? How would I explain why the world had treated her like trash? A throwaway on the Boulevard of Hope. I didn't have it in me. I closed my eyes and called out for my great-grandmother to step in. I pretended I could hear the stirred up seeds of her gourd rattle raising new life within the fallen woman's soul.

It was time for me to move on. After all, it was late, and Mary MacArthur needed to tell her story. But as I took the elevator up to my office, I couldn't put Maria's eyes out of my mind. *"Please help me die. Stay with me."*

I began to imagine the first hour of my day being lightly nutty but manageable. I would hold the space of a plains-dwelling medicine woman on the most fashionable block of Manhattan.

"Relax. Breathe, Mary," I would murmur softly in my great-grandmother's red-brown voice. Then I would raise her invisible rattle and proceed. "You're safe here," I would tell my patient confidently, shaking love in her direction. "No dogs allowed."

28

THE BLOSSOMING OF A BODHISATTVA

"Chinese Kissing"
  by Mei-Mei Chang

My face is property
unowned by anyone
its boundaries are wired
saying beware
there are laws to this land
enter at your own risk

I watch you circle
like some majestic bird
sure of the intensity
of your colors
anticipating the freedom
of an open field
my voice whispers
do not land

you approach me cautiously
caring for the quiet
your eyelashes fall
soundless
a Chinese paintbrush
on the canvas of my cheek
touching here
touching here
here
and here

It had been a very long day with my patients. At best, I felt I wasn't making any headway, at worst I was losing ground fast, and yet through it all I was working so hard. I lit a fire and reclined with a postcard from Callie. She was performing in Rome with Philippe and their new baby, Blossom, having a great time as usual. I looked for the words to hold on to. "I miss you like crazy," she wrote.

"You'll never know," I whispered, lying back holding the postcard over my heart.

Ellington's big orange body lounged next to me on the couch. He wedged himself between me and my manuscript of Mei-Mei Chang's poems. Mei-Mei was one of my most fascinating clients—very sensitive, bright, caught between two worlds. Over the years I had developed a lot of affection for her. But as I stroked Ellington's thick fur, I was deeply troubled by the abrupt turn of events in Mei-Mei's session that afternoon.

As a child, Mei-Mei had suffered from serious neglect and, coming from a similar kind of situation, I related very strongly to her inability to open up and trust. We'd worked hard at helping her confront those early wounds, and attempted to uncover how they manifested in her current life. It was slow going, but I'd been very hopeful.

I'd come to look forward to our weekly appointment. After all, a therapist doesn't feel drawn to all of her patients. Some days, when it appeared that we were getting closer, I felt motherly toward her. Yes, I would have been proud to have Mei-Mei as my daughter, or at least a surrogate younger sister. There was a whole lot going on in her poems that she had a difficult time communicating in our therapy sessions. I liked the idea of traveling into those dark places through her poetry, and it was a safe way for her to know that I was sincerely interested in her world.

Mei-Mei Chang was a first-rate fashion magazine copywriter who had begun to wonder how long she could keep coming up with adjectives for stunning, striking and fabulous. After two years with Saks Fifth Avenue, three years as a junior copywriter for Bloomingdale's and now two years as senior writer for Misha Geisha, Manhattan's fashion Bad Boy, Mei-Mei Chang was fried.

She had chosen fashion because of its drama and sensuality. The culture of the fashion world, with its openness to form and design and color, had brought her great joy in the beginning. "What a contrast to my home life on Long Island," she disclosed to me early on, "where everything had felt . . . well . . . dead."

Poor Mei-Mei. According to her, she had been so conscious of her gorgeous spirit on the day she was born that even now she could remember the guilt passing through her. She remembered laying next to babies in the hospital ward and dreaming happy dreams. But not for long. New mothers passed by and pointed to her beautiful golden skin, her lotus lips, her pale purple eyes. *"A Chinese girl with purple eyes? Must be a crossbreed!"* Within days, her tiny body began to take on a silent rigidity.

"Chang Land," as she called it now, "was an impossible country to prosper in. Tall, stoic creatures paraded in front of my oak wood crib, staring at me wordlessly for hours. I did my damnedest to look adorable and pure, but that seemed to agitate them more. Once a day, around 9:00 A.M., Mama Chang would bend over and pick me up, hold me against her flat chest for a few heartbeats and lay me back down. Oh, how I waited for those moments even though her cool, hard chest scared me. It felt like the Great Wall."

For Mei-Mei, everything after that seemed like a step down on a spiral staircase of self-esteem. Down she climbed, still set on winning her mother's warmth. She knew it was in her mother somewhere, like a lost civilization. By age two, Mei-Mei must have known she was going to spend her childhood digging like one hell of an archaeologist.

So the child spent hours inventing ways to please her mom. At four, she sat at her mother's make-up table and painted her tiny finger and toenails Plum Blossom Pink, just like Mom. Then she clipped a silver dragon-headed hair barrette perfectly in place and eased into her mother's favorite crimson silk, side-slit dress. She sat like a special child, waiting to be ordained into a loving childhood.

"My mother," she said, "tore out the dragon barrette and hurled it onto the floor and rubbed so much polish remover on my nails that my baby skin burned bright red. And all the while she never said a word."

What followed was predictable. Mei-Mei created a life for herself in which she never threatened anyone. Her grades and abilities brought a quiet dignity to her family, but never any excitement or attention to her.

"Attention of any kind makes me terribly uncomfortable and fidgety," she told me one day, waving her beautiful thin fingers in the air.

By the time we met, Mei-Mei had her own life, but she found it nearly impossible to connect with people. After the devastation of her childhood there were no romances or love affairs. No exquisite kisses or words of tenderness. No late nights in intimate jazz joints. No dancing in the spring rain in Central Park. No posh Manhattan wedding. No emotional outlets, period. Except one—stacks of intimate, unpublished poems that gave voice to her unfulfilled wishes, secret desires, her hidden rage.

And now, Mei-Mei had given herself one more thing. It had come into her life like an apparent accident, a whim that would transform her life and our relationship forever. In her two room, sixth floor walk-up, deep in the East Village, Mei-Mei had placed the marble head of a Chinese goddess on a wooden pedestal.

She'd told me about it in what turned out to be a disturbing session earlier that day. "Dr. Bartholomew, in the Chinese culture, there are statues of Quan Yin everywhere. In the house of my childhood my mother had placed a large figure of her at the front door, for protection, she said. For joy. I had been told only that Quan Yin was the goddess of compassion and mercy. Well, where was it? Certainly not in our household. I guess I got disillusioned after a while. My grandmother gave me a little porcelain statue of her, but I stuffed it way back in my closet. I guess, in my way, I was really angry at Quan Yin.

"Anyway, a few days ago I was walking down Christopher Street, losing myself in antique shop windows, when I saw this head of Quan Yin. I started to walk away when I suddenly felt love coming right through the window—from her eyes directly into mine. Her goodness enveloped me. I stood there for a long time, then I began to cry. Tears ran down my cheeks and I felt so alive I thought I was going to start shouting. And you know I never express my feelings. I got a little scared, then I put my face against the cold glass and sobbed. You know how hard it is for me to feel anything, let alone cry!"

I nodded. "Yes, I do know. What happened after that?"

"When I regained my composure, I walked into the shop. The man behind the jewelry case had been watching me, probably wondering if he should call the cops."

"'Are you all right, dear girl?' he asked me gently.

"I apologized and told him I didn't know what had come over me." Mei-Mei smiled ruefully. "I feel guilty for everything. But anyway, this elderly gentleman seemed nice, slightly sad perhaps, but he had all of this wonderful information about the statue. He said the Japanese know her as Kwannon. Why does everyone think I'm Japanese?

"'Millions pray to her,' he explained. 'She dates back to around 500 or 600 A.D. Many believe that Quan Yin still journeys back to the Earth from Lemuria, a civilization that existed before the time of Atlantis, and that exists even now under the ocean where Quan Yin lives.'

"I can just imagine how beautiful it is there," Mei-Mei said. "All I have to do is close my eyes. No stress. No competition. All souls end up there at one time or another to rest and experience a peaceful way of living. I'm *so* looking forward to going there."

I started to get nervous. Was this dementia really a fantasy world that my patient longed to escape to? Or was she really trying to tell me that underneath all this she was feeling suicidal, ready to find heaven?

"Do you see yourself ever going there?" I asked in a measured voice.

"Well, of course," Mei-Mei said matter of factly. "Why wouldn't I want to go there when I'm finished with my time here? Who wouldn't choose Lemuria over New York City?"

"Yes, yes of course," I said, and then added quietly, "When do you have a sense you will go to Lemuria?"

"When it's my time and Quan Yin comes to get me. But don't worry, Dr. Bartholomew. I'm not afraid. I'm excited."

My hands were perspiring in my lap. I pushed further. "Where could I read more about Lemuria? It sounds so inviting. Unrealistic, but inviting."

"I don't think there are any books. And even if there are, I wouldn't trust what's written. From what I understand, Spirit wants to keep it a secret so we earthlings don't ruin it. Anyway, I'm divulging much more than I'm supposed to. I need to tell you more about Quan Yin."

I looked down, feeling I was losing her a little more every minute.

"The shop attendant told me that Quan Yin comes to save our souls. Some say she has been seen in concentration camps, like Auschwitz and Treblinka. Her spirit takes on a body and returns to our planet in order to uplift civilizations that have lost their way."

As Mei-Mei told me all of this, she looked radiant.

"He told me that before she arrives, the air becomes silent and the sky turns deep purple. And then her form appears. Soft, flowing. Very strong, yet very feminine. In her presence, people's souls heal. Their sense of compassion returns. He said she was recently seen in Kosovo, holding the body of a two-year-old boy who had been murdered in the street. People saw the boy's face change and a look of complete peace wash over him.

"She was a disciple of Buddha," Mei-Mei went on, pointing to the portrait on my wall. "But she postponed realizing her own Buddhahood by vowing to return to the Earth until she had answered the cries of the suffering in everyone. They say that all you need to do is look into her eyes and love is awakened."

It sounded to me as though the store owner had been very skilled at making a sale, but I kept that thought to myself. Mei-Mei told me that she had written a check on the spot for $650, money she had been saving for a vacation to Cancun next winter. The store owner agreed to deliver the statue to her apartment early that evening.

"When he arrived, I was so excited. The poor man was gasping when he got to the top of my stairs. He said I should pray to Quan Yin that I'd never have to move. Then he left."

I waited patiently while Mei-Mei paused for a moment as if to gather her thoughts.

"I opened the curtains and let in the twilight," she continued. "Oh, Dr. Bartholomew, I felt so excited! I put on a CD of *Claire De Lune* and sat in my wicker chair studying the goddess's face. The statue was so magnificent that everything else in the room looked wrong. Thank God I knew what to do. I went down the back stairs to my storage room, brought up a bunch of empty cardboard boxes and packed up everything I own. I worked until there was nothing left in the apartment but a table, two chairs, and Quan Yin. I even pulled down my expensive French lace curtains."

She looked at me to see if I understood what she had been feeling. I kept my expression encouraging but noncommittal. She shrugged slightly and went on. And in that instant I knew that something important had shifted for her because, while she wanted me to understand, for the first time she didn't need for me to approve.

"I was totally in tune with the goddess," said Mei-Mei, "and I knew exactly what I had to do. I went out and bought white votive candles and sandalwood incense. I filled a silver vase with mineral water and placed one sterling lavender rose in the center. I lit the candles slowly and sat down in my favorite chair. It was finally done. In the light of the evening, I made my prayers. And Dr. Bartholomew, I have never ever made a prayer before. I guess I've always figured no one listened.

"My first prayer was to be free of my mother."

I nodded again, this time in total agreement.

"I then asked that my father learn how to connect emotionally. And I asked Quan Yin to stop my sisters from being jealous of me. God, wouldn't that be a relief?"

Mei-Mei sighed again, raising her slender hands up toward heaven. I joined her and threw my arms up, too.

"Next I asked her to please remove the guilt from my heart, so that I could let someone love me. Someone really wonderful!"

Where was all of this coming from? I wondered. Here was this young woman sitting in front of me who was undeniably filled with optimism and light. During the years we had been working together, she had been a classic case of depression. I began to suspect Mei-Mei might be bi-polar, and that she was in a state of manic exuberance.

Mei-Mei interrupted my internal dialogue. "And then I did something pretty stupid. I asked Quan Yin if she had someone wonderful to love her. You know, in the romantic way. Man, I felt embarrassed that I said that out loud."

The MollieO part of me wondered why Mei-Mei wasn't feeling embarrassed to be talking to a statue, period. The Lillian part cheered.

Mei-Mei said, "But then I let go of my mistake and I said to her, 'You know, I think I'd be so much happier if I could write about something that mattered to me. I know I would.' And then

I cleared my throat because it sounded like I was making a request, a wish from my heart. I hadn't tried asking for a wish to be granted since I was a very little girl because, first of all, no one ever listened, and second, I didn't think I deserved it. But now, all of a sudden, I felt very clear. So I asked for the big one. I looked much deeper than before into those placid eyes. 'Take me out of my misery,' I requested. 'Please, Quan Yin, help me to be happy.'

"So what do you think, Dr. Bartholomew?" Mei-Mei asked much too quickly.

I didn't have an idea in hell what was going on. I looked at my watch to send a clue. "Mei-Mei," I told her. "I have to think over all of the things you've told me. It's a lot to consider, but overall I'm delighted about how you sound."

"There's something else I want to tell you," Mei-Mei continued, her eyes looking down. "This is my last session. I hope you understand. Now that I've found Quan Yin I don't *need* to come anymore. I would like to invite you to my home so you can meet her, experience her. Do you think you could? We wouldn't be violating any rules or boundaries, because I'm not your client any longer, right?"

"Now, Mei-Mei," I said in my softest voice, "wait a minute. I think you're moving too quickly. I don't think you should end four years of therapy because you've bought a statue."

"You don't get it," she said raising her voice a touch. "What I'm saying is, I've discovered more about myself with Quan Yin in twenty-four hours than I have with you in four years. I'm sorry, Dr. Bartholomew. That's how I feel. But I really would like you to be in her presence."

Suddenly my bruised therapist ego blurted out, "It's a marble head, for Christ's sake!" I struggled to regain some professional perspective. "Look, Mei-Mei, we're not complete here. I'd like you to consider coming here for a few more sessions, so we can have some closure."

She shook her head. "You can't close what never opened. I'm sorry, I don't feel I ever opened up in here. If, after four years,

you really care about me, come to my apartment Thursday evening. Maybe then you'll understand."

"I appreciate the invitation, Mei-Mei," I replied in a calm
voice.

Mei-Mei was putting on her black velvet jacket. I could see
that there was not going to be any further eye contact, so I
quietly said, "I'll think about it. I do want to support you in this.
I care about what happens to you." She was through the door
before I blurted out, "I'm on your side Mei-Mei. Can you hear
me?" Quickly I moved to the elevator and caught her arm.

"The invitation is for 9:00 P.M.," she said, pulling her arm
away. "This is what the goddess told me. This will be your only
opportunity, Dr. Bartholomew."

The elevator door closed. Totally confused, I felt abandoned
and slightly defeated. How could I have not seen this coming?
Mei-Mei needed serious help. She was obviously headed for a
nervous breakdown.

I was more shaken than I dared to admit. Grateful that I had
no more appointments that day, I gathered up my coat and
purse, and then dropped my keys three times as I tried to lock
my office door. As I stood in the stuffy, crowded elevator, I tried
to focus on what was happening in my head. *Now, this is a crisis
and I've got to go there. No one has ever been there for Mei-Mei. It's
going to have to be me. I want it to be me. I've got to help her, and I've
got to think it through. I've got to have a strategy that's correct for this
situation although I'll be damned if I know what it is.*

I walked out into the starless night and across the street, and
absently unlocked my car door. I placed a tape of Marvin Gaye
into the player and drove uptown toward home. Marvin was
singing "Mercy, Mercy Me," and for a moment, remembering
his precious kiss, I let it all go. But then my mind began doing
what it does best, worrying endlessly.

I struggled to find a way to be professional with Mei-Mei
and try to lead her back to a grounded reality—and be open

and compassionate at the same time. I didn't want to come across like a total non-believer, because I knew that would scare her away. Besides, I had to admit I would be lying to myself if I acted that way. Through the years, Lillian had introduced me to a wide variety of spiritual beliefs, many that I had begun to embrace. Like the way American Indians had a reverence for the land and all living things. Like the possibility of reincarnation and the notion that spirit animals come to heal us. My own home and office were filled with relics that were not so different from Mei-Mei's beloved statue. So what was it about this Quan Yin, and Mei-Mei's response to her, that was so upsetting to me? What nerve did it touch that I was too numb to recognize?

I found myself wondering if my great-grandmother was watching over me from somewhere else. I hoped that she was. Maybe I even sensed her, felt her, if only in the remote, dispassionate way I'd engaged her in the past. But now I was faced with an ancient, mythical goddess, speaking from another dimension—under the Pacific Ocean, no less—who had suddenly appeared and totally transformed my patient's reality . . . and in so doing, had given her a connection she had been yearning for her whole life. Was it appropriate of me to fault a situation that was making Mei-Mei feel more alive?

I swung from one extreme to another, from the belief that Mei-Mei's experience was out of the question to acknowledging that there was a side of life that was just plain mystical, and that somehow Mei-Mei had walked through that mystical door. On and on, my mind obsessed. It seemed like there were two Billies chattering within me: my logical personality and my far out soul. I felt like I, too, was going bonkers.

Late into the night I continued to flounder between two worlds as I thumbed through Mei-Mei's manuscripts and watched the crackling fire. The warmth of Ellington's body against my left thigh was the only real comfort I could find.

29

TUNING IN TO THE GODDESS

As I hurried to my office the next morning, I couldn't believe my eyes. There was Maria Milflores still languishing in her garbage bag in the middle of the crowded city. *Can it be she's still alive? Why haven't the police taken her to a hospital? And what in God's name happened to her, anyway?* But everyone in general and I in particular knew full well that the answers to those questions were far too threatening for any of us to be willing to take a closer look.

All through the day, in spite of a busy client load, my mind was torn between Maria and Mei-Mei. These two women were wreaking havoc on my sense of balance. Both of them were in crisis, and yet the two women were pulling me in opposite directions. Or were they?

After work, I walked over to Doubleday Bookstore. I was searching for a psychology classic that I thought might offer some guidance, when I turned down the wrong aisle into the Spirituality & Mysticism section. Before me lay shelf after shelf of books on goddesses.

There they were: Gaia who existed before time; Rhiannon, the embodiment of life, death and rebirth; Artemis, the mistress of animals and goddess of the hunt; Lilith who evokes the dark side; White Shell Woman who created the Navajo people; Isis, goddess of the moon. I was fascinated by the obvious popularity of goddesses, especially because to me they appeared so out of reach as role models, as compared to, say, movie stars. It takes extraordinary courage and wisdom to be a goddess. I think that's why I had never related to them before. They were kind of like long lost legends who moved on to higher ground.

The woman next to me was reading a book about the goddess Athena. Glancing over her shoulder, I read that the author was a therapist. The reader herself was classy-looking, had a scholarly look about her, and she was totally engrossed in the book. I felt comfortable in her company.

"I'm sorry to disturb you," I said, "but I see you're reading a book about goddesses. Have you ever heard of a goddess named Quan Yin?"

"Of course I've heard of Quan Yin. I have an altar to her in my home." *Uh oh.* "But you won't find that much in this section. You might try Buddhism. Quan Yin isn't just a goddess, she's a bodhisattva. She's an awakened being."

"Thank you," I said, and headed for Buddhism. After what seemed like hours of fruitless searching, I asked a salesperson to rescue me and was led to a book—one of only three written in English—that described Quan Yin's history.

"If she's valued by so many different cultures how come there is so little written about her?" I questioned the young man as we scanned the shelves.

"There are many books written about her in China and other countries. Personally, I think it's wonderful that there are only three in English. It keeps her more mysterious, don't you think?"

"I don't know. I guess so," I told him. I felt totally out of my element. "What about a pre-Atlantean civilization called Lemuria?" I asked, a bit embarrassed. "Do you have a section on ancient civilizations like that?"

"Now there's one I haven't heard of," he told me, shaking his head.

In desperation, I headed for the cappuccino counter.

As I sipped from the big round cup, I read up on author John Blofeld's view of Quan Yin. This very educated man was enthralled by her, so much so that he was dedicating his life to studying her. And he was set on reaching enlightenment through her eyes.

I discovered that there is not one consistent story of Quan Yin. Each culture has its own variation. The Chinese believe Quan Yin began as a male force known as Avalokitisvara who arrived from India somewhere around 300 A.D. Of course, it was totally uncool for a female to hold that kind of power back then. So this Avalo person was not only a compassionate soul like the later female entity, but he was a spiritual warrior who would come to anyone who needed his defense. I liked that. By around 600 A.D., Chinese texts depicted Quan Yin in a more androgynous way. I liked that even better. Strong *and* feminine. *Yes.*

It wasn't until 800 A.D., give or take a few decades, that Quan Yin was commonly depicted as a female. At the same time, the powers attributed to her expanded considerably. Ironically, even today some religions still believe that when Quan Yin finishes her work and goes to heaven she reverts to a male form. *Charming.*

The earliest story from China tells of a young princess named Miao Shan who was born into a royal family. Her father, the king, tried to marry her off but the princess refused, begging to spend her life in prayer and meditation. When he saw how strong his daughter's will was, the king gave in and allowed her to go live in a nunnery. Secretly, he arranged with the Abbess to make sure her life was hell by assigning her the most menial tasks while she was there. But Miao Shan was happy to be of service, and she got lots of support from various animals and beings who came from other dimensions to assist her. One of them was a tiger.

Despite all of the king's machinations, Miao Shan still refused to marry. The king sent soldiers to the nunnery, ordering them to kill everyone and burn it down. In the chaos that prevailed, the nuns blamed Miao Shan, who in turn prayed to Buddha for help. In a moment of clarity she pricked the top of her mouth and spat blood into the air. The blood was transformed into rain clouds that saturated the flames and saved everyone. The king was enraged and ordered Miao Shan killed, but even the executioner was moved by Miao Shan's merciful courage and couldn't carry out the king's will. The gates to heaven opened and, as a reward, an incredible, immortal beast—The Earth God Tiger—came to rescue her and to stay with her forever as her ally and friend.

The king fell ill after all of his evil transgressions and was at death's door when a monk appeared and told him that the arm and eye of a compassionate being would save him. A young woman was found who was willing to make the sacrifice, and the king healed immediately. When he went to reward the compassionate soul who had given him back his life and saw that it was his daughter, the king embraced her and begged her forgiveness. In response, a joyful Miao Shan became the Thousand-Armed and Thousand-Eyed Guan Shih Yin.

I looked at the picture of the sculpture of the thousand-armed and -eyed Quan Yin. *The one whose mission is to reawaken love in this world.* For once I couldn't come up with a deprecating thought. Forgiveness is a powerful thing.

There were photographs and illustrations of Quan Yins native to Viet Nam, Thailand, Burma and Tibet. She appeared with pheasants, dragons, temple dogs, elephants, serpents and many other allies.

There were many inspiring tales of the goddess saving the day with her courage, selflessness and high intentions. There were also wonderful stories of pilgrimages made by sailors to Pu To, a South Sea island that holds many shrines to Quan Yin to this day.

Quan Yin, the goddess who answers the cries from the people of the earth. According to Buddhist tradition, she chose to put off attaining her own buddhahood until all of the cries of the people on the planet earth were answered. I had to admit, that was a selfless gesture, and her story was a fantastically well-crafted myth. I couldn't think of a woman alive who wouldn't want to fantasize about a compassionate goddess who would answer her prayers and nurture her weary soul.

As I read on, I learned that Quan Yin appeared to people in many forms: in a human-looking form, as an animal, as the wind, a willow branch—anything that worked. And her repertoire of healing abilities was truly remarkable.

Cures all maladies and counteracts poisons.

Banishes darkness.

Subdues water spirits and demons.

Induces pregnancy and oversees childbirth.

Unites friends and family.

Invokes prosperity.

Protects against oppressive authorities.

Assuages hunger and thirst.

Melts down negative emotions.

Opens hearts.

Casts out self-criticism.

Answers the cries of all who whisper her name.

Protects women.

Reading this last line, my heart began to quiet down in a way that I hadn't experienced in many years. *Protects women. Protects women,* my mind repeated. Inside my heart, the mythical goddess was gaining ground.

That night as I climbed into bed I suddenly started laughing out loud. I was thinking of how my own biography would read.

Has experienced 87,000 lifetimes,
all born under the sign of Scorpio
to make it really challenging.

Millions of lessons to learn, too many
to enumerate here. (See Appendices.)

Will be given many nutty clients to work with.

Always incarnates as a female to truly experience
issues of power.

Prone to midnight anxiety and attacks
of not-good-enough.

On an ongoing excavation to unearth her softness.

Inability to make decisions on imminent issues,
such as facelifts and inner thigh liposuction.

A poet who cannot lift her pen.

Damn good blackjack player.

Does not understand the necessity of masturbation.

A born lover who sublimates through
long walks in the park,
listening to Sting and George Carlin.

A realist who ought to dream just for the fun of it.
But can she?

Never felt safe a day in her life.

A fabulous smile and good teeth.

The gal can't really see herself in the mirror;
only a partial self looks back.

Then more words floated up from my shadowy subconscious.

A failure to herself, no matter how much she achieves.

Must learn to trust and let love in.
This is her soul's greatest challenge.

The years 2000–2001 will be the acid test.

30

TIGER, TIGER

I had considered consulting with my colleagues down the hall about my crisis with Mei-Mei, but I had a feeling I knew what they would say. There was only one person I could discuss this business of Quan Yin and Lemuria with, so I dialed Lillian and explained the situation. I told her I had done some research and that there was indeed a goddess called Quan Yin.

"Well, of course there is!" she laughed into the phone. "What planet have you been living on, anyway?" Then her voice softened. "Why don't you come for dinner, honey? I think I have some information that might help you. You know, though, it could confuse you some, too."

I told her there was no possible way I could be more confused and that I would be there.

Aunt Lillian met me at her door holding an open, leather-bound book. "You sit yourself down," she said, "and let's talk Lemurian! I found this book sitting by a garbage can in the back alley a couple years ago. I swear it called out to me, so I picked it up and brought it home. I put it in the bookcase and just plain forgot about it until now. But I laid back on my old couch and read some this afternoon.

"I'll tell you 'bout what I read. It's pretty interesting stuff. You see, some people think Lemuria still exists, and I don't know why it couldn't. But I'll tell you this—if it does exist, it's a civilization you certainly would love to live in. Very connected to Spirit and the earth like the American Indian ways. Of course, this book is just one man's version of what Lemuria is all about, so I'm not saying it's the truth. Remember, this is mystical stuff. A lot of it has been kept a secret so that folks don't try to ruin it.

"No one really knows when Lemuria rose out of the ocean, but this guy says it was here before Atlantis, and that it was Atlantis that took it down." Lillian stopped briefly and took a sip of carrot juice.

"Billie, we're talking a good sized land mass here, maybe a quarter of the size of the United States—probably located somewhere between Hawai'i, Tahiti and California. This guy says Big Sur, on the coast of California, is the sacred tip of Lemuria, that you can feel the energies when you walk on that land. Also, he says there's a major gateway to Lemuria through the island of Maui. Apparently, you can enter into the next dimension through a little bay on the northwest shore of the island.

"Anyway, politically this is a culture overseen by women, but everybody's treated equal. There isn't a caste system like we have. Everyone is in service and has their own special duties. Incidentally, everyone, no matter who they are, has healing abilities. And there isn't any competition. Sounds too good to be true, doesn't it? Oh yeah, the Lemurians come in all different colors—from milk-toast to sunlight to red-fleshed to butterscotch to chocolate to purple black—every skin tone you can think of. And nobody's looked down on, no matter what color their skin is.

"The earth there is very lush from volcanic ash, just like over in Hawai'i. Norfolk pine, jacaranda, tree ferns, and millions of different kinds of palm trees grow there. The guy that wrote this book says that if we were looking down from an airplane we would see acres of sunflowers, birds of paradise, orchids, hibiscus and heliconia, yellow-be-still and bottlebrush, poincianna and passionflower. Mile after mile of papyrus and wheat.

"I can see it now," she said in a dreamy voice, "just how he's described it. The architecture is just gorgeous. Away from the blue, blue Pacific and powder beaches, the city stretches out. Sparkling white streets lead to the inner structure. Tall, arch-shaped buildings are made of glass, copper, bronze and koa wood. At the end of the street you can see the Temple of the Goddess, The Hall of Records—where the record of your soul's history is sitting—and there's a big open-air market. And there are pastel houses on the outer hills and down in the lower canyons. Light blue lagoons dotted with thousands of colorful koi fish light the entire area. And, of course, to keep it balanced, it's all perfectly feng shuied. Can I say that?"

"What's feng shui?" I asked.

"Oh," Lillian explained, "it's an ancient Chinese way of bal-ancing energy. Anyway, this author says there are statues of the main goddess everywhere. In one, she dangles a strand of Biwa pearls in her right hand. In another, she sits in sweet repose med-itating on an open lotus blossom. A third statue shows her as half woman, half dragon. I wonder how she feels about that! But, like the spirit animals, those goddesses can shapeshift into anything they want to, anything at all. . . . And there are lots of our kind of animals there, too. Whales and dolphins are specially honored.

"The Lemurians are into all kinds of metaphysical sciences, especially astrology and numerology, anything that has to do with the study of the soul. But mainly they're big believers in the power of prayer. All day long they make offerings with prayers of gratitude inside. They light candles and leave roses and iris, gladiolas and gardenias in the name of the goddess. It's quite a scene isn't it?"

"It sounds too good to be true," I said sadly.

"Oh, don't be so negative, honey. It might sound too good for this world with all of its earthly lessons, but after you die I'm sure life on the other side is really wonderful. That's what this old broad is gonna believe, anyway."

"Aunt Lillian, I just don't know what to believe or how to help Mei-Mei."

"Well, I think all you can do is do what you would in any situation, use your compassion and listen. Now, how about some dinner?"

After we finished Lillian's famous tofu casserole she left the table and returned with a small package.

"I have something to give you," she said, handing it to me with a big smile. "But before you open it, remember years ago when I told you about the medicine animals that had come to protect you and help you get through life?"

"Of course. You scared me to death at first, but then the cobra started showing up in my dreams as my friend. Why?"

"Well, because something's changed. Do you remember about the tiger that I told you was in your aura but far away? Well, tonight at dinner, I noticed him lying very close to your left side. Actually, he circled the table several times and sat down next to you. He's definitely come to bring you a message."

"Lillian, you know I don't know how to deal with these kinds of things. I don't have that gift. I can't talk with these kinds of animals. I have to admit, sometimes I actually think I can feel that they're present somehow. But I never really *saw* the cobra or the tiger, you know. I just believed you when you said they were here. What do you think the tiger wants?"

"Well, why don't you just open your gift?"

Inside the paper was a tiny tiger carved out of jade.

"This is what the Indians call a fetish. It's a representation of your medicine animal. I've been holding on to it for many years, until you were ready to own it."

"What should I do with it?"

"You hold it in your hand and shut your eyes and let yourself go. If you relax and let yourself believe, you'll begin to feel the thoughts and actions of the tiger. This way you can actually call the animal to your side anytime you want to communicate with it or want it to protect you."

"It still feels pretty far out to me. And why would a tiger come to me, anyway, at this stage of my life?"

Aunt Lillian looked up with her intense green eyes and smiled. "I don't know what to tell you, honey, but I know your life's about to get real interesting."

31

MEI-MEI

Not at all
like the day
you are free
from the disguise
of your family.
Standing under the awning
of your apartment house
you plant a dragon
hat pin close
against your skull
and underline
your lower lids
with ash.

Alone at 4 A.M.
Manhattan streets are shiny.
It's a game dodging footsteps
wondering if they're yours.

Feeding sugar to horses
your thin fingers
ringed yellow from smoke
shake with cold.

You fool the driver by jumping out of his coach
at a stoplight.
He screams at you
about your epicanthic eyes.
"Eurasian," you scream back.

You wait by the entrance
to Fire Dragon Alley
swaying to a Chinese love song.
Your slender lover climbs through your bedroom window
(his sash dragging across the marble floor).
His chest is slate, the color of wheat.
Your fingers trace the veins of his neck
barely touching.
He rocks you back where
you are safe
in the solitude of trees.
You follow a path beneath a red parasol.
Golden fish half your size swim past in silence.
The wind carries blossoms to your tongue.
They taste like lilacs.

You begin to feel rested
when you are rushed back
by gangs shouting in the street.
You walk on . . .
past the ducks' feet hanging like night shades
in produce windows.
An old man adjusts trays
of yellow chicks
by the side of the road.

You prop yourself
against the gates of China-
town, flashing
neon silk.

32

INVITING QUAN YIN

Typically I was so exhausted at the end of my day that I would skip dinner and climb into my vermilion-colored tulip sheets and die a little death until morning. And believe me, the night after my visit with Lillian was no exception. After spending the day with half of my brain listening to clients while the other half mulled over what my aunt had told me, all I wanted to do was climb straight into those silky sheets. As it was, I stood under the steaming water that poured down my face and I saw my reflection in the mirror, and Callie's ebullient face next to mine. I saw Mei-Mei's beautiful face turn away. I pictured Maria standing under the shower bathing away the filth of the city. I came to a sudden decision. I would go and see Mei-Mei. It was important to her and it was important to me. I would break the rules.

I stayed under the shower until everyone and everything seemed to wash away from me, until I was fully in my body and my mind was still and peaceful in a Manhattan kind of way. I placed my cheek next to the shower wall tiles and breathed. I wondered how this evening with Mei-Mei and her goddess would turn out, how I could bring her back to her senses without talking down to her and losing her confidence forever. I went to my patient "home" files and looked up her address.

When I stepped out onto the sidewalk in front of my building, the evening was melting into shades of peach. I decided to drive my own car instead of waiting for a cab. It had been a long time since I had been in SoHo, and I could use the time looking for a parking place to gather my thoughts. I didn't know what I was going to find when I got to Mei-Mei's apartment, but I knew that I needed to be careful in the way I expressed my feelings, or I'd lose her for good.

A legal parking space was waiting for me right outside of Mei-Mei's building. Any other night I would have had to circle the block a dozen times. Something felt distinctly auspicious. Unpredictable. These are feelings that can send a control freak right over the edge.

By the time I reached the sixth floor, I was already anxious. Where the hell was my Bartholomew cloak of impassivity, not to mention my professionalism? I pushed the doorbell and took a deep breath. The door opened and Mei-Mei stood before me like an empress receiving her audience. She bowed and motioned me in. Her hair was twisted up and positioned at the back by a jade dragon hairpin. She seemed at once eternally young and yet indescribably ancient. Trying to clear the sense of confusion I felt, I shook my head slightly.

The room was semi-dark, lit only by candles placed everywhere. There must have been a hundred purple and white tapers silently dripping their wisdom from every surface in Mei-Mei's living room. The place reeked of rose and jasmine incense. But it was at the center of the room that Mei-Mei had created a lavish altar for her deity. A long walnut table was covered by a white silk shawl, and its fragile tassels fluttered like butterfly wings in the warm air coming from her electric heater.

A silver bowl stacked with floating pink carnations and red rosebuds sat below the head of the goddess. Bananas and oranges filled a neighboring bowl carved with dancing dragons on its sides.

But the details of the room held my attention for only a few moments before my attention fixed on the beautiful likeness that commanded the room. The face was flawless, the eyes unconditional, the mouth joyful, the marble skin animated in the candlelight. Quan Yin's headdress sat high over the crown of her head, sensuous yet simple. Mei-Mei was right, the goddess (*No, the statue,* my mind insisted) had a presence. Whoever had modeled for this amazing sculpture knew exactly who she was. She was mesmerizing. The more you looked, the deeper you breathed. Stare into her eyes and things started to quiet down. She emanated an atmosphere of safety, a feeling that no matter what was happening, you were going to be okay. Annoyed with my flights of fancy, my mind checked in once more. . . . *It's only an inanimate carving of some religious figure. Get real, Billie.*

"Sit down, Dr. Bartholomew," Mei-Mei invited, pointing to the left. "I plumped up my favorite chair for you. Have a seat, please."

Her voice was cordial. Wrapped in creamy, embroidered silk, Mei-Mei was the picture of grace and confidence. This was the first time I had seen her without makeup. She looked so youthful and innocent with her hair pulled away from her face. The slight layer of powder dusted over her features and the outline of her cheeks and lips made her look as if she, too, were cast from marble. I noticed she kept touching a tiny purple jade bottle that hung around her neck.

"Ambrosia," she explained quietly, touching the bottle while looking directly into my eyes. "Quan Yin carries it with her as a healing balm."

Even from across the room, her gaze felt as if it penetrated to my very core. I shivered. Some sort of hypnotic effect, no doubt, brought on by the mood, the candlelight, the odd circumstances.

"We can begin when the moon is high," Mei-Mei went on. "Quan Yin will arrive with the moon. The moon is her ally, as is the lotus."

This is absurd. She's farther gone than I thought.

Mei-Mei retrieved a velvet-covered box from the floor. "Why don't I begin to read to you?"

She picked up a paper out of the box. "All you have to do is listen. Everything your soul needs to hear is right here."

"What is it, exactly?" I asked, feigning an interest I did not feel. I was fairly sure I knew everything I needed to know. My soul did not qualify for a vote. "New poems? I love your poems, especially the one—"

"No, this isn't a poem," Mei-Mei countered. "These are the words of Quan Yin. She is giving me the information I need to be her servant. She will be traveling from her homeland to Manhattan." She paused.

"I can't tell you the other reason she has come into my life until I know you're really with us."

I didn't like it, but something about the energy in the room had started to hook me. I squeezed the arms of the chair, as if reminding myself of something solid, visible . . . real.

"It's all in these pages, Dr. Bartholomew. Are you interested? It's important that you tell me the truth because this is very sacred material. If you're not totally with us, I mustn't share it with you."

Great, my first ethical dilemma. I thought about the question. As a therapist, I didn't want to lose Mei-Mei and that was the only truth I had to go with. Maybe she was on her way to "going crazy" and there was still time to bring her back. Or maybe, like Lillian said, she was having some kind of spiritual breakthrough. It didn't matter. Someone had to be there for her, and I wanted to be the one. Besides, she'd asked if I was interested, not if I *believed* what she was saying.

"Yes," I told her with a determined voice. "I'm honored you want to share the information with me."

"Okay. Well, this is what you need to know. Every night when the moon is high, I sit in front of Her Highness and go deeply inside of myself. When I'm totally relaxed, I place my hands on the sides of her face and I feel the doors of my soul opening. Then I sit back in my chair and wait for her energies to enter me. And I write. I don't ask any questions. I just surrender to her voice, which gets very clear in the first few minutes. The words and images just flow through me, like a river moving from the source. Shall I read you some?"

I sat up and crossed my hands in my lap, adopting what I hoped was an appropriate demeanor. "I'm ready," I told her. My insides felt tight.

"I'll begin at the beginning. In case you don't remember, Dr. Bartholomew, Quan Yin is talking to me from Lemuria."

There was a time, before my meeting with Aunt Lillian, that I would have thought, "Oh shit, she's delusional." But now I was just semi-skeptical, so I closed my eyes in an effort to center myself.

Mei-Mei picked up the manuscript and began to read:

> "*Good evening, Dear One.*
>
> *Thank you for transcribing my words. I am eternally grateful.*
>
> *I am communicating through you today because I have heard the prayers of the people of Manhattan and I am answering your call.*
>
> *I am the one who brushes my lips across your cheek as you sleep.*
>
> *I am the one who envelops you in light during the most perilous of times.*
>
> *I am the one who listens to your prayers whenever you call.*
>
> *I am the one who delivers you from the doorway of death to the gateway of everlasting life.*"

Mei-Mei sure has a way with poetry, I thought.

"Even though I am very close to you, I am light years away. I am speaking to you from Lemuria, a dimension you have visited again and again. It is a realm so peaceful that many have a hard time accepting its existence. And yet, here it sits, awaiting you like an old friend.

I am the mirror of joy that longs to sing within you.
I am the warm, welcoming cradle that holds your bliss.
I am the compassionate one who is destined to love you.
I come to bring you courage.
I come to teach you to forgive.
I will never leave you.

Trust me. Hear my words. And as I say these words, some part of you is opening, remembering Lemuria from the depths of your deepest self. I have loved you for a very long time."

I began to understand why Mei-Mei would create a character like this. Quan Yin was the quintessential earth mother. I couldn't help wishing that my own mother could have been even a smidgen like that.

"Dr. Bartholomew. Where are you?" Mei-Mei asked gently. "Are you listening?"

"Of course I am. I was just resting with my eyes closed. It helps me concentrate. I heard everything so far. Everything."

"It's important that you stay very present. As you might imagine, this information is very confidential, so I can only read it out loud once. Are you ready to continue?"

"Yes," I said in a very grounded tone, hoping my imagination wouldn't take me away again.

I sat like a good therapist, with my hands folded in my lap. Mei-Mei began again.

"I have enlisted my great warrior and ally Tiwa to protect the woman who is ready to die. It will be the great tiger's job . . ."

"Tiger?" I said. "Did you say tiger?"

"Yes, tiger. This is a very special kind of tiger. Quan Yin describes him as a shape-shifter, a creature that can take on any form and move easily between this world and the invisible worlds. He's been her protector and friend for eons. No one can see him unless they believe."

"I see," I said. There were tigers entering my life from everywhere! Things were getting crazier by the moment. Mei-Mei returned to the manuscript for the last words of this evening's reading.

> *"Until we meet again,*
> *Quan Yin."*

Softly Mei-Mei put the paper down. "That's enough for tonight," she told me. "You are always welcome to hear more as Quan Yin divulges more and the story evolves. Well, what do you think? Or as you used to say to me, 'What are you feeling right now?'"

I shook myself out of some sort of hypnotic stupor. Perhaps the warmth pouring in from the heater had gotten to me. I felt out of touch with my surroundings. I forced myself to take a deep breath before answering.

"Well, first of all, Mei-Mei, you're a damn good writer. You really know how to evoke an atmosphere. It's been a long time since I felt interested enough in a piece of fiction that I could sit through paragraphs of goddesses turning to tigers to be their allies. . . ."

From the look on Mei-Mei's face, I knew I must have said precisely the wrong thing. She put her papers back in their box, as if removing them from the reach of a non-believer. When she spoke, her tone was a husky mixture of disappointment and resignation.

"This is *not* fiction, Dr. Bartholomew. This is the truth. This is documentation . . . of what will happen." She looked at the figure of Quan Yin in the center of the room, and then looked back at me.

I started to protest, but she smiled and quietly added, "I understand. I'm sure that lots of people wouldn't allow that a Lemuria could exist, so they probably won't get to experience it. I mean if you don't believe it, how can it be part of your reality? I think I've known about it my whole life. When I was a child I sensed it, I just couldn't put it into words."

For a moment I flashed on that place I went to as a child when Martin was in my room. I thought of the seashells, and the waves rolling in through the center of a place not far away, a place that appeared to be right beyond my ceiling. But that was just my imagination. A fantasy made up by a desperate little girl.

My mind told me that Mei-Mei had bought into an elaborate and complex fantasy triggered by this statue she had purchased. She had opted out of reality and chosen to retreat into this Lemuria place. But in my body, I felt something different.

"I see what you mean," I told her, maintaining an even tone. It was imperative that I not sound worried or condescending. Still, Mei-Mei looked skeptical of my sincerity. My mind raced.

"So, when may I come back to hear more?"

"But you don't believe, do you? You still think it's a fairy tale."

Something told me that she would accept nothing less than the truth. Psychological double-talk would not fit the bill in this situation.

"Mei-Mei, I just don't *know*. Some part of me likes the sound of the place you call Lemuria. And Quan Yin . . ." Once again my eyes strayed to the carving of the goddess figure. "Well, she's a remarkable . . . being. But I don't know yet what parts of this I can truly accept. I want to do what's best for you because you are my first concern. And if part of that is coming to understand Quan Yin, then that's what I will do, insofar as I'm able. Am I making sense?"

Mei-Mei stood silent, her eyes closed. I could only assume she was consulting whatever part of her self now spoke as the goddess figure. Then she smiled with a gentle delight.

"Yes, you are, Dr. Bartholomew. And I thank you for keeping an open mind. We are most grateful. Perhaps now it does not seem so difficult, the idea of aiding Quan Yin, of taking on this task she offers you."

I felt lost. Had a task for me been mentioned specifically? In the story? And why had she dropped that "we" into the conversation? My momentary affection for the idea of a real, nurturing mother disappeared. I started to worry that I was dealing with multiple personality disorder here. But surely I would have seen that coming. At the moment there was nothing for me to do but to humor Mei-Mei.

"Well, of course I want to be of help. I mean, I'm not sure what the task entails, but I will see that Quan Yin gets all she needs on this end. And someone has to help you in this endeavor. After all, anyone who comes into this city needs all the assistance she can get, even if she does have her tiger with her."

"It's Tiwa," she gently corrected me.

"Yes, Tiwa. Sorry. Just give me time to let all this sink in. How about if we meet in a few days, in the evening, same time? Will we be on schedule with Quan Yin?" I asked brightly, even though I felt like giggling.

"I don't know if it will be time yet, but I'll let you know as soon as I communicate with her later on this evening. I'm proud of you, Dr. Bartholomew. I wasn't sure you would be with us." Her innocent trust sent streaks of guilt through me, but I reminded myself that I had to stay objective. I was simply doing what I thought was best for someone who was more than a patient.

Mei-Mei walked me to the door. We bowed toward each other and I began the long walk down to the first floor. The night was alive with people walking their animals (none of them tigers), and I was grateful to be driving toward my desert oasis townhouse on this smoggy, icy-cruel, nutty, nutty little planet.

That night I barely slept. Was Quan Yin a projection of "The Good Mother" that Mei-Mei never had, or a piece of her psyche she thought she was missing? Or was she preparing for the so-called "goddess" to arrive and the "healing" to begin? I assured myself that if I stayed with her we could make our way through it. And besides, I thought, it really was a helluva story, fiction or not.

That night I took out the little tiger Aunt Lillian had given me. What exactly was I supposed to do with it? Clutching it, I dozed.

I was standing under a streetlight watching Maria on Fifth Avenue when all of a sudden a pack of dogs ran to the curb, urinated on the bag, and dug obsessively trying to get into the smelly old covering. I could feel their sharp claws shredding the plastic. The dying woman's body was right against the curb so she couldn't push back or roll away any further. Her eyes froze in total panic. I wanted to protect her but I couldn't move. Suddenly the monsters stopped and ran down the street howling. The sound was horrifying.

Maria put her hand over her chest as if trying to calm her heart down. Even with all of the things she had experienced on the Avenue, I was sure she hadn't envisioned herself being eaten by a tribe of mixed breeds. After a while she regained some composure. She repositioned the slippery bag around her body as well as she could and attempted to close her jumpy eyelids. I felt so bad for her.

Maria seemed to be trying to drift off again, but something else held her attention. She suddenly became as alert as a wolf who was on the scent. She waited as, once again, panic flushed over her face. I watched as a dark shadow skulked long and low and circled her numerous times. Trembling, Maria pulled the plastic over her head as though the thin film would protect her from the menacing form.

The big, heavy presence must have felt truly terrifying. I was holding my stomach I was so worried for her. How would she defend herself? To Maria, whatever was out there was being eerily silent. Inch by inch, she opened the neck of the garbage bag and peeked out. What she saw was a fifteen-foot tiger with yellow eyes. She had no way of knowing he was to become her truest ally. It was Quan Yin's tiger, Tiwa.

Maria screamed. The wise tiger backed a few feet away. He danced toward her and away many times. And then, as if in a moment of insight, he slowly turned, and showed her his north, south, east, and west—the four directions of his body. It felt like a ritual from an ancient ceremony. For some reason this calmed Maria down dramatically, and she dropped back on her side with her cheek resting on her two hands. After all, the cat was probably exhibiting more kindness than most of the other passersby who invaded her street home.

Next, I watched as the cat lay down with his face not more than a foot from Maria's, and engaged her in a steady eye-to-eye communication. It was apparent to me he knew exactly what he was doing. When he felt she was no longer afraid, he moved closer and rested his huge body against hers.

With nothing to lose, Maria stretched out her arm and the great pink tongue began to lick long, deep, holy licks. I thought of Ellington's licks and how good they felt; I could only imagine how healing Tiwa's must be. When he was finished, he stopped and Maria turned onto her other side and he continued. I was fascinated at how loving he was. He penetrated many layers and focused his energy like a parent with his newborn. Maria's forehead, cheeks, throat, chest and so on were bathed until she glistened. The beautiful beast lay next to her, walling her off from the chilly wind with his mammoth torso.

Well, it's all over for me, I thought as I turned over the next morning. *I am now part of a possible psychotic dreamscape that is invading my reality a little deeper every minute. I've got to take it easy and relax, practice what I preach to my clients. I'll get more rest tonight.* But my trembling hands were telling me otherwise.

As I walked to work, I passed Maria Milflores lying in the street again. What the hell was going on? I looked down and tried to let go of her face. Again I felt her trying to connect with me. My mind replayed her words, "Let me be! Let me live in peace!" I speeded up my walk. *She'll be gone by the time I pass by here later this evening,* I reassured myself. I still couldn't believe the cops would let a woman die right there on Fifth Avenue.

33

WHEN THE MYSTICAL BECOMES THE PRACTICAL

Somewhere in all of my confusion I began to shift more into gut reaction. I didn't know what else to do—I had used up all of my professional techniques. Add my day life to my night life with Mei-Mei and my dreamtime woo-woo adventures, and it was easy to see why I thought I was coming apart. Or was I coming together?

When I arrived at Mei-Mei's apartment for the second time, I had no clue what to expect or, for that matter, what I should do or say. Never in any of my textbooks had I seen anything like Mei-Mei's obsession with Quan Yin. Of course, the real issue was that I didn't know what to expect in *any* area of my life. My confusion was not really about my patient. It was about me.

Mei-Mei positioned me in the same chair as she had on my previous visit. The room looked the same, but Quan Yin seemed altered in some way.

"Did you move the statue?" I asked. "It looks different."

"No," Mei-Mei said, "Quan Yin is exactly the way she was last time. It's important that she be positioned in a certain way so that she's in the perfect feng shui of the room.

"This room," she continued, "has perfect feng shui. It must, in order to accommodate the energies of Her Highness."

"Is she still speaking to you?"

Mei-Mei reached behind her and pulled out another stack of paper. "This is the new information, what some people call 'channelings.'"

After talking with Lillian, I knew I had to try to discern whether these transmissions were a symptom of personality disintegration or messages from another dimension. How could I possibly know?

Mei-Mei neatly gathered the sheets of paper together. "As I explained to you the other night, Dr. Bartholomew, these communications from Quan Yin are from another dimension. The energy moves through me and I translate her energy into words."

Feeling nervous about what I was going to hear, and unsettled about the true state of both my patient's mind and my own, I sat back and prepared myself. Mei-Mei looked so beautiful and peaceful, it was hard to stick to my diagnosis that she was in the process of having a breakdown. She didn't display even the slightest evidence of manic behavior. In fact, she was even more together than she'd seemed on my last visit. According to her, she was in service to the goddess. She began to read.

> *"Good evening, Dear Mei-Mei.*
>
> *Thank you for connecting with me again.*
> *Our time is approaching.*
>
> *As you have asked in your prayers, I have uncovered information about your soul's history from the Akashic Records. Let us begin. Your human incarnations originated in China, then Tibet, Mongolia, Eastern Europe, India, and back to China. Your current record reads:*
>
> *Many existences in a female body. The soul longs to be inspired and to inspire others. To write. A challenging childhood. Deep intellectual prowess. A desire to be in service*

before all else. These seeds shall become apparent and must be cultivated by the Earth Year 2000."

Mei–Mei released a bottomless sigh. She looked right through me. I started to speak, then I stopped myself. Actually, it all sort of fit, and Aunt Lillian had prepared me well. Mei-Mei placed the papers in her lap.

"Dr. Bartholomew, let me try to explain in more detail what has happened to me here. I realize now that Quan Yin has allowed an aspect of her essence to travel into my apartment. Her energy enters into her marble image on the table and she becomes animated. From the very beginning, without knowing exactly why, I did whatever I felt prompted to do. I sat quietly before her image immersed in all of this candlelight. I closed my eyes and quieted my thoughts. I knew I must allow the connection.

"I spoke to her, and told her I wanted to know her much better. My intention was so strong that I swear I saw the goddess blink her left eye. Again I closed my eyes and continued to ask her to assist me in my search for inspiration, to help me realize a higher purpose.

"Soon after, I heard a whisper of a voice, and then an energy that was nurturing and warm enveloped me. The words came to me clearly. I heard, *'I am your ally. Our journey is about love.'"*

Mei-Mei's words hung in the air. I sat forward in my seat, hoping to gather clues to the situation from the exact words that she believed she had heard. But, instead of cataloging and analyzing them, I found myself being pulled further into emotions for which I didn't even know I had the capacity. I couldn't interrupt as Mei-Mei continued her story.

"*'There is nothing to fear,'* the voice said. *'Trust me.'*

"I was riveted, Dr. Bartholomew. How could I feel so much connection to a spirit I had never met? Without thinking, my own voice answered, 'Tell me what to do. I will do anything to help you.'

"'*Free the woman,*' the goddess told me. '*Help her leave with dignity. Be a goddess.*'"

Listening to Mei-Mei, I felt a sudden urge to put as much distance between myself and that statue as I possibly could. And what did she mean, be a goddess? As if anyone could become a goddess!

At that moment, a sudden breeze passed through the room, causing the candle flames to jump. Mei-Mei crossed her hands over her heart. Then she got down on her hands and knees, bowed to the statue and touched her forehead to the floor. I was overcome with an uncomfortable mixture of curiosity and, yes, longing. All my life I had wanted to feel connected to something, to someone, just as Mei-Mei obviously was. She had opened her heart and spirit completely, something I had never been able to do.

The breeze swirled around my chair for a brief moment. It was then that I knew with absolute conviction that there was no way I could stop this process, whatever it was.

"She is coming, Dr. Bartholomew, everything is in perfect timing. I don't understand quite how it works yet. But I can feel Tiwa all around me. He visits the statue each night," she said, pointing to a place right beneath the figure of Quan Yin.

"Wait until you experience his energy. And you will experience it, Dr. Bartholomew."

I managed to nod like a good actress, but I couldn't help but ask, "So if I'm a part of this, ask her to tell me something about my own past, or why I'm here. What's going to happen to me?"

Mei-Mei didn't react defensively. Instead, she walked over to the statue and placed her hands on Quan Yin's cheeks. She closed her eyes. She stood quiet for quite a long time.

Then she said, "'*You must leave your past behind. You must forgive and practice compassion. That is why you have been chosen.*'"

I blinked a few times. Could she know anything about my life, or about Martin?

Embarrassed, I told Mei-Mei, "That could be true of almost anyone in Manhattan."

"Yes," she said. "It probably could be. But it's especially true of you."

I sat back in my chair.

Mei-Mei, however, had other issues on her agenda. "Can you imagine what it would be like coming from a heaven like Lemuria and entering into this city?" Her voice was overcome with awe. And then, with some impatience, she prodded. "She needs to know, Dr. Bartholomew. Are you with us or aren't you?"

"Of course I'm with you. Tell me what I need to do."

"Quan Yin will answer all of your questions sooner than you think."

I was more confused than ever.

Mei-Mei left the room for a moment, and I found myself standing in front of the statue. I don't know what possessed me, but I placed my hands on either side of her face. Instantly I felt pleasantly dreamy. The stone was as warm as human skin to my touch. I began to feel the pulse of her cheeks beneath my hands and I quickly jerked them away, breaking contact. I laughed at my imagination.

"Jesus," I thought. "Is it happening to me, too?" Hurriedly I got my coat.

Mei-Mei returned to find me heading for the door and followed, still looking calm and unruffled. I stopped in the foyer and ventured another question.

"The only thing I don't understand is what Quan Yin's and Tiwa's mission is exactly."

"To free the woman, the fallen goddess of Fifth Avenue," she whispered. "But I can't tell you any more. Quan Yin will show you when the time is right."

"What woman?"

"You know. The woman lying on the corner of 57th Street and Fifth Avenue."

I was stunned. How could it be that Mei-Mei was talking about the same woman I knew as Maria? How had she learned of my personal life? How could she possibly know?

"Yes, that woman, and—" Mei-Mei stopped mid-sentence as if she was about to disclose some great secret. Seeing my distress, she bent toward me. "Are you okay? You look a little pale."

"No, no," I lied. "I just want to get one thing straight here." And then I spoke kind of methodically because I was partially losing my mind. "Are you saying that this mission . . . is all about Quan Yin helping that woman . . . who looks very, very sick . . . who is lying in a garbage bag, right on Fifth Avenue . . . die?"

"Yes," Mei-Mei said. "Why are you so shocked? You said you were beginning to believe. Quan Yin is coming here. We told you the story. You must believe, or the miracle will not occur."

I could barely breathe. I opened my mouth, not knowing if any sound would come out. "When will we meet again?" I whispered.

Mei-Mei smiled gently. "I'll let you know."

She bowed to me and pressed a small wooden figure into my hand. I walked out into the hall and heard the door close behind me. I opened my hand and saw a miniature statue of Quan Yin.

As I walked down the darkened stairwell I felt absolutely spooked. I could have sworn there was someone walking behind me. In the corner of my eye, I thought I saw something blurred in the distance. I walked faster. It walked faster. Finally I made it to the lobby, but my heart was pounding. I half ran through the small lobby to the outside door and forced it open.

I ran to my car but the thing was still around me. I shut the door very tightly as if trying to keep something out. I told myself, *Stop it!* but the feeling that something was watching me from the back seat was overpowering. My hands were shaking on the steering wheel as I made my way uptown, so I turned on some quiet jazz in an effort to calm down. I was relieved to see my next door neighbor pulling out as I arrived in front of my house. He stopped, rolled his window down and asked me how I was doing. I said all the right things, and stopped short of telling him that something was following me.

Finally I was alone in my apartment. My hands were still shaking, so I went to the bathroom and rifled through my medicine cabinet till I found some old tranquilizers that MollieO had given me once when I had a particularly bad bout of insomnia. I lay back, and as I was letting go of the craziness of the day I began to slide into another adventure with Maria and her protector.

I marveled as Tiwa magically cocooned Maria in white light, thereby allowing her to relax and feel protected from the policemen who were on her scent. It was Tiwa's job to make sure Maria's body remained right where it was, a hard task to accomplish in Manhattan where there appeared to be no homeless people—just clean, safe neighborhoods. Tiwa was indeed doing "psychic overtime." I couldn't understand what was going on. It seemed he enjoyed confusing the police and the folks from the government agencies by sending out invisible arrows that scattered them in various directions. Usually, twice a day, once in the morning and once in the evening, two cops on horseback would search for the woman several blocks north or south of where she lay. After hours of circling the area they'd finally give up, totally dismayed, and return empty-handed. And still the calls would come in demanding that something be done about the dying woman.

"What's the holdup?" one irate taxpayer demanded. "This is my tenth call. I don't want my children to have to look at that woman one more day. Get her off the street!"

The mayor's office was beside itself.

What was the holdup? I wondered in my dream. Why would a goddess of compassion not answer the woman's prayers and help her die as quickly as possible? The whole thing didn't sound very compassionate to me.

In my dream, Tiwa worked hard to keep the situation as peaceful as possible. His yellow eyes told her to hold on, that soon the goddess would come and she would be released from her miserable life.

"The pain is too much," Maria murmured in a patois of Spanish and English. "Help me to die."

Tiwa licked her swollen hand and placed his paw over it so she could derive energy from his fierce pulse. She was drifting away quickly, but his energy brought her back. As I watched it all through my dream, I was getting upset. "Let her die," I spoke out in my sleep. "Let her die."

34

EVERY SOUL WANTS TO BE SAVED

The night before my fiftieth birthday I came up with a fabulous idea. I would invite MollieO and Lillian to celebrate the day with me by having lunch at a hot new restaurant near the Plaza Hotel.

"Why do you want to ruin the whole thing by inviting her?" MollieO questioned me over the phone. "She'll arrive wearing one of her atrocious outfits and totally humiliate us! For God's sake, darlin', it's your fiftieth! Let's do it right. In style."

Tiwa started showing off to get my attention. In recent days the great warrior and I had developed quite a relationship. He'd begun making his presence known in subtle ways, and so gently and playfully that I soon gave up trying to hold on to my resistance and my fears. I'd decided that, if he was a figment of my imagination, he was a benign and intriguing one that I'd observe and deal with appropriately if I found I was truly losing touch with reality. If, on the other hand, he was real—which to my amazement I was actually beginning to believe—he was an ally like none I'd ever imagined, and I figured I must be in for the adventure of my life.

Figment or not, I never knew when the great cat would arrive. It appeared he'd decided this phone conversation was an event worth showing up for. I still could not see him, but I could sense his movements all around me. Suddenly he picked up one of my rattles off the table and shook it as if to say, "Take control! Don't let her pull that stuff on you!"

"Are you there, Billie?"

"Yes, Mother," I said, but my attention was on a stack of client files that Tiwa had innocently knocked over. His actions were telling me to take a stand.

"You know," I said. "Lillian is one of my favorite people in the world. I don't know what happened that made you so judgmental of her, but that's your problem. I want her to come to my birthday lunch."

"Okay," she finally said with displeasure in her voice. "But don't do a thing. It's your birthday. I'll take care of it."

MollieO arrived annoyingly late, which was typical, and looked absolutely elegant, also typical. "I have found the most marvelous new aesthetician," she told me, fluttering her midnight blue eyelashes at me. "I can see you could use his expertise as well."

Self-consciously I ran my fingers quickly through the sides of my hair and covered my unspeakable nails in my lap as if I was twelve years old again. But she had moved on. Her enthralling monologue consisted of the details and results of her various beauty treatments. I listened patiently, not really caring whether Jean-Claude gave the best haircut in Manhattan, or whether the new facial masques at Elizabeth Arden were miraculously skin tightening and rejuvenating. I sat there, looking at MollieO's perfect face, and all I could think about were Maria Milflores' dark, entrancing eyes. And again I could sense Tiwa moving toward us in the restaurant. I felt his immense body under the table, lying by my feet.

MollieO was perfectly put together: cobalt blue suit to match her eyes and stockings, fuchsia silk shirt and high heels and ostrich feathers to augment the look. Probably no one else in Manhattan could have pulled it off with such "ee-lahn."

"Where's Lillian? She's never late."

"Oh my word, I forgot to call her. Oh well, we'll do it some other time."

I was furious. Tiwa was pawing gently at my leg. "Okay, okay," I said, trying to get him to stop. MollieO heard me.

"Okay, okay, what?" Mother said.

"It's nothing," I said. Then I slammed down my fork and knife, clenched my teeth and said, "Actually, I need to tell you that I can't stay too long, Mother. I have dinner plans."

"Actually, Billie, I was hoping you'd stop by the apartment. I have a little gift for you. But if you have a dinner date this evening I certainly understand. I've been praying you'd meet someone soon and I could marry you off at fifty!" She started laughing at her little joke, but then she saw that her words had actually hurt me. A little too much truth on your birthday can be a terrible thing.

"Actually, I do. And you'll never guess with who!"

She looked up from her bisque.

"With Lillian."

MollieO was not pleased. Her whole demeanor changed into that of an angry, depressed, spoiled child. "You really love that dingbat, don't you?"

"Yes. Yes, I do. She has an incredible heart and she's been there for me in ways you couldn't even imagine. As far as I'm concerned, the only reason I'm alive and kicking is because I've had Lillian in my life."

"Why, Billie! I am your mother! I have always been there for you. Always!"

That was the end of it for me. I asked the maître d' to bring my coat.

"Billie," she said, trying to grab my sleeve. "Don't go away like this! Please come over later. We'll have some good times. Please, I don't want to be alone this evening."

"You know what, Mother?" I said, swallowing my sweetness and stepping close enough to lean right into her face. "Fuck the good times!"

I stormed out of the restaurant and called to apologize to Lillian. "Oh, honey, don't ruin your birthday over this. It's just her way. You know that by now."

At midnight I was still ranting. It felt good to have some power. At first I thought I was the one who was causing Ellington's restless behavior, but then I remembered that Tiwa could show up at anytime. My poor little feline had probably picked up the scent.

"How dare MollieO attack Lillian!" I said out loud, still going on. "She should have one ounce of Lillian's goodness. One ounce! Lillian's the person who saved me. She's my real mother as far as I'm concerned!"

The more I encountered the truth of my feelings the more I could see Tiwa moving toward me. Now he had become an outline of white that was resting at my side. Suddenly he stood and faced me. His eyes were golden, emblazoned in the firelight. It was as if he was saying, *"Ask her what you really want to know. You're a strong woman. Stop protecting her. Get to the truth."*

I knew what I had to do.

35

THE CONFESSION

MollieO stood before me in full regalia, boudoir style. In the atrocious lighting of the outside hallway, after all she had been through, her face still looked stunning.

"Why, Billie," she asked in a drowsy voice, "what on earth are you doing here? It's 1:00 A.M. Can't it wait till morning? C'mon in. You can sleep in your old bedroom. We'll talk in the morning."

"No, Mother, it can't wait until morning. I need to talk now."

"Oh," she said flatly, opening the door and taking my coat. I had to walk a couple feet behind her so I didn't step on the lengthy train of her negligee.

I followed her down the long hallway to the living room where she lit two large pillar candles and a candelabra that sat on top of the grand piano. The room smelled like peppermint ice cream. Frigid and pink. I sank down into the old purple couch. MollieO positioned herself in a velvet straight-back chair. She unclipped her diamond earrings and tossed them across the coffee table. That was her way of signaling me to get on with it.

It amazed me how powerful and subtle that simple signal was. *Stay with your feelings,* I told myself. *Don't fall under her spell.* The truth was, I was floundering because I didn't know where to begin. How do you begin a conversation with your mother about being molested by your father? Where do the right words come from?

"It feels different in here," I said, stalling. "What have you done?"

"It's just the candlelight. It brings warmth to this old room." MollieO covered her mouth and yawned several times.

"Mother, I'm here because I've reached a plateau in my life and I want to move on. I need your help."

Her face looked empty, guileless as a child. "What kind of plateau?"

"I'm tired of being alone." This was not the kind of talk that MollieO liked to hear. She was getting restless and began reorganizing her little Limoge boxes on the side table.

Go on. Don't let her discomfort stop you. You can do this. "Actually, I've felt alone my whole life." My voice dropped. "No matter where I go or what I accomplish, I feel alone. I feel disconnected from my feelings, and then I really feel alone. Do you know what I mean?"

"Sort of. Look at me, waltzing around this humongous place all alone. But I have my flowers, my lunches at the Plaza. Best of all, I have you to keep me company."

I looked down. *She can't hear me.*

I placed my right hand on my heart. "Well, lately, something's been happening, where I feel my heart is opening up and it's bursting like a volcano with all kinds of feelings and images and memories. Overpowering feelings of sadness, so much sadness that sometimes I can hardly breathe."

"That's not like you. You're absolutely resilient. Look at yourself. You're a beautiful, successful, independent woman with a fabulous life. When I look at you I see a force to be reckoned with."

"Yeah," I said, sadness flooding into my voice. "I am those things. I work hard and I have wonderful patients. I have a beautiful home. Great friends. I wear the right colors in the fall and the spring. I know how to appear happy. But underneath this mask is a person who can hardly enjoy any of these things. I seem to be suffering from stuff that happened a long time ago. I guess I pushed all of my feelings down so I could survive. But I can't survive this way any longer. I want a different life."

MollieO was staring at her diamond ring.

"I want to be closer to my friends," I went on, raising my voice a bit. "I want a man in my life. But that's not going to happen until I get closer to my feelings, closer to my Self."

"Well, what's stopping you? You're a therapist. Why can't you figure it out?" MollieO's nerves were on the rise.

I moved closer.

"I need your help, Mother. I need to talk to you about what happened, about why it is that when I was a child I disconnected from my feelings."

"It's late. Let's talk in the morning." She got up and started to leave the room, but I walked over and took hold of her thin arm.

"No, Mother," I said, not letting up. "Now."

With a long, deep sigh, MollieO acquiesced.

"This is very hard for me because I don't want to hurt you. I know how fragile you really are underneath all of your appearances." MollieO looked away again.

"Yes, Mother," I said gently, "I know. I know because I'm that way, too."

The room was dark and silent. The vague smell of Martin's cigar smoke still clung to the curtains. *No matter how you feel, say it now. Come on, you can do this.* I moved away from Mother and leaned against the cold, dark fireplace, trying to steady myself.

"Martin did some bad things to me when I was very little." My voice sounded small.

"I recall," MollieO told me a touch defensively. "I was there, you know. Is that what this is all about?"

For a moment I wondered if she and I might be talking about the same bad things.

"He yelled at you and hit you. I remember."

I nodded. "Mother, do you remember when my bedroom was all the way down the hall, away from everyone else?"

"Sure."

"Well, . . . Martin used to come into my room late at night and do terrible things."

"What kind of things?"

"Unconscionable things. He whispered sexual things to me when I was asleep." I looked over to see if my mother was okay, but she was no longer looking at me. She was walking to the coffee table to light up a Du Maurier.

"Mother, please look at me. This is very hard to say."

MollieO sat back down. Suddenly she looked her seventy-four years, like an aging film actress. The smoke from her cigarette was curling toward me.

"He touched me. He took his hand and—"

"Please! I can't bear to hear this. It's too much!"

"Too much for whom, Mother?" I walked over and crouched by her chair. "I'm the one it happened to, not you."

Her face was shattering before me into a million soundless emotions. I felt guilt flushing into anger, but I went on. *Go on, tell the truth. Do it now.*

"I was three years old, not a grown woman. He continued to come to my room for a very long time, until I was—"

"Five." MollieO said in a resigned, broken voice. "Until you were five. Until I moved Callie into the little study next to your room." She stopped and took a good, long drag. Her hand was shaking. "It was the only action I felt I could take to stop him." Then she put out the cigarette, and hid her face in her hands.

My mind was spinning somewhere out in the universe, but I managed to form the words. "You knew?"

MollieO stood up abruptly and walked toward the hallway to make her escape. I stood, too, and doggedly followed her. "Where are you going, Mother?" I demanded, the years of repressed anger seething through me. "Aren't you going to answer my question? I have never asked one thing from you my whole life, so do me this one favor. Answer my question and I promise that I will leave you alone. Did you know that Father was sexually molesting me all those years?"

MollieO stood in the doorway of her bedroom with her hand clutched on the door so she could close it and lock me out at any moment. Her facial expression was both furious at how far I had gotten into her space and devastated that the hideous reality of her abandonment had finally presented itself. She lowered her head, suddenly lost in the memory of it all.

"I could feel the satin cover lifting and your father quietly getting out of bed. Most of the time I was only half awake, kind of dozing from a sedative, but I'd pretend I was sound asleep. Martin would come back to bed about an hour later and turn on his side, away from me. Once I followed him down the hallway but I was so scared he'd see me, I only stayed a minute—just long enough to hear his sounds."

The reality of her words was swallowing me. I felt lava rush from the volcano within me.

"You mean . . . you knew he was molesting me the whole time and you didn't try to stop him?"

"I couldn't," she said, looking anywhere else but at me. "I thought he'd destroy me."

The lava was dark and fiery, rising.

"Why didn't you call the police?"

"It would've made all the papers. I didn't want our family to be part of a scandal."

All I could feel was rage. "It's always about you, isn't it, Mother? What has to happen to get you to feel something about me?" My voice quieted for a minute. "I used to lie in bed and whisper, 'Mama, Mama, please save me. Don't let him do this to me.' I waited for years, but you never came. I would lie in bed and wish that I would die. I felt so alone, so helpless, worthless, like a piece of trash. I was only three! Why didn't you come?"

MollieO's face was ashen. "I couldn't come. He would've done something terrible to me. I was afraid he would hurt all of us. I'd lie in bed trying to figure out a way to make him stop. And I did make him stop by moving Callie down the hall, next to you."

"That didn't make him stop!" I yelled. "It was Lupe. She was watching from the hallway, too. Only she came into my room. She got in bed with me and took me in her arms. She bathed me and took care of me. And she promised she would see to it that he would never do it again. She saved my life. That's why Martin stopped.

"A woman I barely knew had the courage to save me when my own mother couldn't do a thing. How can that be?" I asked. "I waited for you. What happened? Didn't you care that my world was coming down, that my spirit was being ruined?

"All of those years of his sickening breath and gross body touching me. And then having to get up and pretend I was okay, to sit next to him at your goddamned dinner table and smile like nothing happened. To keep the peace for you. I was your scapegoat." I stopped to let the truth sink in.

"You told me to be quiet. 'Be a good girl,' you said. 'Don't make him angry.' What you were really saying to me was, 'You're not important enough to express your feelings. Play dead.'"

I was crying now, exhausted by my outpouring of emotion. The lights of the city were glimmering through MollieO's bedroom windows. She started to move toward me and stopped. I wondered if she was going to reach out in an effort to somehow try and make things right.

But instead, she closed the door a bit more. "You're just determined to destroy me and make me wrong, aren't you, Billie? All this time I thought you were different. I thought you were the only one who cared about me. But I see now that I was wrong.

No daughter would talk to her own mother this way if she cared even the least little bit about her. Well, you've said what you wanted to say . . . you've humiliated me. You ought to feel quite free to leave now."

The door shut solidly and I was alone in the darkened hallway without wish or expectation. MollieO was right. For the first time in my life I felt absolutely free to leave her.

36

IN WHICH BILLIE LETS GO OF HER BOUNDARIES AND IS FREED

The following evening I was watching the ten o'clock news when they started showing footage about New York's homeless. Mira González was on the street getting viewpoints from different parts of the city. I was surprised and delighted to see how many people were speaking up for the rights of homeless people. Then the scene shifted to a spokesman at the Mayor's office who was talking about how they had been besieged by angry New Yorkers complaining that the homeless were on the rise again, taking over the streets. "We need more cops out there doing their jobs," Carmine Cucinotta, a mechanic from New Jersey, insisted. "Tourists pay a lot of money to come here to have a good time. They don't want to see this! It ain't right."

At the end of her story, Mira mentioned that some of the top politicians were going to be meeting at the Plaza Hotel the next evening. It was rumored that protesters were going to show up and make a scene. I wondered which side they were on.

"It seems everybody's got an opinion on the homeless these days," Mira told us. And then the camera focused on Fifth Avenue in front of the hotel, panning in on a small crowd who had already shown up parading peacefully with their signs.

"It looks pretty good over here," she said. "But just a block away, there's a different feeling in the street, as you'll see right now."

The camera cut to a shot of the crowd gathering further down the street. "There's an entirely different atmosphere down here." Mira pointed her microphone at a middle-aged woman. "Why are you here?" she asked.

"I'm here because I don't feel safe. I want homeless people off the streets now!"

Things were definitely heating up.

The next morning I decided to do something I'd done only twice before in twenty years as a therapist. I canceled my appointments and took the day off. I desperately needed some time—for what I wasn't sure. After my enlightening "talk" with MollieO, a terrible emptiness had overtaken me. In a peculiar way I felt lost, estranged from a part of my identity. I sat floundering in my sadness until the image of Quan Yin's face floated in front of me. The words *Protector of Women* formed a soothing mantra that echoed through me. I closed my eyes. "Quan Yin," I whispered again and again, trying to pull her close.

This one action immediately helped me put aside the confrontation with my mother and redirect my energy. I made a little altar in my living room the way Mei-Mei had done. As I went about gathering items for it, I paused and looked out onto Fifth Avenue and watched the crowds beginning to overflow the streets. I pictured Tiwa lying next to Maria, protecting her.

On my fireplace mantel I placed several golden tapered candles and a picture of myself at age three. The wooden statue of Quan Yin and the jade fetish of Tiwa stood in front. I called Mei-Mei several times but she didn't answer.

I pulled my chair close to the altar and Ellington jumped in my lap.

In the silence I prayed that Quan Yin would come. "I don't know how to begin," I said out loud. I paused.

"The truth is, I want to believe, I want to help you, but you need to show me how. Tell me what to do."

With that, Ellington jumped down and tore out of the room. I sat waiting for Quan Yin's words. Time passed.

I went to the altar and picked up the statue and held it in my hands. It was early evening, hours later, and nothing had happened. I picked up the fetish beside Quan Yin. Dejected, I gave up and went to bed.

Was Tiwa in another world or was I? I kept feeling his absence. A warrior leaving his mission? He wouldn't leave Maria alone. In fact, in my dreams she had become quite dependent on her friend bringing her food, bathing her, telling her stories of what was yet to come. Again, I drifted away. . . .

Tiwa wasn't sure how much Maria really took in, because one moment she was quite conscious and the next she would be almost gone.

"I know you're in terrible pain," he told her. "But you've got to hold on. Soon she will come and you will be released from all this."

Her milky brown eyes looked dreamily into Tiwa's golden eyes and she tried to stay in her body. Remarkably, I could read her thoughts and his.

"Mi amigo," she murmured. "The pain is too much. I need to die. Help me to die."

"I want to show you something," he told her lovingly. "There is a place that is open-hearted, waiting for you. My mentor and I will escort you there. It is a place so lush and healing that every breath you take in . . . well, it makes you ecstatic to be alive. Joyful. No burden. No devastation. No body. Just you as a heavenly being."

Something about the "no body" statement woke Maria up. Yes. Yes. Yes! She prayed for the day she would cast away her shell, and be dusted on the surface of the Hudson River.

"We're going on a journey back home. Your real home, Sweet One," the tiger continued.

She shook her head. What did he mean? The projects? The shelter? The hospital?

"I'm going to show you what I mean. Watch."

Tiwa sat back on his haunches and paused for a moment to plan his sketch. Then, with his big dewclaw, he scratched a wavy line into the New York City pavement and mapped out the way to Lemuria.

As he was drawing he told her, "I divulge this information to you in complete confidence that you will never share it with anyone. Where we're going is an ancient mystery, and must always remain unknowable to humanity. It's part of the larger plan. The magic."

His jagged black claw drew a pretty good outline of what looked like the state of California. In the center he placed an X and carved Bg Sr for Big Sur.

Then he drew a triangle with one point coming out from Bg Sr and connected it to two other points. Hils (Hawaiian Islands) and Tah (Tahiti). In the center he traced a big L. Maria ran her gritty fingers back and forth, tracing the letter.

"Lemuria," Tiwa whispered softly. "As soon as Quan Yin comes we will depart. And you, my friend, will be free. Think of it."

"Lemureea," her tired voice repeated several times. "Lemureea."

The cat supported her head as it fell back in a semi-conscious state.

"Where is everyone?" he wondered. "Let's go. By tonight the stage will be set."

I woke up shaking. My digital alarm clock read 10:38 P.M. I tried to calm down and go back to sleep, but deep in my soul I felt someone calling to me. I got out of bed and began to pace the bedroom floor. I felt overwhelmed with loneliness. My lungs ached and I started to shiver with cold. My heart filled with a terrible longing. "I can't stand this!" I cried out.

I closed my eyes and tried to block out the feelings, but Maria's face kept returning again and again. The more I became lost in Maria the less I could feel Tiwa's presence. When I couldn't take it any longer, I got dressed. Was my dream some kind of projection, or was Tiwa there at her side? I couldn't live with the thought of Maria being alone. I headed for 57th Street.

She was exactly where I knew she would be. My heart was beating fast as I sat down next to her, trying to seem non-threatening. I could hear the voices of protesters shouting just a short distance away.

"Tigre, Tigre," she murmured weakly, but Tiwa's energy was gone.

I moved in closer so I could almost touch her arm. She didn't recognize me, but that was no surprise. Before tonight I had never really known myself, the person she was now seeing. Looking into her eyes, I saw so much emptiness, I felt I could drown. The Great Void. That usually would have scared Billie Bartholomew, but instead I felt captivated.

"Tigre, sí," I told her, mentally chastising myself for not having learned more Spanish. "You and I and Mei-Mei—and my Aunt Lillian—we're the only ones who know he's around."

I could feel someone else watching us from somewhere far away.

Maria moaned and rocked back and forth. She was in so much pain, she couldn't really understand what I was saying. The plastic bag kept falling back, and each time, she weakly gathered it up around her to protect herself. I realized there was very little I could say to assuage her pain—except to let her know that I was right there with her. "Sí, sí," I told her. "El tigre. He'll be here soon."

I took off my camel hair coat and held it out to her. She didn't move. I reached over and gently lifted her, wrapping the coat around her back. I pulled one arm through and then the other, and then bent down a little further and buttoned the coat all the way down. I could smell the dark fumes of the city in her hair.

When it seemed as if she was finally calming down, I reached over and took hold of her hand. Her stiff, cold fingers fastened on to me like a lifeline; I felt the beat of her heart through my hand. *"Stay with me,"* it said. *"Please, stay."*

I looked around to see if there was anything other than the garbage cans to lean against, then finally gave in and let the filthy containers support me. What the hell did it matter, anyway? I had lost my normal life, and before too long I knew I would be holding the woman in my arms, telling her about the goddess who would come to take her home.

Around midnight I felt her body angling close to mine. After a while she rested the back of her head against my chest and I let my hand graze her hair. It felt like a used-up Brillo pad, and for a moment I recoiled. But a tender force was moving through me and I continued to stroke her head.

"It's okay," I told her over and over. "I'm here. You can rest now."

She smelled musky, like mushrooms you find in dark, dark woods, alive but ready to die with the change of season.

I looked at her hands. How strong they were! They looked like a wine maker's hands; the city's dirt was so ingrained that her cuticles and nails were purple black. I placed my hand next to hers and rested it on her leg. She didn't flinch. Next to hers, my hand looked unused and spoiled. Weak. Ridiculous!

The platinum and diamond ring my mother had given me when I turned eighteen sent streaks of light dancing across Maria's face. I traced the wing-like wrinkles under her eyes. Those eyes were quite beautiful, her eyelashes thick and black. I flashed back to the times I had punished myself for my own wrinkles, never thinking to honor the life experiences that had created them. Clearly, the notion of a facelift had never entered this woman's consciousness.

The coat had come unbuttoned and I could now see her wasted form under the thin fabric of her grimy dress, down past her worn out breasts to her sunken belly. Her hip bones jutted out. I reached under her arm and rebuttoned the coat. More and more, I felt protective. Where is her man? I wondered. Where is her child? Where is her life?

I sat holding this woman's hand in mine, seeing her for the first time, and I could feel my heart cracking open bit by bit. As

I realized what was happening to me a wave of anxiety passed through my body, and I flashed back to a dream I'd had over and over for years, the same dream with only minor variations. The most popular rendition went like this: Billie is alone in a city that she doesn't know. She looks in her wallet, but there is no money. She can't remember where she lives, and there are many ominous shadows surrounding her. Her heart is beating triple time. She has lost her glasses and her keys. No one wants to help her. No one can save her . . . she's alone. I can't tell you how many times I woke up from that dream in mortal terror, so relieved to find myself in my comforting bed. And now here I was half lying in the gutter with a woman who was starring in the same dream, only no matter how hard she tries she can't wake up.

Just a few blocks away people were shouting. Several police cars pulled up and parked across the street and turned off their lights. *"Tiwa, come now!"* I cried out in silence.

Maria's forehead perspired. Tiny beads of sweat broke out over the ridge of her nose. Her eyes darted back and forth under their lids. Maybe she was listening to some rhythmic music in her mind. I knew nothing of her history, her culture, her inner life. But did I have to know any of that just to be with her, to hold her?

I helped her turn over. Her head lay against my chest, and I wound my arms around her. I remembered the safety of Lupe's arms. I did what I could to transfer that feeling to the dying woman. Drool slithered onto my coat. For a moment I wondered if I could see death swimming in the liquid. What color is death, anyway?

It was growing cold. The fever in her body was keeping me warm. I rested my chin against her matted hair and closed my eyes. She lifted her head and, for a moment, opened her eyes and looked deeply into mine, but her neck was too weak to support her. Her head fell back onto my chest. I had no words to sustain her. Softly I traced my index finger along her arm the way

MollieO had done to me when I was a little girl. I think she called it feathering.

"I wish I could talk to you in Spanish, but I don't speak Spanish, I speak French." I started to feel helpless again, so I closed my eyes and rocked her. Soon our breathing became one. The boundaries of my fears were melting away.

At last there was no why? where? or what if? There were no "not enoughs," only a wave of gratitude that washed between us. I tried to hold her in ways I yearned to be held. With grace and confidence. To be mothered, fathered, sistered. To let her make the sounds she had been holding back for who knows how many years. Until now I had known next to nothing about this woman. Now I loved her for allowing me the privilege of loving her.

As soon as I let go and acknowledged that there were no barriers between us, it was as if the gates to her being had swung open. A flood of emotions cascaded through her into me. At once, my body released the colors of her grief, her anger, her outrage, her decay, her wild laughter, her divinity, her shattered life.

Filled with the knowledge of who she really was, I realized I felt more connected to her than to any of my "real" family, even my beloved Aunt Lillian. From somewhere down deep inside, I knew that this was the most intimate moment of my life. No boundaries. No questions. I was so joyful to have broken through, to hold someone who needed life when I needed so desperately to feel alive. I knew this would be the only time I could be with her in this way. So there we were, two old souls wrapped around each other waiting for an invisible tiger and Quan Yin to return. It was our secret.

And still nobody noticed.

Except a cop who rode up on horseback. "What's going on here?" he asked in a concerned voice. I didn't answer. He jumped down off his horse. It was then that I recognized a familiar ally.

"Sergeant Fortunato," he said, taking off his cap. "What have we got here? Is this a drug overdose?"

"This woman is dying," I said. "And she wants to die right here. She doesn't want to go to a hospital or a shelter. She wants to die here. She thinks this is her home. I believe she has the right to die wherever she wants, doesn't she? Do whatever you have to do but I am *not* going to leave her."

He placed his hand on her wrist and waited. "Not good," he said. For the first time he seemed to notice how attached she was to me. "It's pretty dangerous out here. It wouldn't be smart to leave you out here unattended."

Then the sergeant squatted down next to us. As I watched him from the corner of my eye he seemed stronger, more imposing, than I remembered.

At that moment Manhattan froze. All the street lights around us blinked out. I saw a lavender sky and the October moon, full and radiant. I had never seen a moon that white before. Apparently, neither had Officer Fortunato, who gazed at the sky, hypnotized.

I turned to wake Maria, who was barely breathing.

"La luna," I whispered, positioning Maria's face upward toward the moon. She blinked several times and then opened her eyes. Her face filled with recognition. Obviously, she saw something not yet apparent to me.

Lying back, we watched in silence. Suddenly, in the far distance, an evening star appeared. And then a ray of purple light began to inch its way toward us. It moved like a piece of silk blowing in the wind. At the very end of it was a figure, walking thoughtfully, slowly. As she approached, I began to make out the gossamer, flowing robes and the beautiful headdress. It was she.

All around us, others were feeling something too. In the distance, demonstrators for and against the homeless lay aside their protests and moved toward the light. Throngs of diners who were lined up at the little bistro on the corner turned their attention to the sky. The Hassidic gentlemen strolling arm-in-arm stopped and pointed. The baker in his kitchen, his loaves lined up on densely floured tables under terrible lighting, bent his head in prayer. The Scandinavian biker lighting a Camel under a streetlight remembered his first love. Rottweilers, Weimeriners and Clumber Spaniels sat without being told, and a young ballet student rose and danced in the violet energy.

All across the town people awoke from their troubled sleeps. Some put on their bathrobes and left their homes. They walked in the direction of 57th Street. Led by their own innocence, they walked toward a pure, purple ray of love streaming from the sky.

As Quan Yin continued her journey toward us, my attention was pulled to where Officer Fortunato was crouching just a few feet away. As I turned to face him, it was as if there were two beings sitting there: one, a caring peace officer, the other an energy so formidable, so unwavering, it seemed to envelop the entire city block. Riveted, I watched a transformation take shape.

Slowly the officer's emotional and physical presence began to dissolve, and in its place came the molecules of pure intention. Where there had been strength and courage sitting next to me, I now felt the impeccable confidence of an ancient warrior.

I glanced up to the sky and saw Quan Yin drifting ever closer in the moonlight. I felt alert yet mesmerized, hanging in the delicate balance of two miracles. I turned again to see the lanky body of Sergeant Fortunato crouch down close to the sidewalk. In what appeared to be slow motion, his uniform faded light, lighter still, until only a vague outline of his human form hovered near the ground. Then the semi-invisible mass stretched into a much grander form.

One by one each arm reached forward, elongating into gargantuan paw, wrist, arm and shoulder. Next the neck and shoulders filled in with musculature bold and sinewy. As the massive neck turned, the head transformed into weighty skull. Snout appeared, pink tongue, and fang. I felt the heartbeat empowered. I heard a fierce purring.

But it was the eyes, revealing themselves amber and clear, that rendered me, once again, full of hope. It was in those eyes I found the cop who had delivered me from unspeakable dangers in my life. It was in those eyes I discovered the immortal tiger who had done the impossible: He had taught me to believe.

I could see him more clearly than ever before. Stiff white whiskers, creamy eyelashes and jowls, and a perfectly symmetrical butterfly shape imprinted in white on each ear. Tiwa was no longer an image, a vision, hanging like a veil in front of my eyes. There, on that cold dark street, he was as real as the lamp post. Exhaling long, steamy breaths, he lifted his massive body from the pavement and slinked passed me in the night. I could see him, smell him and, if I wanted to, I could reach over and touch his elegant coat. The warrior of my dreams had walked out of a dedicated cop's body and appeared, flesh and fur, right here on the Avenue. *Tiwa, Tiwa,* I heard my soul whisper.

Finally it all began to make sense.

"Oh, my God," I whispered to Maria, shaking my head. "They exist in this world!"

The majestic cat walked out to meet the Goddess. Quan Yin stroked the back of the tiger's neck, and together they floated toward us in a cocoon of amethyst light.

The street was thick with humanity. Body to body, New Yorkers pressed together in the winter night. No one strayed.

We all watched Quan Yin's approach. Most people would not let themselves see her . . . and yet many could feel her, and that was wondrous enough.

I noticed the little bottle around her neck, a light jade bangle around her wrist and the serenity on her face. She looked directly into my eyes and her mouth formed the loveliest smile. Not sure I could receive the wealth of love she was transmitting in my direction, I looked away. But then I remembered a moment under the ocean. Had I dreamed it? At that moment I knew that to survive I needed to trust and give in to Quan Yin's love, to surrender to the experience. What was I remembering? I didn't know. I took a deep breath and smiled back.

The whole thing had become overwhelming for Maria. She had now lost consciousness and was dancing in the emptiness. The goddess moved closer and delicately placed a cool kiss on Maria's cheek. Maria sat up and looked into Quan Yin's eyes. Feeling the intensity of Quan Yin's love, Maria's soul had begun to ease its way out of her body. She lingered on the cusp of death, but then I felt her pull back. She looked at Quan Yin as if to say, "How do I know when it is time to go?"

Reaching down, Quan Yin took Maria's hands in her own. She touched my hand too. An inexpressible softness reawakened inside me.

Now that the veil between life and death was lifting, I could see the electromagnetic field around the woman's body shift from vibrancy to nothingness: greens to blues, to peaches, to whites, to golds, to open space. Finally, Maria was at peace.

Looking down at the lifeless shell that lay in my arms, I wept.

As she departed, the goddess Quan Yin lifted a silhouette of platinum light all the way out of Maria's body. She cradled the soul securely in her arms. Tiwa, the mighty tiger, moved to her side, then turned and nodded to me. Quan Yin bowed her head. I bent my head and closed my eyes. I bowed back. When I opened my eyes, the three had vanished.

The moon was sinking in the twilight of early morning. Slowly the street was emptying again. Now curious onlookers approached. I rushed to a pay phone.

"There's a woman lying on Fifth Avenue and 57th Street against the curb," I told the precinct operator.

"Do you know anything about her? Does she have a family? Do you know her name?" she asked.

"Her name is Maria Milflores," I said.

"Who are you? Are you the person who found her?"

"Me? I'm just someone who walked by and tried to help."

"I see," she said. "How hurt is she? Do we need to send an ambulance?"

"No," I said, "she doesn't need to go to the hospital." I lay my forehead against the wall of the telephone booth. "She's gone home."

"I'm afraid I can't hear what you're saying. Are you saying she's dead?"

"Yes," I said. "*Perfectly* dead."

The dispatcher told me someone would be there shortly to pick up the body and take it to the morgue. I walked back to the curb and sat beside Maria's abandoned form. Maria Milflores, the woman of Fifth Avenue, was gone.

By now the corpse was creating quite a stir. I took her hand to show the crowd that everything was being taken care of. I closed my eyes and imagined all the stories passersby were making up. Soon, thousands would be stepping over the place where the body now lay, never realizing that someone precious had surrendered her life right here, that an incredible healing had taken place.

When I opened my eyes Mei-Mei was sitting on the other side of Maria, holding her hand. Soon the ambulance arrived, and a couple of young attendants covered the body and delicately placed it on the gurney. Mei-Mei and I watched the vehicle disappear through the excited crowds.

Before I could speak, Mei-Mei turned to me. I opened my arms. We hugged like old friends. In our silence, everything was spoken.

Part Three

SWEET SURRENDER

"I am remembering forever, where we Belong."

—Alma Luz Villanueva

37

DONE

Callie was still on tour in Europe. She was always on tour.

"You're not coming home, are you?" I had asked her over the phone.

"Paris is a blast this time of year. You know how that is. Why don't you come next spring and stay with us? We have plenty of space in our villa, and our little one, Blossom, can't wait to meet you. Please come. I miss you, sister."

"I miss you, too, Callie. I'll think about coming. Really, I will."

"Okay, but I'm counting on it! Oh, by the way, I'm singing all the songs you like so even if I can't be with you *there,* I can be with you *here.* I'm killing them with your favorite songs, kiddo. I love you. I love you. *Je t'aime.* Talk to you soon."

I wanted to tell her about Quan Yin, about Maria, but before I could even begin she was gone. Callie was like that, running, hectic, ephemeral as hell. To most, it was enchanting, but it never left me space to share myself or to tell her of my disappointment. I had hoped her new family would slow her down, but it didn't seem to be happening. But then, when it really came down to it, I liked having Callie with me any way I could.

Walking down Fifth Avenue, the season's first snowflakes sparkling in front of the streetlights, I thought of that amazing

October night I knew something had shifted in me. An old part of me had died right along with Maria. I knew that my days as a therapist were numbered.

But I needed something. Someone. A mentor? Simone Signoret belonged to my life as an actress, in my role as MollieO's caretaker. I longed for a community where people looked after each other, where connections were deep and long term. I wanted to live in a place where cultivating a connection to the earth was a top priority. I longed to be treated as if my soul was important.

I missed Callie, but there was no way I was going to look for her on the southern Riviera. So I called the city's jazz station when I got home, and requested a couple of songs we used to sing together. I needed Callie close to me. I closed my eyes and listened to Johnny Hartman, and pretended it was Callie singing.

The lyrics of a beautiful 'forties love song drifted through the window out into the winter sky. My eyes dropped to the street, down the Avenue, the place where Quan Yin had released Maria from her suffering. It was true, the adventure had ended, but I had been forever transported out of my everyday life. And I never wanted to go back.

My mind felt as clear as one of MollieO's crystal champagne flutes. I took advantage of the moment and raised an imaginary glass of Dom Perignon.

"I'm done," I said, toasting the city.

Surprisingly, I was sure of what needed to happen. I picked up the telephone and dialed my Aunt Lillian. I told her about what had happened with Maria. She laughed and told me that the newspaper had a different perspective about the event. Apparently, the authorities were relieved that the whole "homeless ordeal" had been put to rest, and the mayor's office was taking credit for the commendable crowd control and absence of violence.

"Lillian, I need to ask a favor of you."

"Anything at all, honey."

"I want to leave New York and start over. I want to go to Maui and create a simpler life."

"Why, that sounds just wonderful, Billie."

"But they have a quarantine for animals, and Ellington has gotten pretty old. I think he's getting ready to pass, and I don't want to make him go through all of that."

"I would be honored to take him. When are you leaving?"

"Next week!" I said excitedly. "As soon as I can. But I need to say some important good-byes, first."

"Good for you, honey! It takes a lot of guts to do what you're doing."

"All I know is I *have* to go. I want a vacation. I want to be immersed in all of that softness."

"Softness?"

"Yes, you know."

"Oh, like Quan Yin's softness."

I felt so thankful for Lillian. We made plans to meet for dinner in the next couple of days.

"I want to book a flight to Maui for a week from today," I told Isabella, the ticketing agent. "Non-stop. The earlier, the better."

"Round trip, ma'am?"

Shocking myself, I said, "One-way. God, it feels scary saying that."

"I can't even imagine," Isabella said, and I could hear both excitement and envy in her voice.

That night, with the tiny carved image of Quan Yin tucked under my pillow, I smiled an easy smile as I closed my eyes to sleep. For the first time in a long time I was trusting my own decisions. I would go to Maui and heal in the softness. And if it felt right, I would be as open as possible with no expectations— at least that's what my conscious mind promised. My unconscious mind created a fantasy that had me believing my journey to Maui had quite another meaning.

I began to doze off, and before I knew it I was having one of my technicolor dreams. Quan Yin and I were sitting with our legs dangling over the lava rocks by the reef of the bay.

"I have questions about this goddess thing," I told her. "The only thing I know about you is what I've read and what Mei-Mei told me about her conversations with you. And you know how cynical I was before."

"Yes, Billie, I recall."

"Well, since the night you came to take Maria, everything has changed for me. I'm very curious. I guess you could say that I'm in awe of you. Is that okay?"

"The truth is always okay."

"Okay," I said, "here goes. First of all, I'd like to hear from an expert about what a goddess is. In our culture, goddesses are part of an ancient mythology. They aren't real. So, that's my question: What is a goddess? And are you real?"

Quan Yin smiled.

> *"A goddess is a real soul who has left the planet and holds the sacred energy of peace within her. Her main job is to transmit that energy out into the world. A goddess is someone who is in constant communication with the Divine, in service with the creator of all things.*
>
> *"A goddess is also a mirror of all of the wonderful aspects of the feminine that are deep inside you. As goddesses, we manifest into a human-like form and radiate love, compassion, forgiveness, courage, hope, trust, healing energy and so on, to remind you of who you really are—to help you remember the magic of your soul. Do you understand what I am saying?"*

Her face mirrored me in such a feminine way.

"Quan Yin, how does someone become a goddess?"

She closed her eyes. Waves crashed against the lava rock.

"Every woman is on the journey of becoming a goddess. Goddesses come in all different colors, sizes, shapes and attitudes. But they all have one thing in common: They honor love above all else."

"That's comforting," I said, feeling there might be hope someday even for me. *"What does it take to become a goddess? Is there a special training?"*

"It takes an open heart. It takes the courage to trust in the power of love, and that is a challenge on this planet because of the poverty, wars, illness, greed and lack of connection. All of these scenarios create opportunities for you to discover ways to communicate love through generosity, forgiveness and compassion. So, your times on earth may serve as an introduction to the goddess training. In truth, every moment is a part of that training, every lifetime. Everything you experience and the way you handle it brings you closer to the final graduation."

"Oh," I said, putting my head in my hands. I considered my lack of patience, my anger, my resentment, my parents.

"Imagine all of the possibilities women have to become goddesses. Think of the life of a beauty queen. Imagine the experiences a woman farmer has working the earth. Consider the woman who engages in sexual relations for money. Or the woman who miscarries. Each has her own evolutionary program: the addict, the judge, the one who swims with dolphins, the cellist, the one who lies dying in the street, the one who is molested by her father. All of these women are in training at different levels. Each one is making choices that move her along or detain her."

"So . . . did my molestation advance me or detain me?" I said, not wanting to hear the answer.

"It advanced you and it detained you."

I could feel my confusion surfacing. "Quan Yin! Are you telling me that my father molesting me was a good thing?"

> *"I am saying that one incident with all of its horror created many possibilities for you to grow, to evolve toward your goddesshood. I know this is hard to hear, but try, listen. Every female enjoys more than one opportunity to explore the depths of her being, and with many, these opportunities have to be grueling or you do not grow. Then, what good is the test?*
>
> *"Yours was particularly difficult. So much so that to survive, you closed your heart. You disconnected from your personal life and you blamed others for your demise. But thank goodness you didn't close your heart forever. You made the choice to trust again. Now it is time to find love. And to do that you must release your negative thoughts about your father's illness and your mother's self-obsession. It is time to let go, Billie. Try seeing your parents as two old souls who floundered terribly as parents. They made mistakes that you are not willing to carry. Forgive them now and let go of your burden. Move on.*
>
> *"Live your life with gratitude—as a goddess!"*

This certainly was a lot to take in, and I noticed that I was sighing deep, cleansing sighs. Finally, I relaxed again and looked into her eyes. My mind got quiet and the next question surfaced.

"If you are the Goddess of Compassion, who am I? The Goddess of Neurosis?"

> *"Be gentle, Billie. Soon you will be known as the Goddess of Pure Love."*

"Really? This is a joke!" But her eyes said something different. "What will my duties be?"

"Whatever it takes to assist your sisters in accepting who they really are."

"I guess I've been doing that all along, but I feel like I'm light-years away from being a goddess. Is someone watching my everyday activities and keeping score along the way? And if so, how am I doing?"

"You tell me."

"Comme çi, comme ça."

"From where I sit, you are doing just fine."

Overwhelmed by all of Quan Yin's attention, I changed the subject. "Are there any other wise tidbits to help me along the path?"

"There is always more to learn, much more than I can explain here. But to start you off: Be friendly. Smile a lot. Engage eye-to-eye. Hug as often as possible.

"Remember that you are not your mind. Don't get caught in limiting thoughts and their accompanying emotions. Your true Self is elegant, soft and powerful. Emanate those qualities.

"Above all, trust your intuition. Listen to your body.

"Live larger than thought, closer to heart."

"Wow, I really do feel like a beginner."

"The soul of Billie Bartholomew a beginner? Hardly."

"You're not just saying that?" I said, my insecurities getting the best of me.

"Billie, . . ."

"I'm sorry. May I go on?"

"You have my full attention."

"How many lifetimes does it take to become a goddess?"

> *"That depends. It can take hundreds or it can happen in an instant. It all depends on self-acceptance and forgiveness. As soon as you know that you are a goddess then that journey ends and the next one begins. If you do your work, Billie, pretty soon you will be ready for your first assignment. And we have quite an assignment in store for you."*

"How can you tell how far along you've come?"

> *"Some are more giving, already committed to service. Others take greater care with themselves. Find a balance of the two, then you know you have found the way."*

"I have so many more questions. Can we meet again?" I asked.

> *"I will be honored to be a part of your training."*

"How come girls aren't taught a kind of goddess training in school?" I said, feeling a great clarity coming over me. "And why is there so little literature that describes the life of the goddess? I think all of this information should be mandatory. Girls and women need to know how much there is to look forward to, and that all of the crazy, painful experiences we endure have a payoff. I think if my women patients had been given this information right off the bat, they'd have gotten off mood elevators in a heartbeat."

> *"So what are you waiting for, Pure Love? Come to Lemuria. Learn. Practice. Return and teach them."*

I thought of my bulimic patients and the ones who were teetering with manic depression. I thought of the ones who had lost all hope, those who'd split their personalities. I thought about reading them the adventures of my life, starring Quan Yin. I saw them standing up and smiling, then dumping their narcotics in the nearest trash bin.

"One more thing, okay?"

"Okay, but just one until we meet again." She looked out in the distance, no doubt hearing someone else's prayer.

"I'm embarrassed to ask you this, but I have to."

Quan Yin waited while I found the words, the nerve.

"Will I find true love in this life? I'm sure you've seen that I have a pretty bad record."

"I have, and you are making progress. Do not stop. Risk it all for love."

"Okay, this is the final question. Really! What comes after being a goddess? Do I get another body? Am I light? Or do I take a final breath and vanish into eternity?"

"You will see."

Her voice was fading like fog through sunlight.

"You will see, Dear One. All in good time."

38

SAYING GOOD-BYE

How do you leave fifty years of a life behind?

I'd never worked as hard as I did that last week of my life in Manhattan. Friends' reactions were mixed, but most of them urged me to follow my intuition. They couldn't wait to visit me as soon as I got settled. I knew they would come, and a part of me felt protective about taking my time and setting up a new life before they descended. Every one of my friends immediately assumed I had met a man. What else could inspire me to make such a leap? "What's his name?" they kidded me. "Why are you holding out?" But I assured them that my decision came from my ancient feeling of exhaustion, and fascination with the idea of a softer life.

My most difficult task, of course, was to help my patients make their transition to a new therapist. Inevitably, I found myself talking to some of them about leaving therapy altogether. Each of my patients knew something was going on when they walked into my office. "You look different. What's up?" Tom Barger, a widower who had been with me for ten years asked. "You look so happy." One after another, they sat in the comfy chair and listened with various levels of distress to my reasons for ending therapy with them.

"I know this is difficult," I told them, passing brownies and madeleines. "We've come so far. But it's time for me to leave New York. I want to see if my real home is in the Hawaiian Islands. I have two wonderful colleagues that I admire who've opened their practices to my patients. They're fresh and full of energy and very smart." I watched faces fall.

"I feel so honored to have worked with you, and I will miss you. But I have to go."

Michael, my depressed patient of fifteen years, complained about having to start his "story" over with a stranger. But he added that, as of late, he was beginning to feel more joy and he wanted to thank me for that.

One of my newer patients, Sally, who suffered from obsessive-compulsive disorder, gave me a wonderful hug when we said good-bye. Carla, my bulimic patient, brought me a good-bye gift of all the utensils she had used to make herself vomit. She wrapped them in a little velvet box that she asked me to bury in the earth on Maui. I gave it back and thanked her for letting me know that she had moved on. I also let her know what an act of power she would bring off if she buried her past herself.

And then there was Mary, prey of the terrorizing terrier whom she had finally put to sleep. Sweet, sweet Mary of the "Dog-Bitten Bouffant Casserole Set of Scarsdale." Mary outdid herself and brought me a pineapple upside-down cake to usher in my new life in Hawai'i.

Eight hours a day they came and surprised me with their big-hearted understanding and loving critiques of the work we had accomplished. After my last appointment, I shut my door and sat in the office that had been my second home for more than two decades. As I boxed up my pictures and vases—the accoutrements of my old life—I felt proud of my work, and not the least bit apologetic about my decision to leave.

I looked out the window that faced Fifth Avenue. The night was bombarded by taxi horns and distant sirens. For a moment I felt nostalgic about the evenings I had dined alone at the wonderful deli down the street. I thought of Mike, the flower vendor who had given me a gorgeous orchid for my birthday, one of many plants I was going to deliver to Mei-Mei.

"I'm sorry I'm late," I told Mei-Mei as I placed the plants on her kitchen table. "I've had so much to finish."

"I'm glad you could come," she said, smiling. "I thought we'd meditate and have a bite to eat, okay?"

Mei-Mei's place looked just the same as it had a few weeks before when I'd been introduced to the illustrious goddess of mercy and compassion. Again, wavering candlelight and the fragrance of papayas filled the room. The statue looked even softer than I had remembered. I walked over and touched Quan Yin's cheek.

"She has changed our lives," I finally said, "hasn't she?"

"I don't think I had a life before I met Quan Yin," Mei-Mei said.

I shared that feeling.

"I know I was short on compassion, but that is changing every day.

"I almost forgot," Mei-Mei went on, "did I tell you I got accepted to one of the big writers' conferences in New England? Only ten poets got scholarships. I'm going in the spring."

As I looked into her bright, animated face, I thought back to the young woman I had met originally. I could hardly remember what she was like.

We sat across from each other with our eyes closed, holding hands in the healing energies of the room. Later, as I buttoned up my heavy winter coat, Mei-Mei said, "Don't forget me." I wrapped my arms around her one last time.

"Whenever I think of Quan Yin, I will think of you," I whispered. "You have been a great teacher. Truly an elegant goddess." Our eyes were tearing, and I told her I would write to her if she promised to send me a copy of her first book of poetry.

The following evening I decided to watch the news while I was packing up boxes of the stuff I was giving to Lillian. One of the major networks was airing a special on New York City's homeless. They weren't too far into the show when the same automaton journalist appeared who had been interviewing protesters on the street the night Quan Yin came and released Maria. I was flooded with frustration at the way the show was being handled.

"This is Mira González reporting from 59th Street. We're here, right in front of the Plaza Hotel where, not long ago, what began as a protest turned into a non-violent happening. I've been out here talking to various folks trying to get a clearer picture of what really did happen, what it was that changed the whole atmosphere from one of chaos and uprising to . . . to . . . well, peace."

The camera zoomed in close on an elderly woman who looked well-to-do.

"I don't understand, really. All of a sudden I felt this warm sensation in my body and I felt drawn to go outside and walk. It was way after midnight. And I never go outside after seven!"

"Man, it was *weird,*" a skinhead with lizard-slit eyes told Mira. "It was definitely a freak of nature."

A little boy kept trying to give his point of view, but his mother kept pulling him off to the side. "Stop that!" she snapped. "Behave yourself right now." Finally he poked his head through the crowd. "There was a big tiger!" he told Mira. Everybody laughed.

"We're talking about a big, balmy fog that rolled in," said a pinstripe-suited gentleman, biting into a croissant. "That's what we're talking about here!"

I watched Mira grab the arm of a middle-aged man working construction on the corner.

"Well, it's hard to put words to it," he said, looking directly into the camera, "but I saw a miracle happen here that night."

"A 'miracle?'" Mira repeated, weighting the word with a note of cynicism.

"Oh, lady," he continued, "you wouldn't believe it if I told you."

"Try me."

"Well," he said, "I saw an angel come from heaven and take the soul of a homeless woman who had died here. That's what I saw."

"Whew," said Mira, shaking her head. "Now there's a guy who could use an early retirement." She turned abruptly away from him and continued her search.

"Let's go to Tony Giaconna," she said quickly, but the camera was following the worker into the network of ladders and scaffolding. "Tony, I believe you've brought us a credible source from the mayor's office. . . . Tony, can you hear me?"

39

KEEP FINDING ME

As I was closing up my life in New York, I realized that I could not leave without saying farewell to my father. It had been five years since our explosive confrontation, and things had changed. Radically. Somehow the whole experience with Maria and Quan Yin had opened my heart in such a way that I no longer needed Martin to be kind or understanding, or even to take responsibility for what he had done to me. For the first time I was able to let go of the horrible memories, on my own and by myself, with no mandate for my father or anyone else. Finally, I was at a place where I felt I could forgive him. And I knew that without total forgiveness I would never find myself, or the kind of partner I'd dreamed of, or my real work. I would never find inner peace. None of it would be mine.

I phoned Martin's apartment and told his nurse I wanted to visit. Sounding delighted, she offered to send the limo to pick me up. I declined.

I couldn't help chuckling to myself when I noticed how calm I felt as I showered and dressed, ate a small meal and prepared for my visit. On my way out the door, I noticed the little Brownie camera that Martin had given me so many years before sitting on top of one of my storage boxes. Remembering how much joy it had brought me, I smiled. I thought I would let him know today how much that camera had meant to me. Of course, in the years that had passed I had gone on to other cameras, like a slim little high-tech Nikon. I packed that in my purse.

Without fantasy or expectation, I left my apartment. MollieO had let me know that Martin had suffered numerous strokes and was now confined to a wheelchair. He could barely speak. I wasn't worried. Lillian had taught me that if you want to, you can always find a way to communicate.

I rang the doorbell and waited. Jeanne, the nurse, opened the door. "I told him you were coming. It's the first time I've seen him smile in weeks."

She led me down the long hallway. Gone were the family portraits and flowers.

"Where are all the flowers? Father used to love white carnations. He used to put them everywhere."

"He stopped all of that awhile back when he started getting sick. But I know how good flowers can make a person feel, so every week I put some fresh ones in his room." She opened the door. "Here she is, Martin. Here's your daughter, Billie."

Martin had lost the use of his facial muscles, but he attempted a smile. I could feel something in him I'd never felt before. It was an absence of the edge of hostility he'd always carried somewhere not too far from the surface. It was an openness, a sense of calm that I'd never before felt in his presence. It was—to my amazement—a simple, quiet happiness.

"I wanted to see you because I am leaving New York," I told him, pulling over a chair. "I'm moving to Hawai'i. I know how much you love it there."

Martin nodded.

"How are you feeling? You look pretty good."

His eyes continued to blink at me as he strained to stay connected to what I was saying. I told him how I was leaving everything behind—my home, my practice, my friends. Everything.

"I'm a little nervous," I said. "It's pretty risky. But I remember when I was a little girl, you gave me that Brownie camera. Do you remember, Father? You told me not to worry, that you knew I could do it. You told me I could do anything."

Tears were slipping down his face. I held his hand. "I will always thank you for that."

We sat and looked into each other's eyes. I remembered a time before the bad times, when we had walked together down a quiet little beach near Miami. I could feel, again, how happy and safe I had felt in my father's arms. And in those moments I actually felt love for the man I had been afraid of, the man I had felt tormented by nearly all my life. The man I had shown, a few years before, a vengeful side of me, a side even I hadn't known existed. Now nothing in our past mattered.

"I brought another camera with me today," I said and pulled the Nikon from my purse.

"Do you think Jeanne would take a picture of us?"

Father nodded.

I stood in back of the wheelchair, then bent over until my face was next to his.

Jeanne pointed the camera and came in for a close-up. She snapped the shutter again and again.

"This way we can remember each other in this moment forever," I told him.

It was early evening and I needed to finish packing all those boxes. I buttoned my coat. "It's hard to believe," I said. "In a few days I won't be needing this."

Martin swallowed hard and tried to find the words. Again our eyes met.

"It's okay. I think I know what you're trying to say. I love you, too, Father. "

I walked down the corridor feeling lighter than I could ever remember. As I opened the door I thought of Quan Yin and prayed that, if Martin wanted, she would come to his side, too, and take him home.

40

LEMURIA, HERE I AM

Driving in her old Chevy convertible to La Guardia, Lillian turned to me and said, "I wish I had the courage to do what you're doing, honey. But the truth is, I don't. I've been complaining about this damn city for too many years and look at me—I'm still here!"

"You're the best part of Manhattan, Lil," I said. "You created a normal life for me." Then we both turned to each other and shouted, "Normal?!!!" and laughed.

"As soon as I get situated I'll send you a ticket and you can come and hang out with me, okay?"

Lillian pulled over to Hawaiian Airlines and I jumped out and grabbed my carry-on. I went around to her side of the car. Taking her face in my hands, I said, "Keep Ellington warm, okay? Until we meet again, I'll see you in my dreams. Right?"

"Right." Lillian said in a voice rich with feelings. Looking deeply into me, she said, "I knew from the beginning you were a special one." Then she grabbed her purse and dug down to the bottom and pulled out a wrinkled piece of paper. "Here," she told me. "You're incredibly intuitive, but even so you might need this." She passed me a map of Lemuria that she'd torn from one of the books in her library.

"You always take such good care of me," I said.

The flight attendant served me a cup of guava nectar. I looked out the window, down at New York. Through my mind's widening aperture, I followed Aunt Lillian down Manhattan's streets heading for the Village. I pictured my clients moving through their day and prayed that they were making it okay. Mei-Mei sat, writing at her little oak table, directly across from the marble head. I envisioned MollieO dressing up for a game of Canasta and fastening in place her prettiest charm bracelet. I saw Martin sleeping in the sunlight of another afternoon.

I set the music dial on a Hawaiian station and relaxed into the sweetness of slat key guitar and romantic island melodies. I pictured the popular resorts and pristine, crowded beaches stretching for miles. Suddenly the thought of relating to *anyone* seemed overwhelming. I wanted nothing more than to be a woman who had left it all behind. A woman with no past. A nobody.

The "fasten your seatbelt" sign went off and I reached down into my bag and pulled out a small velvet box that protected the miniature statues of Tiwa and Quan Yin. I held the carvings against my chest. A faint scent of plumeria blossoms wafted through the cabin. When I put the statues back in my purse, I found the neatly folded map of Lemuria down near the bottom. I laid the torn out page on my lap. As I relaxed deeper into the yellowed blueprint, an odd thing occurred. At first I thought it was just my imagination, but soon I realized that hieroglyphic symbols were emerging through the paper. They seemed to reveal themselves like lost artifacts that formed a secret language appearing instantaneously, only for me. *"Come closer,"* they whispered. *"Closer, still."*

I began to sense the presence of the invisible civilization, the lost dimension beneath the ocean where I might begin a very different kind of adventure: my apprenticeship with the goddess. I closed my eyes and felt the black lava rocks of Maui reaching out to me. . . .

EPILOGUE

The sky is marbled turquoise and the palm trees are blowing gently all around me. I am making my way down the stairs to the little beach of Napili Bay. I sense Quan Yin close to me now, her loving arms outstretched and waiting.

I begin the slow wade in. The lackadaisical waves gently slap my legs and hips. Angelfish and tang bob below. I take in a long, beautiful breath and then I dive deep. Deeper. I am gliding toward Lemuria.

Suddenly, as if waking from a long dream, I recognize the magnificent city floating in the distance. I let my body go as the currents carry me along to the shimmering gateway.

Soon I will trace the great cat's paw prints, through the wet rainforest teeming with life, by the mystical birthing pools, into the crystalline city where sensuous structures of mahogany and koa wood curve through the streets. Perhaps I will pause, inhaling the inebriating scent of mango and jasmine, coconut and starfruit.

The sultry wind caresses my face. A misty, open gardenia is poised behind my ear. I am draped only in a piece of lavender silk. In the distance, a mother whale breaches, her baby at her side.

Luscious. Ripe. The sun, the water, the volcanic red earth breathe out of me from every pore. I am becoming the woman I have looked for all my life.

I see a Lemurian woman in the marketplace dyeing cloth moon color in the midday sun. As I approach she lowers her head and bows, graciously welcoming me to her home.

Now I feel the smooth marble stairs beneath my feet. I am at the door to the ancient temple where Quan Yin resides—the sacred space where I will learn to celebrate the timeless art of compassion and joy, of ultimate softness. My trembling hands push the heavy door open. I sense destiny all around me.

I will meet Her today.

BIBLIOGRAPHY

Austen, Hallie Iglehart. *The Heart of the Goddess.* Berkeley, Calif.: Wingbow Press, 1990.

Blofeld, John. *Bodhisattva of Compassion: The Mystical Tradition of Kuan Yin.* Boulder, Colo.: Shambhala, 1978.

Boucher, Sandy. *Understanding Kuan Yin.* Boston: Beacon, 1999.

Boulet, Susan Eleanor—Trust, and Babcock, Michael (text). *Goddess Knowledge Cards.* Rohnert Park, Calif.: Pomegranate, 1998.

Graham, Lanier. *Goddesses In Art.* New York: Abbeyville Press, 1997.

Palmer, Martin, and Ramsay, Jay. *Kuan Yin Myths and Prophecies of the Chinese Goddess of Compassion.* London: Thorsons, 1995.